Strictly On Ice

Strictly On Ice

Helen Buckley

Where heroes are like chocolate – irresistible!

Published 2022 by Choc Lit Limited
Penrose House, Crawley Drive, Camberley, Surrey GU15 2AB, UK
www.choc-lit.com

A CIP catalogue record for this book is available
from the British Library

ISBN 978-1-78189-478-1

Printed and bound in Great Britain by Clays Ltd, Elcograf S.p.A.

For David, Donovan and Richard –
who make me smile every day

Acknowledgements

I'd like to thank everyone at Choc Lit and Ruby Fiction for deciding *Strictly On Ice* was a story worth sharing – especially the Tasting Panel readers: Julie Lilly, Anne Eckersley, Joy Bleach, Amy Nordon, Jenny Kinsman, Kirsty White, Rosie Farrell, Alma Hough, Deborah Warren, Honor Gilbert and Sharon Walsh.

Thank you to my enthusiastic and supportive family, friends and readers, who give me the encouragement and confidence I need to keep writing, in particular: Mum, Helen Bowen, Amanda Gee, Rachel Raine, Danielle Desanges and Sarah Duke. Thank you also to blogger Vikkie (Little Miss Book Lover) who gave me useful feedback on my draft, and who is a tireless champion of authors both new and established.

Thank you to Amanda Horan and David Mansfield – your editing and proof-reading skills helped me get *Strictly On Ice* ready for submission.

I consider myself extremely fortunate to team up with a brilliant Choc Lit editor, and I am thrilled with the final version of Katie and Jamie's story that we worked on together.

I'm hugely grateful to friends and family who read my last novel and are eagerly awaiting this one. Your support, freely offered and so generously given, means the world to me.

Finally, thank you to my husband David, for everything.

Prologue

Then

Katie was pillowed in a silent soft cloud of white. Heavy and calm, her deep breaths like the ebb and flow of a regular tide. No matter how much she tried to wake up, her eyes resisted, keeping her in stasis in the quiet dark.

The roar of the crowds had stilled around her and she didn't understand how so many people could be so quiet. The warmth confused her – the ice should be cold and unyielding. She gently grazed her fingers over the slippery surface and felt starched dry cotton where the freezing moisture of the ice should have clung to her fingertips.

She shuddered as the darkness became lighter and a pain spliced its way into her consciousness, piercing the depth of her dreams with white-hot flashes of agony coursing through her leg. She could feel it more now as the pain came regularly, crashing into her like waves.

Figures hovered over her, chasing in and out of her vision, their voices puncturing her sleep. She didn't understand most of what they said, but one comment echoed through her mind again and again and throbbed like an ache through her entire flesh.

'She may never skate again.'

Katie tried to fight the encroaching blackness, but she slipped into a hazy sleep with one thought in her mind. She would never forgive Alex for this.

Chapter One

The voicemail notification stared at Katie like an angry red eye as she checked her phone. Ignoring the message, she tucked her feet up on the sofa underneath her favourite blue blanket, worn and frayed from years of use, and opened her banking app. She chewed her lip anxiously as the numbers appeared, hoping that somehow there would be more than she imagined, but it was worse than she feared. Overdrawn, again.

Katie shivered, feeling goosebumps ripple across her arms as she snuggled further into the blanket. Her studio apartment felt dank and cold, but she resisted the temptation to turn the heating on and burn through money she didn't have. It didn't help that the windows were ill-fitting rickety sashes, one of which refused to close properly. No matter how much duct tape she used, the tiny crack was still letting in the winter chill from outside where Storm Doris howled like a demented banshee.

She flicked through the TV channels to see if there were any storm updates, wondering if she should have paid the heating bills instead of her TV licence. She knew it was pathetic to admit the TV kept her company, filling long empty hours with the familiar faces of presenters jabbering at her. She would rather be cold than sit in silence.

Katie finally remembered to check her voicemail after watching an interview with a *Love Island* contestant. Katie snorted in derision as she dialled her voicemail – she never could understand people who sought fame, so desperate to be seen, to be liked. She remembered her dad's warnings about over-exposure when she won her gold medal. He had been right, of course, although the money from interviews and adverts certainly would have come in handy. The automated message greeted her, announcing a new message, and Katie hoped it was someone signing up for lessons or looking for some private coaching. She could really use the income.

'Hi Katie, this is Hannah Samson from All Star Productions. I'm phoning to speak to you about an exciting new TV show we think you'd be perfect for. Give me a call back, I'd love to chat to you about it!' Hannah's high-pitched voice was irritatingly perky, and Katie winced and held the phone slightly away from her ear.

Katie's finger hovered over the off button for her phone but then she hesitated, the overdrawn figure from her bank account flashing in her mind. She sighed and stabbed at the phone to return Hannah's call.

'Hannah Samson.'

'Hi, it's Katie Saunders. I got your voicemail message,' Katie said, warily.

'Hi Katie, thanks for calling me back. How are you doing?' Hannah asked.

'Fine thanks,' Katie said curtly, not in the mood for small talk. 'So, what's this new show?'

'Well, it's called *Sport Star to Skate Star*, and we'll pair top athletes from various disciplines with professional skaters to see how they do each week at performing a routine. The public alone decides who wins,' Hannah said breathily.

Katie frowned and couldn't keep the irritation from creeping into her voice. 'That's not new. Isn't that just imitating *Dancing on Ice*?'

Hannah sighed dramatically, as if she were peeved at the accusation of imitation. 'It's building on the public's love of a tried and tested format and making a few tweaks. We feel it's time for a newer, fresher approach,' she burbled.

'Well, I've always refused to do *Dancing on Ice*, so what makes you think I'd be interested in ...' Katie paused, unable to remember the name Hannah had said just moments ago. 'Your show?' she said eventually.

'We're paying much more money,' Hannah said, triumphantly. 'And we would be willing to give you the freedom to choose and choreograph your own routines if you wanted that option.'

Katie thought about her overdraft and the last offer she had turned down flat. She hesitated for a moment, torn between her dire money situation and her desperation to avoid the public eye with all the gossip and intrusion she hated.

'Can you send me the details?' she said finally, thinking she could take a look, just to see what they were offering.

Hannah ended the call with a wide smile and waved her croissant to get Marsha's attention, who raised a perfectly tweezed eyebrow. Hannah hadn't really expected to hear from Katie Saunders at all, given her reputation for stonewalling the media. Getting her on the phone was a big deal, let alone getting her to agree to look at the details.

'I take it that went well?' Marsha asked, and Hannah could hear the envy in her voice.

Hannah nodded, running her fuchsia nails through her short blonde hair, the crisp strands perfectly straightened and glossed with serum. 'I'll get Katie, and then Donald will have to give me a promotion. Watch this space,' she said knowingly.

Marsha laughed. 'The ice queen on our show? I'll believe it when I see it, Hannah. She's hardly done any media since the accident.'

'Well, maybe she's changed her mind,' Hannah said, refusing to allow her positivity to be blunted by Marsha's pessimism.

She started tapping frantically at her keyboard to draft the email to Katie with the details, and pressed send, her fingers crossed.

Jamie glared at his phone as it buzzed insistently on his bedside table, rudely interrupting his sleep. Blearily, he raised his head slightly off the pillow to check the time and a throbbing pain at his temples quickly morphed into a stabbing pain behind his eyes.

His fingers scrabbled past used tissues and empty pill

packets, before finally finding the phone. He jabbed at the answer button while blinking fiercely.

'What?' he rasped, his dry tongue sticking to the roof of his mouth. He licked his lips and winced at the taste of stale kebab and booze.

'Jamie, please tell me you're not still in bed,' said Matt. 'It's midday already, you lazy slob.'

'You're my agent, not my mother,' Jamie said, rubbing his gritty eyes and desperately wishing someone would bring a bacon roll and a coffee to him right now. 'What do you want?'

'I've been asked if you'd like to take part in a new reality TV show,' Matt said, cheerfully.

'No,' Jamie said, firmly. 'I don't do reality TV.'

'You don't know what it's about yet,' Matt said, sounding slightly exasperated.

Jamie rubbed his forehead and sighed. 'Make it quick.' He groped for the glass beside his bed and drained the small amount of water.

'It's a new show where sports stars and athletes try their hand at figure skating. It's called *Sports Star to Skate Star*.'

Jamie groaned and leaned back on the pillow. 'Isn't that just *Dancing on Ice*? It's not even original.'

Matt paused and Jamie could practically hear him clench his jaw with annoyance. This was the first offer Jamie had been given since his disastrous performance at the World Cup eighteen months ago. He knew Matt was keen to get some commission flowing back to his pockets. 'They're offering quite a bit of money for the first series, and they'd really like a rugby player.' Matt spoke curtly, trying to sound patient.

Jamie paused and tried to force his dusty throat to swallow. He knew his savings weren't going to last forever and he had to find work soon. 'Send me information by email. I'll read it when I've woken up properly.'

'Great.' Jamie could hear the smile in Matt's voice.

'No promises,' Jamie warned him, and hung up so he could

order some McDonalds for home delivery. After he ordered, he rested his head back on the pillow, turning the idea of being on a new show over in his head. He hadn't had any work in months and as the time stretched on, he started to feel more stir-crazy, rattling around in this ridiculous house, surrounded by happy images of his former life. He was about to turn thirty-one and knew he needed something new to drag him out of this deep rut he had dug himself into, but ice skating? He shook his head and winced at the idea.

'Stupid idea,' he muttered, turning over and waiting for his delivery to arrive.

Chapter Two

Katie waited for the download to complete. The free Wi-Fi in the café was slow but it was cheaper than paying for it at home, and the café was warmer too. The blue download bar remained stuck on thirty-seven per cent. It didn't help that reminders to update her laptop kept flashing up and it would barely open anything without freezing. She jabbed angrily at it and stared around the café as she waited for the file to load, tapping the table impatiently.

Katie had chosen a bad time to come. A group of new mums had gathered in a corner nearby for their weekly catch-up. Their tiny babies mewled while they laughed and chattered, proudly displaying the fruits of their fertility, discussing the best holiday resorts for new parents and how amazing maternity leave was. Katie stared across at them with envy, knowing that some of the women must be her age, perhaps even younger, yet their circumstances couldn't be more different. One of the mums caught her eye as she stared and Katie looked away quickly, embarrassed. She re-read the email from Hannah while she waited for the download to complete, her fingers anxiously kneading a packet of sugar.

"We understand that you're offering coaching services now, and we're hoping that your injuries from the accident have healed sufficiently over the past couple of years to allow you to take part in our show. It'd be an honour to have a former gold medallist on the team."

Katie felt anger rise in her gut like acid when she read over the words "accident" and "injuries". To Hannah, those were throwaway terms, but to Katie, they were weighted with the devastation and the loss of everything she had ever worked for. Her fists clenched and she had the urge to throw her mug against the wall and watch it shatter, just like her ankle on the ice those years before. Her jaw ached and she knew she was grinding her teeth.

The download of the contract completed, and Katie clicked on it violently, trying to breathe deeply.

Jamie looked out of the windows to where his nieces were playing in the garden, though they were so bundled in thick downy jackets that they could barely move their arms. His mum, Susan, was bustling in the kitchen behind him, in her element as hostess.

'You look tired, love,' Susan said softly, before checking on the roast lamb. She brushed her short blonde hair away from her face as the heat from the oven fanned her forehead and reddened her cheeks. Her hair used to be the same sandy blonde as Jamie's but it had lightened as more and more grey hairs made their inevitable appearance.

'Hmmm,' Jamie replied, running his hand over his unshaven chin. He knew he looked a mess, but he didn't see the point of making much of an effort just for Sunday lunch with his parents and his sister.

One of his nieces waved at him to come outside, her chocolate-brown hair streaming behind her as she ran in the pale winter-sunshine. 'Maybe later, Alice!' he yelled to her, and she looked disappointed.

He was in no mood to play and felt listless and lumpen. He got out of puff so easily now. It was probably all the extra weight he had put on since his rugby days, he thought. He regretfully touched his waistline, feeling it softly bulge against his trousers where he had once proudly sported a defined set of abs.

'Tell me about this show,' Susan asked, coming around the counter, dressed in a flowing blouse in soft tones of grey and looking much younger than her sixty-five years.

'They pair sports stars with professional skaters and get them to perform each week. Public vote, a judging panel, you know, the same old thing as that other skating show.' He sighed and turned to her. 'It's nothing new or exciting.'

'Except that all the participants are actually athletes?' she asked.

'I suppose that's the main difference.' He shrugged. 'They want to see how athletes from different disciplines adapt to skating.'

'Maybe you should give it a try,' she said hesitantly, squeezing his shoulder. 'It would be a good distraction. You might even enjoy it.' She smiled at him, her dark green eyes the mirror of his own, though slightly more crinkled at the corners.

Jamie pressed his lips together. 'I'm not keen, Mum. I'd be a laughing stock – can you imagine me ice skating? And I bet they'd make me wear Lycra or sequins.' He grimaced at the thought.

She laughed. 'You know, I hear skating is actually pretty tough exercise. It'd certainly get you into shape.'

He tried not to flinch. Most of the extra weight had piled on quickly since leaving rugby, but then it had carried on accumulating, especially after the divorce was finalised. He wished the papers hadn't printed those awful pictures of him on the beach last year. The public humiliation was bad enough, but he winced inside when he thought of Cassandra seeing them, thought of her laughing at him and congratulating herself on deciding to leave him.

'I'll think about it, Mum,' he said to her, trying to shake off the thought of Cassandra and strolling out to the garden where Alice and Isabelle greeted him with cheers. He scooped them both up in his arms and whirled them around, loving the way their cheeks were bright from the cold and how they clung trustingly to his arms, never thinking for a moment that he would let them fall, never judging him.

He wouldn't admit it to anyone, but it wasn't just the loss of rugby and his reputation he was grieving for. It was the chance of holding his own children in his arms, a chance that seemed to recede further every year; a possibility that Cassandra took with her when she left him two years ago. And the worst part was he had only himself to blame.

'Katie Saunders signed!' Hannah exclaimed, slamming the phone down and fist pumping the air, not quite believing the good news.

A few of her colleagues gave her a smattering of applause.

'You proved me wrong after all,' said Marsha, holding up her hands. 'How the hell did you manage that?'

Hannah pushed her chair back and straightened her clingy blue dress, slipping on her heels that she had kicked off underneath her desk. 'Who knows? I guess she's desperate,' she said to Marsha, and strolled towards Donald Major's office in the far corner; where the fat gold letters on the door trumpeted "Producer".

Hannah rapped her knuckles on the door a few times before opening it and poking her head around. Donald looked up from his desk and gazed at her coolly. A thick-set balding man with steely grey eyes, he had a reputation for being a ruthless ratings chaser. It was Hannah's first chance to work closely with him on this new show and she was keen to make sure he knew how capable and ballsy she was. If she could get in with Donald, her career path would be paved with gold.

Knowing this was her chance to impress him, she boldly entered the room, shoulders squared and head held high.

'Hannah. How can I help you?' he said in bored, level tones, having reverted to looking at his computer screen.

'I got Katie Saunders to sign,' she said, delighted to see his instant reaction to her news.

'Excellent, well done!' he said, his expression changing from bored to pleased. Hannah hovered hopefully before his desk, but he didn't invite her to take a seat.

'Have her doctors confirmed she can definitely handle the skating?' he asked.

Hannah nodded firmly. 'She's good to go. It'll be a brilliant comeback story, especially as they thought she would never skate again. The doctors have been pretty amazed at how well her ankle has healed.'

Donald pressed the palms of his hands together gleefully, as if imagining the headlines.

'And she still looks good? Hasn't gained too much weight I hope,' he said.

Hannah slapped down the most recent photo she had of Katie and Donald looked pleased to see she hadn't let herself go since being out of the public eye. She was still petite, with a tumble of wavy dark brown hair and pale blue eyes that matched the ice she had once mastered.

'And what about …?' Donald let the question trail off and raised his eyebrows hopefully.

Hannah's grin widened, her perfectly whitened teeth shining against her gentle golden tan. 'He's looking over the contracts now. Telling him Katie had signed up definitely piqued his interest.'

Donald gave a smug smile. 'We need to make sure we tell the press straight away that Katie has signed up – make it public knowledge so she can't back out. Hopefully, that'll persuade our boy to sign up as well.'

'Leave it with me.' Hannah turned and walked back to her desk, heels dragging slightly on the thick carpeting, her head dancing with anticipation as she picked up the phone to talk to the media team.

Katie hurried home from the corner shop, leaning into the force of the wind which drove the rain into her face, stinging her skin. She dashed past the row of shops, passing through small clouds of heat from each doorway, first the steam of the barbers' then the hot greasy air from the fish and chip shop.

The faded façade of the second-hand shop contrasted with the beaming lights of the new Tesco Express directly opposite, shining out in the gloom beneath the heavy rain.

She wrapped her arms around the plastic bag she was carrying and leaned forward, her feet becoming wetter with every step, until she finally reached the safety of her block of flats. The building loomed before her, the wet grass in front churned up from where someone had driven over it, the thick muddy channels now filling with rainwater. Tugging on the entrance door, she dived into the hallway and took the stairs two at a time, knowing the lift was likely to either be broken or smell of urine.

Her damp feet slapped against the cheap vinyl flooring as she hurried up to her flat, keen to get inside and rip off her wet clothes; her jeans clung stiffly to her. Shoving her shoulder against the peeling white door, she pushed her key into the lock and jiggled it till the door finally gave way. She slammed the dripping bag down on the kitchen counter and kicked off her shoes, hoping they wouldn't take too long to dry in her cold flat.

She peeled off the wet socks and jeans and luxuriated in the dryness of her cosy jogging bottoms, making a steaming cup of tea and curling up with the paper, now sodden from the rain. She never could get out of the habit of reading newspapers. It seemed so old-fashioned, but it reminded her of sitting with her dad, wiping the ink stains from their fingers as they read the news together.

Blowing gently on her tea, she turned the page and flinched. There, in stark bold letters on page four, was her name. Clearly, the TV company was keen to make sure the public knew who would be taking part, but Katie was mystified why they would highlight her signing up. She knew she wasn't particularly popular with the public. Katie thought for a moment about turning the page and not reading any more, but curiosity got the better of her and she started reading the article, sighing when she saw the old cliché of calling her the "ice queen" being trotted out again. A few years ago, the media had used the phrase "ice princess" to describe her, which sounded ethereal and romantic. Ice queen sounded so hard and bitter. Still, Katie had to accept that's how she had come across in the few post-accident media interviews she'd done, so she could hardly blame the papers for the caricature.

She read the rest of the article with interest, as the show had released a few names of participants who'd already signed up and Katie wondered who she would be paired with. Theo Jarvis and Rory Henderson had been announced as participants and she hoped they might pair her with Theo. He was a silver medal gymnast and heartbreakingly handsome. If I'm going to skate with someone again then it might as well be with someone who's easy on the eyes, she thought.

Only a couple of the professional skaters had been announced so far, all ice dancers rather than Olympians. She knew some of them vaguely. At her peak she could literally skate rings around them, out-do any of them on the ice when it came to skills, speed and performance.

It just isn't fair, she thought angrily, scrunching her fists in the paper and blinking back hot tears that burned her eyes. She was a world-class skater, and yet here she was, in her freezing studio flat with a gaping overdraft – and preparing to go on a reality TV show with amateurs. She was only twenty-three and already she was at the bottom of the skating heap.

She wiped her cheek roughly with the back of her hand, knowing her fingertips were already smudgy from the cheap newspaper ink. Her head had started to throb gently at the onset of her tears, and she tried not to think about all the hours of practice and the sacrifices she had made since she was a little girl only to wind up in this position. She took a breath through her nose, sniffling, and told herself firmly not to give in to self-pity. She would just have to make the best of it.

She ran her finger gently over Theo's picture, drinking in his tanned skin and caramel-hued eyes. Maybe if she got a decent partner they could win and it would help her to get some more work and more money and move out of this dump.

It would also be rather nice, Katie thought, to be liked by the public again.

Then

Katie sailed around the ice, twirling happily, her dark ponytail streaming behind her. She knew her dad was watching and she turned her head to see him, waving at him while he chatted with a tall man at the side of the rink.

He waved back and she turned to pay attention to the skating coach, who asked the girls to line up. They lined up, one by one; little girls neat as a pin in their skating outfits, hair tightly plaited or twisted into buns. Katie stared at them and put a hand self-consciously to her hair. Her dad had bunched it into a high ponytail and jammed various hair grips around it to keep it in place. Katie glanced at the girl next to her, comparing and feeling messy and ugly. She bit her lip and looked back at the coach.

'And well done, Katie. You're the only one who is really getting this so far,' coach Daisy Leeson said, with a serious nod towards her. Katie smiled proudly at the praise and grew a little taller as the other girls looked at her enviously.

They could have the best hairstyles in the world, thought Katie, but they could never be better than me on the ice. She met their eyes with a cool stare.

'I'll see you all next week,' Leeson said, dismissing them. The girls departed, some arm-in-arm, giggling, to find their parents at the edges of the rink.

Katie turned and skated over to her dad who greeted her with a grin. He grabbed her hand and pulled her towards him, the familiar woody scent of aftershave and cigarettes lingering on him.

'Sweetheart, meet Ivan Somerville. He's a private coach,' Brian said enthusiastically, his eyes gleaming.

Ivan gave Katie a polite nod. 'You're very good out there. Do you like skating?' he asked, leaning down slightly.

Katie tilted her head up to meet his eyes and nodded. 'I love it,' she said. 'When I skate, I feel ...' She stopped, searching for the right word. 'Like I'm flying,' she said eventually. Ivan nodded sagely, as though he understood exactly what she meant.

The two men turned away to continue talking as Katie undid her skates and watched as the next class started on the ice. She watched them thoughtfully, knowing she could do better than even the older, more advanced students. She could outshine them all, fast and fearless, even with her scruffy hair. She wanted to skate back onto the ice, but instead, she sat quietly, her fingers tugging at each other with impatient energy that hadn't been spent by the exertions of the class. She couldn't help but overhear the conversation between Ivan and her dad, though they talked in low voices.

'Do you think Katie is promising?' Brian asked Ivan, a hopeful lilt in his voice as he glanced at his daughter.

'I do,' said Ivan, smoothing a hand through his thick blond hair, the occasional white strand glinting through in the rink lights. Katie beamed at the stranger's compliment, though she kept her back towards them, fascinated by the spins the students were trying.

'How old was she when she started skating?' Ivan asked Brian.

'Four. She kept asking about it after she saw skating on the telly. She's been skating for two years and she just can't get enough.'

Brian turned to Ivan. 'How old are your students?'

'It depends on the student. Any age, if they show promise. Better to start them young,' he said, rubbing his chin with a large, rough finger.

He glanced at Brian. 'If she wants to skate, and I mean skate to compete, then it's a lot of time and a lot of work, and I warn you, it is an expensive undertaking with no guarantees,' he said, in a low voice. 'There would be my fees, many hours of training per week, the cost of using the ice at the rink, not to mention boots, costumes, travel ...' He trailed off. 'I'm not trying to put you off, but I've had so many promising students drop out due to the lack of funding for figure skaters in this country. Some parents end up spending thousands per year, even up to £30,000 at the more elite levels.'

Katie turned around and caught her dad's eye. She didn't know what it would cost, but she hoped her dad could afford it. She looked at him hopefully, with a half-smile.

'Let's talk numbers, Ivan,' Brian said, his mouth firm and decisive. Ivan raised his eyebrows, his face impassive but his eyes smiling as he saw a triumphant look cross Katie's face before she turned back to watch the students trying things she couldn't wait to do.

'Just five more minutes, please Dad,' Katie begged, clasping her hands together.

'Come on pet, the rink is about to close and you still have homework to do,' Brian said, folding his arms, signalling he meant business. A shimmer of irritation creased his forehead and Katie realised he had been standing at the rinkside for hours. Her dad always joked that he should live at the ice rink, so much time had he spent watching and waiting for her there since she started skating six years ago.

She obediently skated to the edge and came off the ice. Her cheeks were glowing with warmth after several hours of practising the new moves Ivan had taught her yesterday. He had told her not to repeat the moves too many times, but every time she made a mistake it lingered in her mind like an unbearable itch. The Young Stars competition was fast approaching, and she wanted to try again and again until she had her routine perfect.

Brian tapped his watch at her as she unlaced her skates carefully. 'Homework calling,' he said, hurrying her along, trying unsuccessfully to stifle a yawn.

She shoved her trainers on and scrunched her sore feet inside them, feeling the relief of being off her blades. 'Ready to go,' she said, jumping up and promptly wincing at the heat of the pain that blazed in her knee.

'Still giving you trouble, kid?' Brian looked at her, his eyes creased with concern.

'Just a bit. I'll ice it when I get back,' she said, shrugging. No matter how much it ached she would never miss a practice. The only time she had ever missed a session with Ivan was two years ago when she had glandular fever, and even then her dad had to force her to stay home.

'Ivan always says not to repeat the jumps too many times in one session,' Brian scolded her as they walked out to the car park, Katie attempting to walk normally, albeit stiffly, so he wouldn't realise how much pain she was in.

'I know I know,' she held up her hands. Katie knew her dad was right, but she had almost perfected the jumps and couldn't wait to show Ivan. Her knee would heal itself; the injuries always did. Katie had always felt invincible on the ice, as though nothing could ever really damage her when she was on it. Sometimes after a fall, when she would raise herself up, she would be surprised and delighted to find only minor injuries, and often wondered if she was specially made for taking hard falls without breaking.

As they drove home, she looked out at the summer sky, only just beginning to darken with bands of deep blue spreading above the red and orange horizon. The freedom of skating was starting to wear off and she turned her thoughts to school tomorrow with a slight dread. If she could avoid school completely and skate all day she would. She felt so trapped behind a desk, forced to sit still and regurgitate facts. Katie knew she belonged out there on the ice, not in school where there was no one to eat lunch with and the other girls stood in little groups, laughing shrilly together at things she wasn't interested in.

All that mattered to her was the next session, the next practice, the next competition. Ivan wasn't an expressive coach, but she knew when he was pleased with her as he would give a small restrained nod, a single clap of his hands, and say "Good" in a low voice. When she first started skating with him four years ago she had wondered if his muted response was because he wasn't pleased with her progress, but she soon learned that it was just his typically restrained manner. She now counted her success in terms of how many "goods" she had per session. Yesterday there had been four "goods" and tomorrow she was determined to chase more, to show Ivan she was ready for the next level. She knew her dad wasn't pleased about her current marks at school, but who cared about that when she could already land a double axel at age ten?

Chapter Three

Jamie walked towards the ice rink, hefting his gym bag over his shoulder, and drumming his fingers on the strap in nervous anticipation at meeting his skating partner. He had been told by a dour woman from the production company to meet his partner at Slough ice rink at six in the morning, so he had dragged his protesting body out of bed and gulped coffee when the sky was still pitch dark. The world was silent and slumbering as he blearily drove the short distance to the rink. Even now, dawn still felt far away, just a distant promise over the horizon where a faint glimmer of blue sky began to seep into the blackness of the night.

Walking swiftly towards the ice rink, Jamie stood still for a moment, impressed by the swooping wooden curves of the entrance. The warm tones of the wood contrasted with the shimmering grey of the windows, the large panes of glass staring blankly back at him. He traced his reflection growing larger as he walked towards himself, hefting the doors open with a pleasing swoosh.

He was glad that at least he didn't have to travel far to the rink. He guessed that perhaps his skating partner was staying or lived nearby, which would save them both a hefty commute.

His custom skates lay heavily in his bag. He'd run his fingers over the gleaming narrowness of the blade, and couldn't imagine balancing on anything so thin, let alone whirling around on a slippery surface on top of them. He was more nervous about trying a new sport than he thought he would be. Rugby was all he had ever known; the thud of the ball against boot, the slide of wet grass against bodies, the jarring thrust of the scrum. The blank emptiness of the ice; cold, forbidding, and exposed, scared him.

Jamie's footsteps echoed around the still, frigid air of the rink, the sound bouncing off the hard plastic chairs and barriers surrounding the ice. The harsh fluorescent lighting illuminated the cylindrical metal ceiling, and made it seem colder inside. At this hour there were very few people around, just a sour-faced teen at the front desk with a smattering of angry acne and an attitude, a few staff members milling around, and a handful of dedicated skaters there to make the most of the time before the rink opened to the general public later in the day.

As he approached, Jamie could hear the gentle swoosh of blades gliding over the ice, the slight crunch of turns and pivots over the frozen surface. His partner was already there, a low barrier separating a portion of the ice just for her and Jamie to use.

He strapped on his boots, lacing them up tightly around his ankles, wincing at how uncomfortable they were, and walked clumsily towards the rink, pushing open the barrier. He could already see his partner as he approached the ice, could see her gliding around with perfect grace.

Oh no, he thought, nerves bubbling in his stomach. It was the skater who had refused to forgive her partner for the accident that shattered her ankle and had left him broken-hearted. Katie Saunders. Jamie had seen she had signed up for the show and had hoped he wouldn't be paired with her. After all, she wasn't known as the ice queen because of her sunny and welcoming nature. From what he'd read, she sounded like a bit of a cow.

He was grateful the "first meeting" segment would be filmed at a later date, when they would pretend to meet for the first time, and this early morning would be just for them, away from the additional awkwardness of the cameras.

Jamie grimaced and stumbled towards her, feeling the pinch of his new skates on his ankles. He hoped she wasn't as harsh as the media made her out to be.

Katie didn't notice Jamie arriving. She leaned into the turns and glided over the ice, warming up her muscles, feeling the familiar sense of freedom that came with being able to move so far and so fast with a single flick of her ankle. Her titanium-patched ankle, full of metal rods and screws. She had been skating on it during coaching sessions for the past year and it seemed to be holding up well, though there was a stiffness there that was new to her, a rigidity that came from the metal parts holding the bones neatly in place. Still, she was grateful to be able to skate at all after the fall two years ago. Sliding smoothly to a stop, she turned to see Jamie.

Oh no, she thought, her heart sinking. She didn't know Jamie Welsh personally, but she could see instantly that his former rugby-playing bulk was now additionally beefed up, to put it kindly. She stared coolly at him as he clomped over the ice to her. His clumsy gait didn't fill her with confidence, especially as she knew he would have already had hours of private lessons, as promised by the show's producers.

They would be voted out the first week for sure, she thought, nibbling on her lower lip. Trying to fight her disappointment at not seeing Theo skating over to her, she met Jamie halfway and extended her hand.

'Hi, I'm Katie Saunders,' she said, raising an eyebrow as he shook her hand and wobbled dangerously on his skates. He towered over her by at least a foot so she had to tilt her head up to look at him. Underneath his baggy maroon hoody, she could see the broadness of his shoulders, more used to the aggressive heat of a scrum than the cool precision of lifting a partner on the ice.

'Jamie Welsh. Great to meet you, Katie,' he said, politely. 'I'm really looking forward to working with you.' He gave her a tentative smile and the corners of his dark green eyes crinkled slightly. Despite his unshaven face and the bags under his eyes, Katie could see that he was a good-looking guy. It was a shame he had let himself go so badly, she thought.

She gave a short nod. 'It'll be ... fun.'

Jamie nodded hesitantly. 'Sure.'

'Have you ever skated before?' Katie asked him, eyeing up his feet, already turning in from the pressure on the blades, his ankles probably starting to burn.

'Nope,' he said, shaking his head. 'Only the sessions I've had to prep for the show over the past month, to get to grips with the basics.'

She pressed her lips together into a thin line. 'Then we've got a lot of work to do.'

He shrugged. 'You're the expert.'

Katie skated around him, eyeing up his posture, her hands tucked behind her back and her head tilted to one side, her long hair neatly tamed into a high ponytail that swished around her slender neck.

'We'll need to work on those basics, get you standing right and moving across the ice gracefully, both backwards and forwards,' she said.

'Standing right?' he asked, trying to turn his head to look at her as she circled him. She could see he was already slouching with the effort of standing on the blades.

'Yes,' she said. 'I can't believe you've already had private coaching. You're very ... awkward looking. And quite slumped,' she added, feeling a little guilty when she saw his cheeks flush under his four-day stubble. But she was in no mood to mollycoddle a washed-up rugby star who had got himself sacked over his drunken antics. She was here to win and restore her reputation, and feelings and emotions had to be thrown out the window when it came to winning. Ivan had always told her that.

'Well, then, let's get to work,' Jamie said, and Katie was surprised at the firm determination in his voice. She hoped he would match it with his actions.

Just thirty minutes later, Jamie was forced to plead for a break, puffing heavily, his face rapidly turning a mottled shade of red like corned beef. Katie tried not to make a face and nodded curtly.

'Sure, take ten,' she said, secretly wondering how the show could claim to only have "sports stars" as participants when Jamie was clearly way past his prime.

They skated to the barriers and sat on the plastic chairs. Jamie dug out a Red Bull from his gym bag and took a few desperate gulps as they sat in silence and watched some of the other early-morning skaters at the far end of the rink.

'I had no idea people went ice skating this early in the morning,' Jamie remarked, observing a young teenager in deep discussion with his coach.

Katie sipped from her water bottle and gently tucked a loose strand of hair behind her ear. 'It's the best time. The rink opens super early, with fresh ice, and it's not open to the general public, only serious skaters,' she said. 'I've always trained here so it kind of feels like a second home to me.'

Jamie looked at her. 'You're local then?'

'Yep. I grew up in Feltham, not far from here.'

'I know Feltham, vaguely,' said Jamie. 'I'm from Windsor.'

Katie smiled. She could tell by Jamie's accent that he was from a pretty posh area.

'So, why this show?' Katie asked him curiously, as he mopped his face with a towel, a damp sheen on his forehead.

He draped the towel over the back of his neck. 'The money's pretty good. And this is going to sound sad, but my mum was really excited by the idea. She's always loved watching ice skating.' He shook his head and smiled at his mum's enthusiasm.

'Really?' Katie looked surprised. 'I assume she would be more of a rugby fan.'

Jamie laughed. 'Well, of course, rugby, but she also loves the winter Olympics. She was a huge fan of you and Alex.' He paused awkwardly. Katie looked away and didn't respond. Alex was the last person she wanted to talk about.

Katie leaned down to rub her ankle, loosening the tight white boots and flexing her toes, then turning the ankle around in small circles, her fingers probing and testing for pain or signs of weakness. There were none but it was something she repeated after every skate, fearful of what she might find. She sat up, relieved.

'Is your ankle fully healed from the accident?' Jamie asked, watching her.

Katie flinched at the word accident. 'It'll never be quite the same as it was, but the extent to which it's healed has surprised the doctors,' she said, quietly.

'It must have been pretty traumatic,' Jamie said.

Katie guessed he saw her flinch, and she wished he would take the hint and stop talking about it. She nodded and shuffled uncomfortably in her seat, and they sat in awkward silence for a moment.

'It's great that you can skate again,' he said, finally.

'It's all I've ever wanted to do,' she said, and busied herself lacing up her skates so they could continue their practice.

Then

'We must get a photo, Dad!' Katie grabbed Brian's hand, the medal swinging around her neck. She loved the way it felt, the weight at the end of the smooth ribbon, gleaming gold and all hers.

Brian laughed and pulled a bulky old camera out of his pocket, adjusting the lens and winding on the film, looking around for someone to take the snap.

'Would you mind?' he asked as a woman walked past him. She looked like she was in a hurry, but she glanced at Katie and her frazzled expression softened into a smile. 'Of course,' she said graciously. 'Congratulations,' she said to Katie as she took the camera from Brian.

Katie beamed as her dad put an arm around her, squeezing her close so she could smell the scent of Old Spice and the cigarettes he refused to give up even though she continually nagged at him for smoking. She held up her medal proudly as the woman took the photo.

'Thank you,' Brian said as he pocketed the camera, the woman hurrying on her way.

Katie revelled in the congratulations as people passed her by, patting her on the back and shaking her hand. She rubbed her fingers over the cool solid medal and breathed deeply, feeling the joy of triumph flow from her heart through every part of her. She had won – she was World Junior Champion, at age sixteen. She had won medals at plenty of other international events, but this was the one she had coveted and dreamed of, the most prestigious international competition for junior figure skaters. It was even more exciting that she had won it in front of a home audience, as the competition was held in the UK that year.

Brian watched his daughter soak up the praise, brightening at the victory as though the sun itself were shining through her eyes. 'I'm very proud of you,' he said, and kissed her on the forehead. She beamed back at him.

'It's time to go, kid, so get changed. I'll treat you to anywhere you'd like for lunch.'

Katie was reluctant to take off her favourite costume and put on regular clothes again. It was like being a superhero who had to resume her drab civilian disguise to cover up her real identity. She slowly packed away her things in the changing area, gently folding the purple layers of tulle that had danced around her as she skated her way to gold that morning. She ran her hands lovingly over the smooth material as she tucked the costume into her bag. It had been ridiculously expensive – most ice-skating costumes for competitions were. She had accidentally seen the bill for this one in her dad's coat pocket when he had lent it to her one afternoon and had gaped aghast at the £1,000 it had cost him. Katie tried to push the guilt out of her mind about how much money he spent to help her pursue her dreams, of the lump sum he had been awarded after her mum's death that was now being chipped away.

She had tried to speak to her dad about it once but he had told her firmly not to worry about the money, that he would make sure there was enough to pay for everything she needed. Katie had printed some advice on funding opportunities, but he had folded up the papers roughly and tucked them away without a glance, snorting at the idea of such "charity". He was a very proud man and stubborn as an old goat, so she hadn't talked to him about it any further and thought it best to let the subject lie.

As she packed away her costume, Katie could hear agonised sobs coming from a far corner of the changing rooms. She kept her head tucked down but looked out of the corner of her eye at the young girl sobbing to her coach. Katie recognised her as one of the competitors – a pretty girl named Anna who had fallen three times during her routine. Her coach was trying to console her as tears dripped down onto her skates. Katie sighed, feeling a wave of pity for her. Anna looked up and caught Katie staring at her. Katie flashed her a sympathetic smile, but the girl scowled at her through her tears and Katie looked away, busying herself with packing her bag as Anna left with her head hanging dejectedly and disappointment etched onto her face.

As the last footsteps echoed around the changing rooms, Katie put on her jeans and a sweatshirt but kept her medal around her neck, tucked inside her clothes and close to her chest, the metal warm from her body heat. It had been hard-won. That medal represented hours of training, injuries suffered, Ivan chastising her, homework incomplete, and her mum's money. Katie felt the weight of what it meant to her, so much more than just a clean routine on the ice, and was determined to make sure her dad's sacrifices would be worth it with this and so many more victories to come.

She headed out to the car park, back to life on solid ground.

'After you, madam.' Brian held the door open and she slid into their trusty red Corsa she had affectionately named Rusty.

'Where to?' he asked her with a smile.

'The next Olympics,' she said firmly, with a flinty gleam in her eyes.

Chapter Four

It was only 9 am when Katie and Jamie left the rink after their three-hour session. The sky was an insipid blue and the promise of an early spring danced in the air, with tiny pink blossoms studding the frosty tree branches like gems.

Katie walked briskly to her car, a very old red Vauxhall Corsa which Jamie eyed disdainfully.

'That's what you're driving?' he asked incredulously, as she popped the key in the lock to open the door and it squealed in protest as she swung it open.

She frowned at his tone. 'So?' she snapped.

Jamie held up his hands in a mollifying gesture. 'Sorry, I just didn't know cars that old were still roadworthy,' he said.

'Well, it gets me from A to B,' she said curtly, sliding into the driver's seat. 'I'll see you at the next training session.'

He nodded and watched her drive away, the engine unhappily emitting a high-pitched squeal, and walked to his own car, a BMW with supple leather seats, and takeaway boxes littering the back. The first training session had been hard work and not at all enjoyable. It wasn't just the physical discomfort from the exertion, but also the awkwardness of trying to talk to someone who clearly wanted nothing to do with him – unfortunately someone with whom he was now going to have to spend a lot of time over the next few months.

He took a deep breath as he put the car in gear, trying to clear the exhausted fog from his mind, and headed for his sister's house in Brighton. He was shattered and all he wanted to do was catch a few extra hours' sleep, but it was his niece's fifth birthday and he knew he should make an appearance, even if it could take a few hours to get there.

He drove in a slight haze, the miles passing quickly as he wound his way towards Maddie's house, stopping at a service station on the way. The practice had left him starving and stiff, and he winced with pain when he got out of the car, the muscles in his thighs protesting every movement he made. The basic training he'd had in the weeks before clearly hadn't prepared his body well enough, although he couldn't say that he had tried whole-heartedly, and had missed a few sessions due to some late nights out. He hadn't thought it would matter but clearly, it did.

The party had started when he arrived, the children running around excitedly with frazzled-looking parents trying to keep an eye on them. Jamie felt a pang as he realised many of the couples there were younger than he was, while he was turning up alone. Again.

His sister greeted him with a kiss on the cheek, and Jamie hoped the change of clothes and the deodorant he had drenched himself in would be enough to cover up the exertions of the morning's session.

'Coffee?' Maddie asked, as she took the present for Alice from him and laid it on a table already straining under the weight of numerous brightly-wrapped packages.

'Thanks, that'd be great,' he said.

'I need some too,' Maddie said with a yawn.

Jamie smiled at her. 'Those night shifts must be tough,' he said, feeling proud of his sister's dedication to nursing.

She nodded. 'They can be, but my current shift pattern gives me more time with the girls, so I can't complain.'

Jamie followed her into the kitchen where his mum and dad were chatting with a few guests as the children swirled around them in the throes of a sugar-induced half-term high, their socks sliding on the polished wooden floors.

Susan clapped her hands excitedly when she saw him. 'Jamie love, how did it go this morning?' she asked. 'I'm just dying to know who you've been paired with.'

Maddie handed him a black coffee and he sipped it thankfully. 'Katie Saunders,' he said.

His dad looked pleased. 'Excellent. A gold medallist. Can't get much better than that!'

Susan nodded eagerly, her pale hair bobbing gently. 'What's she like? I'm surprised she can skate after that awful accident in the Olympics.'

'She's an amazing skater and she says her ankle seems to be okay now,' Jamie said shortly, unwilling to go into too much detail about Katie's rather prickly demeanour.

Maddie sensed his tone and raised her eyebrows, looking amused. 'But …?'

Jamie gave a half-smile and shook his head. 'Something tells me she's going to be hard work.'

Maddie laughed and started pulling paper plates from a packet. 'Just don't mess about Jamie, we don't want to see you voted off in the first week,' she said sternly, waving a plate at him.

'Absolutely dear, you must give it your best shot. I'm sure Katie is going to be an excellent teacher,' Susan agreed.

'We'll see,' said Jamie, remembering Katie's disapproving gaze, and feeling doubtful.

Katie clicked on the YouTube video. The footage was slightly shaky but the view of Jamie on the pitch was clear as he prepared to take the conversion kick. He looked a lot fitter in his rugby days, she thought, admiring his physique when it hadn't been abused by several years of bad habits and unhealthy living.

The hope of the fans, of the nation, rested on Jamie's powerful shoulders as he prepared for the kick to convert the try and win against Australia by the narrowest of margins, in the closing moments of the game. He looked anxious and sweaty as he lined up the ball and Katie shuddered as she watched the tension gather in his jaw. If there was one thing Katie understood, it was the pressure of being in front of a crowd that was waiting for something amazing, the weight of their expectation bearing down on you like a closed fist.

She knew what would happen next, but she had never actually seen the footage before. Nerves clustered in her stomach as she watched the clip even though it had happened a couple of years ago, only weeks after the Olympics when Katie's ankle was broken.

The steam was rising off the players in the rain and Jamie wiped his forehead with his hands, his hair dripping with moisture and his sodden kit clinging to his body. Katie watched him approach and kick the ball, powering it up and over towards the goalposts. It was sailing towards the bar. The ball went wide.

The look on his face was one of choking disbelief at first, then utter despair filled his eyes. The World Cup victory he had held within his grasp moments before, had just died. He put his head in his hands as the crowd cheered, jeered, booed, and mourned the loss of the World Cup with him. The England players milled around with the shroud of lost glory hanging over them. Right now, the players were consoling him with kind words and sympathetic slaps on the back. The fans and the players were generous with their forgiveness, but Katie knew that would change when the damning photos of his drinking session the night before the final would emerge a few days later.

Katie shook her head in judgement as she stopped the video, wondering what on earth possessed him to behave so stupidly before the final. It was hard to feel sorry for him when the disaster was so clearly self-inflicted.

She stretched out her calf muscles. The first training session today had been child's play for her. She had been building up her stamina on the ice for months now, testing out her ankle and gaining back her flexibility. Muscle memory truly was a beautiful thing, she thought.

Katie leaned forward, resting her elbows on the table. The plastic tablecloth was sticky under her hands and she picked at the edges as she stared at the photo frame on the windowsill. It was a photo of her and her dad, just after she won gold at the World Junior Championships. He looked so proud, a broad grin on his face and bright blue eyes shining, just like hers. She closed her eyes and remembered the feel of his old coat under her fingers, the faint smell of Old Spice marking the memory.

'What would you think of me doing a TV show like this, Dad?' she muttered to the picture, wishing she could hear his voice respond to her, but there was only the sound of the cars outside. She could imagine what he would think, given his often-expressed scorn of reality TV stars and athletes who courted celebrity status. She drummed her fingers on the table and thought about how different things would be if her dad were still around.

It was a long drive home and Jamie felt heavy with fatigue. He could feel his body begging for rest, but he had already agreed to see Greg. Sleep would have to wait a few more hours.

He passed block after block of identical apartments lining the Kingston riverside. Their clean modern facades reflected the street lights and the river flowed nearby, smooth and dark and silent. He pulled up outside one of the blocks and hurried to the door, the cold air enveloping him on his way up the carefully manicured path. He rang the buzzer to Greg's flat, feeling the cold start to permeate through his clothes and prick his skin, teasing the warmth away from him. Greg was one of his oldest friends, a friendship carved out on the playing fields of Eton riverside and solidified when they both played together for Harlequins. Greg hadn't made the national team, but he had succeeded where Jamie had failed – he'd invested wisely in property and married a beautiful American woman called Clara. Jamie had been honoured when they had asked him to be the godfather to their little girl last year, but he was glad that tonight Clara and Annabelle were away so Greg wouldn't be on call for fatherly duties and distractions.

Greg opened the door to let him in. Jamie picked his way

carefully through scattered childish debris and sank into the comfy sofa that hulked in the middle of the living room.

'I already ate half the pizza,' Greg said, sitting next to him and switching on the match. He, unlike Jamie, had managed to stay in shape since leaving Harlequins. He had Clara to thank for that – she was a health food junkie and regularly made Greg her guinea pig for various new diets that she then featured on her popular blog. Jamie knew a takeaway pizza was a rare treat and he would be sworn to secrecy to make sure Clara didn't find out about it.

Greg handed Jamie a cider. 'I needed that,' Jamie said, taking a few gulps and sighing. He shrugged his shoulders to ease the aching muscles that were clenched, vice-like, around his upper back.

'Tough day?' Greg asked, with a sideways glance.

'You've no idea,' Jamie muttered, and he steeled himself for what he knew was coming.

Greg grinned playfully. 'Have they got you twirling around in sequined jumpsuits yet?'

Jamie scowled at him. 'It was only my first session today, and no one is getting me to wear sequins. Ever.'

Greg laughed and leaned back on the sofa, his hands behind his head, his palms rubbing against the buzz cut that served to disguise how quickly his hair was thinning.

'I heard you've been partnered with that Olympic skater?'

'How'd you hear about that?' Jamie asked, surprised.

'It was online this afternoon,' Greg replied. 'If you're going to do something humiliating like figure skating at least you have the chance to do it pressed up close to someone fit I guess.'

Jamie shook his head. 'Trust me mate, there's a reason they call her the ice queen.'

'Pretty cold-hearted from what I hear.'

'Seems that way,' agreed Jamie.

'Maybe you could, er, break the ice?' Greg said suggestively, grinning gleefully at his joke.

'I may be hard-up since Cass and I divorced but I'm not looking for further humiliation, thanks,' Jamie said, starting another bottle of cider. Even though the divorce had happened almost three years ago, he still felt a stab of hurt every time he thought of his failed marriage.

Greg's expression turned serious at the mention of the divorce. He shifted about in his seat and leaned forward awkwardly. 'Listen, Jamie, there was something I wanted to tell you, kind of why I invited you over here. You know Clara and Cass are still good friends, right?'

Jamie tensed, wondering what was coming next.

'Well, er, there's no easy way to say this but Cass is engaged,' Greg said quickly, looking at his feet.

Sadness sank through Jamie's gut, a lump rising in his throat. He forced his expression to remain nonchalant while his heart pounded under the surface of his skin. He swallowed hard and his grip on the bottle in his hand tightened.

'Oh right. Well, good for her,' he said casually, though his mouth felt strange and stiff and dry as he formed the words.

'Sorry mate,' Greg said, sympathetically. 'I wish it could have worked out for you two.'

Jamie nodded. 'Me too.' He stonily turned his attention back to the game, munching gloomily on a slice of pizza. He soon started on the beers, and tried not to think about Cassandra with someone else, someone other than him.

Then

Jamie couldn't understand why she was screaming at him, her words lost in a high-pitched sob-choked fury. Her nails dragged into his cheek, her stinging slaps rained down across his chest.

'Cass!' he yelled, trying to hold her arms back, not wanting to hurt her as she clawed at him, crying.

'I saw those pictures of you. How could you, you cheating

bastard!' she screamed, hot flecks of spit flying from her mouth to his face. Her fingers tore desperately at his shirt. Jamie had never seen her so out of control.

'I didn't do anything!' he said pleadingly, hoping she would stop, but she wasn't listening to him over the tide of rage that coursed through her.

Cassandra began to reach out around her and grab items to throw at him, her hands blindly seeking any missile she could use, her bright blonde hair loosening from her chignon in the frenzy. Strands of hair stuck to her wet cheeks as she whirled around and threw a photo frame at him. Jamie ducked but the sharp silver corner of the frame caught his shoulder. He winced.

'Cass! You need to calm down. Please *listen* to me,' he yelled.

The photo smashed behind him, the tiny fragments of glass sputtering violently over the wooden floor. Cassandra bent over the sofa and drew shaking gulps of air as she sobbed, putting one hand to her mouth, her trembling legs sinking into the sofa cushions.

Jamie looked on in anguish at seeing her in such turmoil, her cries tearing through his heart. He approached her tentatively, hands outstretched as if surrendering. 'Sweetheart, please,' he said softly as he gently placed a hand on her back. She shuddered and pulled away, her brown eyes dark and liquid with despair.

'Leave me alone, Jamie.' She turned her face away.

Chapter Five

Katie waited. The rink was empty and echoing as she warmed up, the only sounds her breathing and her skates scraping on the smooth surface of the ice. She had always relished the early morning patch sessions when the ice was fresh and hadn't yet been churned up by amateurs. The ice-hockey markings glowed under the lights. Katie hated the way their garishness marred the perfect white surface, carving the ice up into segments, goals and lines. She wanted the ice to be pure, unblemished, her own unmarked canvas, for her use only. Alex was the only one she had ever deigned to share the ice with.

Jamie was late. After forty minutes she stopped skating and slid to the barriers. She checked her phone and took a few gulps of water, crinkling the plastic bottle in her hands and looking around the rink in frustration. Katie would never have dared to turn up late to Ivan's training sessions – it would have been incredibly disrespectful.

It was 7 a.m. by the time Jamie stumbled in. He looked pale and unkempt, tufts of hair sticking up erratically from his head and his eyes shadowy from lack of sleep. He shot her a sheepish smile. 'Sorry, I'm late. I, er, overslept.'

She glared at him, unable to hide her annoyance. 'Get your skates on. Literally. We have *so* much work to do,' she said, her voice taut.

He sat down and forced his skates on his feet, still blistered from yesterday. He winced and fumbled clumsily with the laces.

Katie looked over at him. 'You're not wearing suitable socks, and you didn't cover up those blisters,' she said, accusingly. 'You can't skate if you don't take care of your feet. You'll just end up cutting them to ribbons and filling your skates with blood.'

Jamie scowled with irritation. He stood up and folded his

arms. 'You don't hear me complaining, do you?' he said, his voice still husky from lack of sleep. 'I've trained with sprains, fractures and even a dislocated shoulder. I'm sure I can handle skating with a few blisters.'

He turned and walked towards the ice. Katie followed him as he clomped to the rink, her shoulders rigid with annoyance, and wondered if there was still time to ask the producers to reassign partners.

'Updates?' Donald looked around the table expectantly, his eyes resting on Hannah. She hated the way he always made his team sit for meetings while he loomed over them with his arms folded in his tailor-made navy suit.

Hannah and her colleagues sat around a large glass table, hot drinks steaming and iPads poised as a cold rain spattered against the large windows framing the meeting room. The pastries in the middle of the table were ignored, even though more than one grumbling stomach was heard during the meeting. Donald didn't approve of eating during meetings, and his team didn't dare disobey by enjoying the free catering provided for them.

Hannah checked her notes. 'All the pairs have started their initial training sessions,' she said. 'Most have been announced by the press now, but of course, we're keeping a few surprises up our sleeves in terms of the judging panel.'

The people around the table chuckled, exchanging knowing glances, and Hannah gave a small satisfied smile. She was thrilled she had managed to sign up the participants Donald had most wanted. He didn't seem to care that the format had been tried before by another TV channel. Hannah admired his determination to get the ratings he wanted by any means, and she knew she could help with this. The tactic was simple enough – exploit the public's obsession with celebrity romance. They had in their hands a couple destined to be together and Donald had given her the strings and allowed her to play puppetmaster. If she could make it happen, the headlines and the ratings would be stratospheric, and a promotion would be on the cards for sure.

'Let's run through the plans for the next few weeks,' Donald said, as the team nodded and Hannah sat up in her seat with excitement. She couldn't wait to get started.

'Please don't turn up late again,' Katie said. Her eyes were looking at the floor and she spoke quietly, but her voice was firm.

Guilt gnawed at Jamie. He knew turning up an hour late was a rubbish thing to do. The news about Cassandra's engagement had left him in turmoil so he had drunk too much at Greg's and had to kip on his sofa. He had woken up with a Lego brick stuck to his face and no time to go home and change.

He nodded. 'I'm sorry. I did okay today though, right?'

'Sure.' Katie gave him a nod and walked out of the rink to her car without another word to Jamie. It seemed like she was still annoyed at him, and he couldn't blame her. He knew he needed a shower too, and it probably hadn't been that nice for her to skate with someone smelling of stale sweat and last night's beer.

Jamie sighed and sat down to remove his skates. Katie had been right about his feet – they were a mess of bloody grooves and watery patches of skin where blisters had swollen and burst. He rolled his socks over them, groaning as he put on his shoes, and hobbled to his car.

Jamie pushed open the door of the café, which announced his arrival with a gentle chime. Katie waved at him from where she sat towards the back, away from the door letting in wafts of cool air from outside. He walked up to her, his hair misted with rain.

He screeched back the chair opposite hers, the white paint

flaking off the back and the plastic-coated seat cover fighting a losing battle with the foam innards that had forced their way to the surface.

'This is an interesting place,' he said, looking around, raising his eyebrows at her.

She smiled. 'I know it seems a bit rough around the edges, but I used to come here with my dad a lot.' She wrapped her fingers around a large mug of tea, her skin gently turning pink as it warmed, and she hoped Jamie couldn't see the shiver of sadness that came over her at the memory of her dad, so ingrained in this place.

Jamie ordered a coffee and ripped open three packets of sugar, pouring them in and stirring vigorously.

'Thanks for meeting me here anyway,' she said. 'I thought it would be a good time to size up the competition.' She flipped open her laptop to show Jamie what she had found. She had spent some time researching the other participants and wanted to motivate him to try harder by showing him the competition. Katie was relieved that her laptop had decided to work today – it was old and chunky and the battery life was non-existent, but she couldn't afford another one.

Jamie nodded and leaned forward, grimacing a little at the stickiness of the table under his hands.

'You've really done your homework,' he said, looking impressed as Katie clicked through the documents and weblinks, poring over the details, pointing out the participants' weaknesses and strengths.

'It's obvious to me that Theo is going to be a favourite,' Katie said, pointing at a photo in *The Sun* of Theo Jarvis with his partner Maria, a statuesque Russian ice dancer who made Katie look like Tinkerbell.

Jamie shrugged. 'Maybe he's a terrible skater,' he muttered sullenly as he scanned the webpage, taking in the gymnast's incredible physique.

Katie raised her eyebrows at him. 'Maybe so, but he's young, good-looking, probably very flexible, fit, and will get a lot of votes from female viewers,' she said. 'He's the eye candy of the bunch,' she added, slightly wistfully.

'Eye candy, huh?' he said, teasingly.

Katie laughed and looked down at the table. 'For the viewers, not the participants,' she said, feeling a slight blush warm her cheeks. She hurriedly clicked off the page and onto another.

Jamie and Katie leaned closer to each other to share the screen, their elbows touching, and agreed there was some stiff competition. Not just from Theo, but also Lara Jenson, a young footballer from the England women's team, and Derek Hayward, a sprinter who was in amazing physical shape and had buckets of charisma.

Rory Henderson, a former footballer, and Vicky Fordham, a retired Olympic swimmer, were well regarded by the public, although Katie didn't think they would be able to pick up the skating as quickly, plus they had at least twenty years on the younger participants. Rory would be skating with Anna Warwick – a perky brunette ice dancer that Katie already knew from their younger competition days. While Katie had won at Olympic and World Championship level, Anna had stayed on the regional and local circuit, never quite able to progress. Katie remembered her agonised sobs after the Junior Championships one year when she had taken some hard falls on the ice.

Katie studied the information on Angela Graves, a female boxer. 'She looks incredibly fit, but I wonder if she'll have grace and rhythm for the dancing,' she wondered out loud, tapping a finger thoughtfully on the keyboard.

Then there was snowboarder Jo Harte. 'She'll probably have really good balance, being a snowboarder,' said Katie. 'And unafraid of lifts too. She'll be fearless.'

'She's also great to party with,' Jamie said, with a grin. Katie looked curiously at him.

'I met her at the Sports Personality of the Year after-party,' Jamie explained. 'She's hilarious, the life and soul. Completely drunk me under the table. It'll be great to see her again.'

'Yes, well we're not interested in her drinking skills,' Katie said primly, pursing her lips. She wasn't at all interested in hearing about Jamie's drunken exploits.

'Do you know any of the pro skaters personally?' Jamie asked, changing the subject.

'Yes, I've met some before, and we've already had several meetings for the show preparation,' Katie said, draining the last drops of tea from the pot into her mug.

'Oh? How come?'

'We've had to all meet a few times for choreography discussions, training tips, stuff like that,' she said. In truth, she hadn't enjoyed the meetings. She wasn't good at small talk and socialising, and she had always hated the underlying rivalries and professional jealousies among fellow skaters that simmered beneath the surface of their rehearsals.

'What do you know about the judges?' Jamie asked her, taking a sip of coffee.

'Tate Wilmott – he's a former Olympic medallist for the USA.' Katie chewed on her lip thoughtfully. 'I've never met him but he's pretty legendary. I've heard he's a real sweetheart, so maybe he won't be too harsh.'

'And there's Deborah Mercer,' Katie continued, pointing at a photo of a chic older woman with glossy silver hair and a waistline about the size of Jamie's hand. 'She's a figure skating choreographer. I've met her a couple of times, though I've never worked with her directly. She's well regarded and fair, but I've also heard that she can be brutally honest.'

'I'm surprised there are only two judges,' Jamie said.

Katie nodded in agreement. 'I know what you mean. I wonder if they tried to get someone else and they turned it down.'

Jamie drained the last of his coffee and checked his watch.

'Sorry Katie, I've got to dash,' he said. 'It's my mum and dad's twenty-fifth anniversary and we're taking them out for a special lunch.'

'That sounds nice,' Katie said, feeling a small wave of envy. 'Who's we?'

'My sister, her wife, their kids, and me,' he replied, grabbing his jacket from the back of the chair and checking his pockets for his car keys.

'Sounds fun,' she said, running a finger around the outside of her teacup.

'Yup. Gotta go.' He shrugged his jacket on and headed out into the grey mist that hung in the air outside, steam rising from his breath as he walked away.

Katie watched Jamie through the large window, foggy with warmth, and looked down at her watch. She was kind of glad the meeting was over already. She and Jamie weren't getting on too well, and it was pretty clear that he was unimpressed with the café. Still, it would have been nice to have had something else to do, someone else to see. There were plenty of empty silent hours to fill for the rest of the day, with nothing and no one requiring her attention. She ordered another tea and sneaked another look at Theo's profile.

The week before the first live show was full of activity and Jamie was pretty pleased with himself for turning up to every practice session on time, and not hung-over either. The mornings were beginning to lighten from winter's dark grasp so it was getting easier to get up at the crack of dawn, though he certainly didn't enjoy it.

Katie had been a reliable and patient teacher, though she hadn't warmed up much to him in the past few weeks. They trained together, she instructed him, corrected him, and then they went their separate ways.

On a few occasions, the producers sent a TV crew to film parts of their practice sessions and shoot interviews with them to use in the show. Jamie was sure they had managed to get lots of footage of him falling and generally looking clumsy and awkward on the ice, but at least he gave a good interview. He couldn't say the same for Katie. Under the gaze of the camera, she became even more stiff and awkward, so Jamie had offered her some interview tips. 'I'm a skater, not a TV personality,' she had snapped angrily, and Jamie didn't offer again. She had also refused to do any interviews on morning TV, so Jamie had to go on his own. It was a relief really, given how bad she was at being in front of the camera.

They had their opening routine more or less ready and had practised it at the purpose-built rink in the studio that week, with the show's head choreographer Jacob Raine making some last-minute changes.

'Are you nervous?' Katie asked, as they finalised their last practice before the dress rehearsal with everyone the next day.

'Maybe just a bit,' he said. 'I'm still wobbly on that leg work in the middle section. And my turns aren't as quick as yours so I feel like I'm lagging behind.'

'You've done well though. Really. You're not that bad,' she said, grudgingly.

Jamie laughed, and it echoed around the rink back to them. 'Wow, high praise indeed. I think that's the first time you've said something nice to me.'

She looked startled. 'What? I'm a very encouraging teacher. All my students have said so. Although to be fair,' she said, tapping a finger on her chin thoughtfully, 'none of my students ever turned up hung-over and late like you did.'

He chuckled, and he was surprised that she actually smiled back at him – a genuine smile replacing her usual tense expression.

'Honestly Jamie, you've really knuckled down, and it shows. You can stay upright, you're strong, and I think that'll be enough for the first show,' she said.

He nodded. 'I hope you're right.'

'I'll see you tomorrow at the fitting and dress rehearsal,' she said, turning with a wave.

Jamie smiled, feeling satisfied and rather smug with the way his body had responded to the training. He was regaining his fitness, the additional weight around his torso melting away with each strenuous training session. Alice had put her arms around him last week and exclaimed, 'Uncle Jamie you're not so fat any more!' Maddie had been mortified and had told her off, but he had laughed at her childish honesty, and the praise of the five-year-old gave him a boost.

He finished putting on his shoes and zipped up his gym bag, heading out briskly to the car park. He was due to check-in at the hotel near the studio this afternoon and he still had to get home and pack. As he passed by Katie's car, he could see her at the wheel, her head bowed and the engine silent. He paused, unsure of what to do. Hesitantly, he approached and rapped on the window, hoping he wasn't interrupting some strange meditative ritual.

'Everything okay?' he asked, as she cranked the window down slowly, the old car lacking the swift luxury of electric windows.

'No,' she groaned. 'It won't start!'

She hit the steering wheel in frustration, a red flush high on her cheeks and her eyes shining with tears. Jamie dropped his bag to the ground and indicated for her to pull up the bonnet, but he couldn't see any obvious problems. She hovered over him, her eyes wide with anxiety.

'I think you'll have to call the AA.' He turned to her and sighed. 'You know, it'll probably cost more to fix the car than it's even worth. Why don't you get a new one?'

She looked down at the gritty black surface of the car park and nudged a small stone with her shoe. 'You're probably right,' she murmured.

'Want me to wait with you?'

She shook her head firmly. 'No, I'll be fine. Thanks though.'

'No problem, see you tomorrow.' He walked to his car, feeling guilty about leaving her there and wondering if he should stay regardless, but the way she had said no and the resolution in her voice had told him there was no point offering again.

Katie sat in the driver's seat for a while, sliding her thumbs over the wheel, half-heartedly trying the ignition every few minutes, hoping it might shudder into life. She knew the car had been on its last legs for a long while, but it reminded her so much of her dad that her heart ached to think about getting rid of it. There had been so many miles of driving to and from competitions and sessions in that car, just them on the road together, winding down the windows and listening to Iron Maiden and singing at the top of their voices. The car was a little piece of her dad she still had left and she didn't want to let it go.

Eventually, she resignedly punched in the number for the AA on her phone, blinking away the tears.

Chapter Six

The studio echoed with shrill nervous laughter as the participants prepared for the opening show. A competitive tension crackled in the air, each couple stealing furtive glances at the others, sizing up, comparing, as they completed the dress rehearsal.

Jamie stood awkwardly in his tight trousers as they waited for their practice turn. He had noted with satisfaction his new waist measurement, but the trousers clung to him and made him feel rather exposed. Katie had looked him up and down and given him a nod of approval, herself clad perfectly in denim blue and diamante, her hair braided back from her face and her eyes luminous.

Their run-through was smooth enough, though he still stumbled on one or two of the turns. The first live show was tomorrow so there was no more time to hone the routine. Jamie shrugged at Katie by way of apology and she shook her head gently at him as they skated off the studio rink. It had felt a lot smaller and more enclosed than the one they used for practice sessions. Jamie eyed it nervously, feeling his errors would look even bigger on a smaller patch of ice.

'Try not to stress about rehearsal errors. You can still pull this off tomorrow night,' Katie said reassuringly, as they both headed for the dressing rooms.

As Katie and Jamie were the last to rehearse, they arrived last at the pre-show briefing that was taking place at the studio after the dress rehearsals. Pushing through the heavy wooden doors to the conference suite, they entered into a hubbub of voices, a throng of participants and producers mingling over lukewarm wine and canapés. Jamie spotted Jo Harte and headed over to her. She grinned at him as he approached, brushing a hand through her peroxide-blonde hair, still sticky from the hairspray applied for the dress rehearsal.

'Jamie!' she said, greeting him happily with a kiss. 'Good to see you again.'

'How's things, Jo? Your routine looked pretty good from what I saw in the rehearsal,' Jamie replied.

'Thanks.' Jo gave a self-conscious smile. 'It surprised me how nervous I was. I'm so used to skating on a flat board – this is so much harder than I thought it would be.'

Jamie nodded. 'I know what you mean. I'm just constantly trying not to fall flat on my face.' He looked around at the group. 'Have you met everyone properly yet?'

Jo scanned the room. 'Mostly. There hasn't been much time to chat, but everyone seems pretty nice. How's it going with your skating buddy?' she said, with a nod at Katie, who was across the room deep in conversation with Carmen, a stunning Latina ice dancer who had been paired with Derek Hayward, the sprinter.

Jamie looked over at Katie. 'She's all right.' He leaned closer to Jo and said in a low voice: 'We're hardly best friends though.'

Jo chuckled. 'I'm not surprised. She has a reputation as a tough cookie.'

'What about your partner?' Jamie asked, realising he couldn't remember the name of the guy Jo had been paired with.

'Andy? He's a sweetie,' said Jo, referring to Andy Gilkov, her American skating partner. 'He's so funny, cracks me up all the time.' She smiled and was about to add something but was interrupted.

'Everyone, a moment of your time please,' a commanding voice boomed out over the chatter. 'I'm Donald, the lead producer, and I'm delighted to welcome you all as we enter the final countdown to our first show.' Donald's steely eyes roved the room as a few of the people cheered excitedly. He cleared his throat to continue.

'We're thrilled you've decided to join in our new venture

of taking seasoned professional athletes and asking them to turn their natural physical giftings and competitive edges to the unique and challenging sport of figure skating. We're so excited to see what you can do!'

He paused, placing the tips of his fingers together carefully.

'Most of you will have met already and if you haven't, I'm sure you'll get to know each other very well in the coming weeks. However, due to some contractual wrangling, we were not able to reveal everyone who would be involved ... until now.'

He grinned widely, tiny beads of sweat gathering on his forehead and round his temples.

'We're delighted to announce the final professional skater joining our family for the next few months and forming the third and final member of our judging panel – Alex Michaelson!'

An astonished murmur rippled through the room as Alex stepped forward through the door behind Donald. He grinned and gave the room a wave, his other hand nonchalantly in his pocket. In tight black jeans and a white T-shirt, he looked more like a rock star than a figure-skater. His hazel eyes gleamed as he looked around the room, his raven hair artfully ruffled to look as though he had just rolled out of bed.

Oh, this'll be interesting, thought Jamie, as many eyes turned knowingly towards Katie. All the colour had left her face, leaving her already pale skin alabaster white. She pressed her lips into a thin line, her arms crossed and head lowered as Alex stepped forward to address the room. Her hair curtained her face so Jamie couldn't see her expression while Alex spoke.

'Thanks for the warm welcome, Donald,' he began. 'I'm so thrilled to be part of this new show and to bring my experience as an Olympic and World champion to the judging panel. I can't wait to see how you all perform each week and whether or not you'll find skating as tough, or perhaps tougher, than your other disciplines.'

He paused with a smile, his eyes coming to rest on Katie. 'Some of you I already know very well, and others I look forward to getting to know over the coming weeks. Good luck everyone!' He stepped back and shook Donald's hand while the room applauded warmly and people scattered to murmur in their huddles.

Katie's heart stuttered as Alex addressed the room. She had sworn never to have any contact with him after what he did, and to stand in the same room as him and hear his voice once again, made her shake with anger. She could feel the weight of people's stares on her as she stood tense and still, tracing the patterns in the carpet, her chest tight.

Carmen touched her lightly on the arm. 'Are you okay?' she asked, her eyes full of concern.

Katie looked up at her. 'Fine,' she said, through gritted teeth, her hands tucked into fists underneath her armpits. Carmen was about to say something, but Katie knew she'd seen Alex gliding through the room towards them out of the corner of her eye. She gave Katie a polite smile. 'I'm just going to chat to Derek,' she said, and drifted away to look for her partner.

Katie took a deep shaky breath and turned around just as Alex reached her. They hadn't seen each other properly since the accident but Alex hadn't changed at all. He was still lithe as a puma, a half-smile on his lips as he tilted his head to look down at her, an intense adoration lighting up his eyes so they glowed like liquid gold. She tried not to flinch as he leaned in towards her and extended his hand hopefully. 'Katie ...' he said, softly.

Katie knew people were watching as Alex stood for a moment with his hand outstretched, a wistful smile on his face. With her chin tilted up, she glared at him with silent rage, her jaw clenched. She had so much she wanted to say to him, but her throat was so tight she knew she couldn't speak a single word. She spun on her heels and walked away from him and out of the room, feeling everyone's eyes on her, sensing the hush that had come over the room at the awkwardness of the meeting. She knew people would pity Alex for her coldness and her lack of forgiveness, but she didn't care.

Katie walked as fast as she could through the vinyl-floored halls of the building, pushing on every heavy wooden door as hard as she could so they swung open before her, and practically ran through the glass doors of the exit. She took deep hard breaths of the cold winter air, dragging its purity into her lungs to cool her furious thoughts.

She had made up her mind. She was quitting the show.

Then

Katie felt completely lost. She tried to hang onto the music in the background, but it faded and skipped in her mind. Her eyes were unfocused, and she was losing time. She tried to focus on the ice, but waves of grief threatened to engulf her and her chest was too tight to breathe properly.

She checked out of her triple axel too early and fell heavily, pain shooting through her ribs and her hip, as she slid to a stop. The music carried on echoing around the rink as she curled up by the barriers and a warm river of salty tears ran down her cheeks. She shivered as the chill of the ice seeped through her clothes and into her skin.

There were very few people there that morning at the patch ice session. One skater looked across with concern and started towards her, fearing she might be hurt, but she waved across at him roughly. 'I'm fine,' she called out shakily, and pushed herself up before skating sore and trembling to the seats. She had the right to have her music playing that morning, but she cut it short and sat in silence, leaving the ice to the handful of other skaters as a thousand thoughts crashed in her head.

Her hip throbbed and burned. She tried not to let the panic rising from her stomach clamber into her throat, otherwise, she feared she would start sobbing hysterically there and then where she sat on that plastic chair. In the space of a few weeks, everything that had filled her life had melted away and she felt utterly alone and completely helpless.

Ivan's decision to retire after she won gold at the Olympics wasn't a shock. He had been open about it with her and her dad from the moment he'd chosen to move back to Canada. Seeing him leave cast a long shadow over the victory of winning but she knew she could find another coach. She could have coped with that change – as huge and scary as it seemed at the time – if that had been the only curveball she had to deal with.

It had been in the throes of her Olympic success and amidst the mania surrounding her victory that her dad's heart had also decided to retire from active service. Katie put a hand to her head and tried not to rerun the details of that day, though they replayed behind her eyes every time she closed them and every night when she tried to sleep. She relived his death, again and again, the scenes in her mind indistinct like a nightmare but always with the same outcome – he was gone and would never come back.

She had to shut out the world's demands on her as she struggled to get through the probate paperwork. Interviews and sponsorship deals, and looking for a new coach, felt utterly impossible. She ignored press and media requests, shunned agents, simply deleted emails and voicemails. She was only eighteen and felt entirely alone and completely incapable of coping, and it felt easier to bury her head in the sand.

And then there were the bills. She was shocked when she found out how much money her dad had spent on her skating – all of the hospital settlement money from her mum's death plus money stacked onto credit cards over the years she had been skating. She waded through maximum limits, overdrafts and overdues with mounting horror at the debt her dad had built up while she had thought only of winning and only of herself.

Her dad was buried but the demands on his estate remained for her. She would shut the door and turn out the lights, ignore the phone calls and pray she would wake up in a different time when this wasn't happening. Katie knew she had to find solutions, accept the interview requests, start looking for sponsors, but she couldn't even find the energy to brush her teeth some days. Picking up the phone seemed like climbing Everest. Skating was an impossibility until recently and even though she could get down to the rink some days, nothing seemed to work any more.

She had no idea what she was going to do.

Katie dragged herself from bed, her head pounding and her throat dry from sobbing into her pillow all night. Grief held her in a tight grasp – it had taken up residence in her heart and invaded her body so even simple movements felt impossible. Her limbs felt heavy and uncoordinated as though the blood had been squeezed out of them.

The only routine she had left was going to the rink, and she knew if she didn't force herself to go, there would only be empty hours to fill and she couldn't bear the silence of the flat that she and her dad had shared, couldn't bear to be immersed in his memory all day with no respite from the ghost of his presence. She kept expecting him to walk in any minute, to hear his key turn in the door followed by him strolling in with milk and a packet of custard creams from the corner shop.

She ignored the pile of unopened letters and unanswered voicemails and hurried out of the flat, slamming the door on the memories crowded behind it, begging her to stay and wallow in them.

She had a slightly better day on the ice than last time. Other skaters were there with their coaches, so she kept to the edges of the rink and worked on her spins, imagining herself to be like wet clothes being wrung out in a spin cycle, drops of pain and sadness flying out from her, leaving her crumpled but clean.

Katie's hair was damp against the nape of her neck when she took a break and stretched out her muscles. She sipped a Lucozade and closed her eyes for a moment as she sat by the rink, trying to keep her mind clear and blank like water, batting away her worries as they tried to intrude on her thoughts.

'Katie?'

A small man stood before her, his oversized jacket crumpled at his shoulders, his thinning grey hair parted neatly to one side. Katie vaguely recognised him, wracking her brain for a moment to remember his name. Sergei Varnier.

'Hello,' she said, warily.

'I saw you practising your spins,' he said, his accent clipped and crisp. Katie wasn't sure where he was from; she thought maybe somewhere in Eastern Europe. 'It was good. I hope you don't mind that I watched.' He looked out over the ice and the other skaters, shaking his head with a small amused smile.

'Not at all. What brings you here? I didn't think you coached anyone here?'

He smiled at her. 'I was told this was where you trained and I wanted to introduce myself.' He extended a hand and she shook it, surprised at the coarseness of his skin, which seemed out of place next to his neatly trimmed nails. 'I am Sergei Varnier, and I am Alex Michaelson's coach.'

She nodded. 'It's nice to meet you properly,' she said. The memories had filtered back to her in that moment, and she could recall that their paths had crossed at various events where Alex had also competed, but she hadn't spoken much to either of them at the time.

'I was sorry to hear about your father's death,' he said carefully, observing her with dark watchful eyes.

'Yes, thank you,' she murmured, looking at the floor, not really in the mood to talk about it and bring up all those emotions, just when she had managed to keep them in check for an hour.

'So, what are your plans now, Katie?' Sergei asked her, shuffling his shoulders inside his jacket.

She shrugged and twisted a loose thread on the hem of her fleece. 'I'm not sure.' It wasn't a question she wanted to be asked, as she had no idea how to answer it. Sergei nodded, and they were both silent for a moment. Katie felt there was more he wanted to say and waited expectantly, wondering what he could want.

'Alex is looking to skate in pairs now.'

She looked up at him, eyes wide.

He chuckled softly. 'I can see that news is a surprise to you. Well, Alex is very unpredictable.' He shook his head, grinning at the whims of his protégé whom he had coached since the very beginning of his career. Sergei continued, drumming his fingers gently on the barrier to the rink. 'He is the best male skater in the world. You are the best female skater in the world. Imagine what you could do together ...'

Katie sat mutely for a moment, unsure of what to say. She hadn't considered turning to pairs skating at this point in her career, although she had always thought of it as an option and Ivan had told her never to rule it out. Pairs skating opened up a whole new set of things to try. The thought of being able to do a quad throw made her shiver with just the thrill of the idea, not to mention the lifts; the chance to soar over the ice and truly fly. The daredevil in her was enticed by the very thought of it.

'I don't know what to say.' Katie didn't know how to make this kind of decision, not without her dad, not with the way she felt now. She could barely answer the question Sergei left hanging in the air, let alone make any concrete plans.

'Look, why don't we get you, me and Alex to meet for a coffee, and we can have a little chat, yes?'

She nodded, suddenly feeling tired out from the effort of making even minimal conversation.

'Tomorrow?'

'Sure.'

'Good. Give me your number and I will text you where and when.' He extended a pen and a scrap of paper and she jotted down her mobile number for him. He gave her a polite nod and walked away, his steps echoing around the rink as her mind raced with possibility and her body ached with fatigue from the weight of her grief.

Chapter Seven

'Did she take it badly?' Donald asked Hannah, as they sat in his office discussing final plans for the show.

'It took about ten minutes after Alex's reveal yesterday for her to email telling me she was quitting,' replied Hannah, an amused smile on her face as she studied her nails.

'Well, that didn't take her long!' Donald said, laughing.

Hannah chuckled. 'Not to worry. I told her to check the small print and said we would be in touch shortly with a breach of contract case and that she better consult a lawyer.'

'And …?'

'And she backed down. I guess she doesn't have the money.' Hannah's lips curved into a satisfied smile. 'I would feel sorry for her, but Alex is *such* a sweetheart, and she was so rude to him at the briefing. He genuinely looked like he was going to cry.'

She leaned closer to Donald over the substantial wooden desk, her eyes wide as she lowered her voice confidentially. 'You know he's still totally hung up on her,' she said. 'He practically told me so himself.' She sighed and put a hand over her heart. 'It's so sad.'

Of course Alex hadn't been honest with her about something so private, but she knew from the wistful tone in his voice and the forlorn expression in his eyes that he wasn't over Katie. Hannah knew there was plenty of drama to work with, lots of things they could do to bring those two back together again and maximise interest in the show. Hannah only hoped Katie wouldn't be so cold-hearted and would warm up to Alex once the show started. She could only imagine what the headlines would be like if they could somehow get those two to fall for each other again.

Donald's forehead creased as a frown flitted across his face. 'What I don't understand is why you paired her with that rugby oaf,' he said, sternly. 'I want Katie to stay in the competition as long as possible, but you've given her a terrible match with Jamie Welsh.'

Hannah cringed inwardly at her mistake. She knew she had screwed up on the pairings, and her brain scrabbled for someone more junior to blame. 'Marsha mixed up the pairs. Before I knew it, they were training together and it would have looked suspicious to switch for no good reason.' She kept her voice steady and her eyes level with Donald's, hoping he wouldn't realise it was actually her mistake.

'Still, imagine if she was skating with Theo Jarvis, how jealous Alex would be ...' Donald said, wistfully, imagining the additional layer of drama it would add to the show. 'Plus, Theo's bound to have a good run in the show, and she wouldn't be in danger of leaving us too soon.'

Hannah tapped her fingers together, trying to think of a solution. 'I'll talk to the votes team. We'll make sure Katie and Jamie stay in.'

'Good.' Donald nodded. 'Do what you have to do.'

Katie sank down onto the bed as she scrolled through the headlines on her phone, her thumb swiping anxiously up and down the screen.

"Alex Michaelson to Judge New Ice Dance Show"
"Skating Stars To Be Reunited"
"Can Katie and Alex Finally Break the Ice?"

Alex's face was everywhere she looked, that cocky half-smile and those perfect cheekbones staring at her underneath news stories that trumpeted his involvement in the show. The rumour mill was in full swing and Katie saw her and Alex's names, side by side, again and again, across the gossip pages. She couldn't read any more and was about to slap her phone down when a message buzzed through from Jamie.

Are you okay? You left pretty quick yesterday.

Katie was dreading the live show that evening. The thought of having to be on camera and be judged by Alex was sickening, and she couldn't back out, the producers had made that very clear. She was trapped and she had to go through with it.

I'm fine, she texted back to Jamie, her shaking fingers tapping out the letters, barely registering that he had been concerned enough to ask her how she was. *'See you soon.'*

She stood up to gather her things that she'd spread over the cheap polyester bedcover in the budget hotel near the studio. She was grateful to be in a hotel close by, especially with her car still busted, though the sports stars had been put up somewhere much more extravagant than the pro skaters. Fortunately, Alex was also staying in the much nicer hotel along with the sports stars, so she didn't have to worry about bumping into him over the noxious breakfast buffet or running into him in the garishly carpeted hallways.

Katie had never really enjoyed staying in hotels, as her sense of loneliness was always heightened when she was in one. She would sit in her bland room, hearing the voices chattering in the corridors as the other guests passed by, and feel small and contained in her little carpeted box with only the TV for company. She didn't particularly like her flat but at least it was home, and she felt less lonely there than in the hotel. It was only for two nights each week, she consoled herself, already looking forward to checking out the day after the first show had been completed. She just had to get through tonight's ordeal first.

She sighed and grabbed her bag and her room card as her phone pinged to let her know her driver was waiting outside. She thought sadly of her trusty old Vauxhall that couldn't be fixed, and headed downstairs to the waiting taxi, the hours till the first show closing in.

The atmosphere in the studio pulsed with urgency and excitement. Katie watched from the edge of the rink as the lights were tested, the neon pinks and luminous greens dancing over the ice, choreographed to go with each routine. She glanced over at where the judges would be sitting, and shuddered. She knew this had been a bad idea right from the beginning and wished with all her heart she could find a way out of it. She had even considered pulling out because of her ankle injury, but the doctors for the show were checking on her each week so they would know she was lying.

Jamie tapped her on the shoulder and she swung round, feeling tense and edgy.

'Hey,' he said. 'Are you getting ready anytime soon?'

She sighed, trying to exhale away some of her tension. 'Sure, just about to head to get changed now.' They turned and walked together. 'Are you nervous?'

Jamie gave a half-grin. 'A little,' he said. She gave him a look and he laughed. 'Okay, a lot.'

Her gaze softened. She knew what it was like to feel nervous before competing. 'It'll be okay,' she said, patting him gently on the arm. 'You can do this.'

He smiled and walked away to get himself ready. Katie walked down the corridor past the dressing rooms, where the sports participants had a large room each to themselves, and where the professional skaters were sharing two to a room. The metallic tang of hairspray hung in the air, mingled with the unmistakable earthy smell of fake tan. Katie was glad she had refused to take part in the tanning – it had never complemented her look.

A slightly frazzled woman with a clipboard approached her. 'Right Katie, let's get you in costume, please. Hair and make-up are scheduled in for you as well.'

Katie followed her obediently to get ready.

Jamie stood looking at himself in the mirror, his costume on. A touch of gel in his hair darkened the roots and kept it slicked back so it wouldn't turn into a sweaty mop during his performance. He was thankful they'd allowed him to wear dark colours so the sweat wouldn't show through, as he was already damp with perspiration. He didn't know if it was the warmth of the changing room or nerves, but he could feel an increasing clamminess at his lower back and under his arms. He was looking fit and toned again though, he thought, as he checked his reflection. His muscle definition was returning from underneath the layer of self-pitying bingeing damage he had wrought on his body in the past two years.

'Jamie, it's nice to meet you.'

Jamie looked round to see Alex standing behind him, lounging in the doorway of his dressing room. They were roughly the same height at six foot two, but the similarities ended there. Alex was slender, his muscles toned and lithe under his tightly fitting shirt. His features were like pale carved marble, his jet-black hair and his golden eyes giving him an almost vampiric look.

Jamie shook Alex's outstretched hand, the fingers long and tapering, his skin cool to the touch. 'Good to meet you.'

'So, you're skating with Katie,' Alex stated, his eyes scanning Jamie carefully.

'That's right.'

'How's she doing?' Alex asked, leaning nonchalantly against the doorframe.

Jamie wasn't quite sure what to say and shrugged awkwardly. 'Good. She's a tough teacher.'

Alex laughed, two rows of perfectly straight white teeth appearing behind his lips. 'I'd expect nothing less. She's …' He paused and ran his hand through his hair, smiling. 'Hard work.'

Jamie nodded. 'Right.'

'Well, good luck with the show tonight,' Alex said, putting his hands in his pockets and sauntering away. Jamie watched him leave and hoped he wouldn't be drawn into the middle of Alex and Katie's weird dynamic. He had enough to deal with as it was.

*

'Stop fidgeting,' Katie murmured to Jamie as they readied themselves at the edge of the rink, preparing to skate on and perform their routine.

'Sorry,' he whispered back, and tried to settle his limbs, which shivered with anxiety.

They both waited in silence as their introductions were played, including the interviews and clips of them in the practice sessions. Jamie felt Katie flinch as she watched, and knew she must be aware of how stilted and cold she came across.

Laughter murmured around the audience when they showed footage of Jamie stumbling again and again and Katie berating him, again and again. Jamie burned with humiliation at how the clips were edited to make him look like a graceless, uncoordinated idiot.

'Fuck 'em,' he said, glancing sideways at Katie.

She nodded firmly.

He slipped an arm around her waist and grabbed her hand as they propelled themselves forward to the centre of the rink as the show's presenter, Faith Mansfield, announced their names. Jamie's stomach jumped and suddenly he desperately wanted to show them all he wasn't a joke contestant, that he wasn't some bumbling fool and was sick of being thought of as a loser. He gritted his teeth and breathed hard through his nose, determined to try his best.

They faced each other in the centre of the ice, Katie's eyes like a calm sea, her lips softly outlining the count in to the routine. He focused on her and tried not to think about the laughter of the audience or the shaking in his knees.

Somehow Jamie managed to keep it together all the way through their dance, though he could barely remember a moment of it. He allowed his limbs to take over while his mind focused on keeping him breathing. Jamie's face must have gone blank with the effort of it all as Katie kept murmuring 'smile' to him each time they were close enough for him to hear her voice over the music.

He clung to her and he could feel her pulling him along, helping him when he nearly fell, a shudder of his ankle causing him to wobble dangerously. Katie saved him from falling, her calm hand gripping his arm, her momentum pulling him out of his unsteadiness. In rugby matches the anxious energy was easy to shake off as he ran up and down the pitch and smashed into the scrums, but here he had to control every muscle and force the nerves down so he could keep them contained. It was one of the most nerve-wracking and draining experiences of his life and he was gratefully stunned when the bright lights shone on them at the end and they awaited the judge's comments.

'Well done, Jamie,' said Tate kindly, in his Nebraskan drawl. He was wearing a sparkling black ensemble that glimmered in the studio lights every time he moved, which he did regularly as he spoke, his long arms emphasising each syllable. He was a strange and slender man, with thinning hair atop his pale pointy head and a quirky sense of style.

'You had some wobbles in the middle section, and you're pretty stiff, but I thought it was ... a good effort,' he concluded, smiling graciously at them both.

Jamie nodded but he could barely hear the words for the rush of adrenaline that was still pounding through his veins. Katie seemed composed by his side, not even out of breath, and she smiled up at him encouragingly as she heard Tate's comments.

Tate looked at Deborah for her to start her feedback. She pursed her lips and looked at her notes, her steel-grey hair gleaming in the light, not one strand out of place. 'Jamie, I thought you made a good effort, though I think your nerves came across, and yes, you did make some mistakes.'

'I thought the choreography was fun but neither of you particularly looked like you were enjoying it, I must say,' she continued. The audience laughed and Katie's mouth tugged down slightly at the corners, a tacit acknowledgement that Deborah was right.

Jamie felt Katie stiffen and take a deep breath as it came to Alex's turn to speak.

Alex opened his mouth but before he started, Deborah interjected quickly. 'And Katie, it's so lovely to see you back on the ice,' she said, with a smile, to cheers from the audience and solemn nods from Tate and Alex.

Katie gave her a wan smile in return as Alex began.

'Jamie, that was a really good try. It must be tough to switch from rugby to skating, so well done and I think you gave it a good shot. Your turns and footwork were a little … flabby, so try to tighten them up,' Alex said, a hard gleam in his eye. He paused and leaned forward over the judging desk, hand on his chin and an impish grin on his face. 'You're very lucky to have such a talented and beautiful partner to skate with.'

Jamie thought he could actually hear Katie's jaw bone grinding as she twisted her hands together behind her back and looked impassively at Alex.

The audience loved it and cheered and a piercing wolf whistle rang out over the top of the din. Alex leaned back and chuckled. Jamie and Katie turned and skated off the ice, waving to the audience. Jamie could see Katie smiling but it looked tight and unnatural to him, and she clutched his hand so fiercely that blood squeezed from his fingers.

'That was okay, right?' Jamie murmured to her as they skated back, but Katie didn't respond.

'Hey,' he poked her on the arm.

'Sorry, what?' She turned and looked blankly at him as they came off the ice and undid their skates.

'That was okay wasn't it?' he asked again, irritated by her distraction.

'Yes, you did well,' she said, but her eyes weren't encouraging and Jamie's heart sunk.

They walked to the interview area, and Faith Mansfield was there with her supercharged smile, brandishing a microphone at them both to conduct their interview. Jamie tried to be positive, and not get distracted by Faith's magnificent cleavage, but he was pretty sure that neither he nor Katie came across as quite sincere.

The dancers and athletes gathered on the ice to hear the results of the public vote, and Katie was sure she and Jamie would be in the bottom two. They stood between Theo and Maria, and Vicky, who was skating with Eric Bowen. Katie could hear Theo murmuring and Maria giggling, but she stared rigidly ahead, waiting for the results to be announced by Faith. Angry thoughts about Alex were still crashing around in her mind and it was hard to focus on anything else.

Some of the skating pairs held hands or looped their arms around each other. Jamie and Katie's arms touched but they stood stiffly side by side. Katie could feel how jittery Jamie was as he waited to hear if he'd done enough to stay in the show. She imagined he was probably desperate to avoid the humiliation of being the first one voted off and she felt a pang of sympathy for him as he shifted nervously beside her.

Faith turned to the camera and turned on her megawatt smile, her perfect black curls shining and crisp in the studio lights.

'And now we have the results of the public vote. You have decided who will get to skate another week and who will go in the skate-off. Here we go.'

She listened into her earpiece.

'The first pair to be saved by the public is ...' She paused for dramatic effect. 'Theo and Maria!'

Maria squealed next to Katie as Theo picked her up and celebrated. Katie wasn't at all surprised – their routine was good. Theo was already extremely confident on the ice, and he and Maria made a gorgeous pair. Their sizzling chemistry was obvious even at this early stage in the competition, and the gossip columns were already buzzing about it.

Faith continued. 'The second pair to be saved by you is Rory and Anna! Congratulations!'

Jamie looked over at Rory and gave him an approving nod as Rory fist-pumped the air in triumph, laughing. Katie raised her eyebrows. Rory had skated terribly, but he was so sweet and jovial, she guessed the public had really warmed to him despite his lack of control on the ice.

The remaining pairs stood tensely as the third result was about to be announced. Katie felt that if Rory was voted through, surely the audience would spare Jamie too? After all, he had done pretty well that night. She heard him breathing deeply and she gently placed her hand on his wrist to give him a reassuring squeeze.

'The next pair to go through to the second week is … Jamie and Katie! Well done!'

Jamie grabbed Katie's arms with his large warm hands and grinned at her as she gaped in surprise. 'Yes!' he exclaimed, and she had to laugh at his delighted face. They left the ice to applause from the audience, greeting the other saved pairs at the edge of the rink.

Katie was genuinely surprised and the rest of the results passed her by in a haze, leaving Angela and Derek as the final two athletes who would have to go to the skate-off. The two pairs dashed off the ice to prepare as the others headed backstage to sit down.

Katie walked to the changing room she shared with Carmen. It was a sparsely furnished room with two chairs and a coffee table, space to change and store their clothes, and a large mirror on the wall. Katie sank into one of the black leather chairs, grateful for the relative stillness and quiet.

She could hear the audience and the studio gearing up for the next section of the show with the skate-off, but she stayed still, running through their routine in her mind, like she used to do immediately after a competition, obsessively analysing her performance again and again. She was deep in thought when Carmen bounded in.

Katie looked up, startled at the silence being broken, unaware the show had finished and that she had completely missed the result.

'Angela got voted off!' Carmen exclaimed, throwing her skates down carelessly and stretching a slender leg out in front of her and onto the coffee table.

'I thought she might be in danger – she was so stiff on the ice,' said Katie, smiling at Carmen. 'I'm so glad you and Derek are staying in.' Katie meant it – she didn't know Carmen particularly well, but she seemed kind-hearted and Katie would rather be sharing with her than the others.

Carmen nodded. 'I'm so glad Derek and I can stay another week.' She fanned herself dramatically.

For some reason, Anna had followed Carmen into their changing room, and went straight to the mirror, checking her reflection and stroking her sleek hair. 'I can't believe Rory and I are still in the competition,' Anna interjected, reapplying her lip gloss and turning round to check her reflection.

'Neither can I,' Carmen said, grinning at Katie, who tried to suppress a smile as Anna scowled, looking peeved.

'Katie, a bunch of us are going out for a few drinks – you wanna come?' Carmen asked, smiling over at her. 'If your partner or family are around you can invite them too – my boyfriend's coming.'

Katie thought for a second. It might be nice to relax for a bit, throw off the stress of the show, maybe chat to Theo …

Anna looked over quickly. 'Yeah, it'll be a great chance for all the skaters and the *judges* to get to know each other,' she said, pointedly.

Katie knew what she meant. Alex would be going, which meant there was no way she would. She shook her head, feeling disappointed.

'Thanks for the invite, but I'm wiped out,' she said. 'Maybe next time?'

Carmen shrugged. 'Sure.'

As Carmen left the room Anna hovered, eventually sidling awkwardly closer to where Katie sat. Katie looked at her, wondering why she was still there in her and Carmen's changing room.

'It must be so nice to skate again, Katie, after that terrible accident,' Anna said. 'Even if it is just on a reality show and not the Olympics.'

Katie couldn't tell whether or not she was being sincere or gloating; her dark brown eyes were inscrutable, a small smile played on her freshly glossed lips.

Katie sighed and ran her hand over her hair, still tight and crisp from the hairspray the stylist had loaded it with. 'Yes, well, it's nice to be back on the ice at least,' she said.

'And how lucky for you that you're so well acquainted with the judging panel. I bet that'll make life easier,' Anna said, raising an eyebrow with a smug grin.

Katie frowned at her. 'What's that supposed to mean?' she snapped. She had always hated snide comments and would rather people just say what they meant.

Anna plastered on an innocent expression. 'Oh, you know, only that Alex would surely never mark you down, with all your history and all, and with the way he still feels about you …' She trailed off, fishing for gossip.

Katie glared at her sharply. 'You have no idea what you're talking about.'

Anna shrugged and bounced out of the door, her shiny brown bob swishing neatly, calling out over her shoulder, 'See you next week!'

The thrill of not being voted off was starting to wear off and Katie's heart sank as Anna's words brought reality back home – she would have to skate for Alex again next week. She rested her head in her hands before she roused herself to pack up and return to the budget hotel.

Then

Katie walked into the coffee shop. She was dead on time, but Alex and Sergei were already there, Alex with his hands wrapped around a large steaming black coffee, Sergei with an espresso. Alex unfolded his long slender legs from underneath the table and stood up eagerly to greet her as she approached.

'Hey Katie, so nice to see you.' He leaned in and gave her a loose hug. He tilted his head to one side and looked at her earnestly. 'I'm so sorry about your dad.'

She gave him a weak smile. 'Thank you.'

Sergei hadn't risen and he pointed to the empty chair at the table. 'Please, sit. I'll get you a coffee?'

'Just tea would be fine, thank you,' she said, carefully putting her jacket on the back of the chair and taking a seat.

Alex leaned back in his chair, his raven hair swept back from his face. 'How are things?' he asked, with a concerned expression.

'So-so,' she said, unwilling to go into detail about how despairing she actually felt. She rubbed her hands on her jeans and tried to keep her voice light. 'Trying to keep busy. You?'

He grinned at her. 'Things are pretty good with me.'

Sergei returned with a mug of tea and set it before her, a small amount of it sloshing over the side. 'So, let's get down to discussions,' he said, his voice clipped and curt.

Alex interrupted him as he was about to start talking. 'Katie, I'm sure this is a tough time for you, and you know, this is just an idea. So, no pressure.' He smiled warmly at her and held up his hands.

Sergei made to speak again and Alex carried on regardless, leaning towards her over the tabletop, pushing his coffee to one side.

'See, I want to be the best in every aspect of skating, as I'm sure you do. And I'm looking for a new challenge, with a partner. I want to do jumps and lifts and throws that no one else dares to do or can even try,' he said intently, gazing into her eyes as he spoke.

'I know it's a lot to ask, and some would think it was crazy to give up individual competitions. But we're already at the top of our game individually,' Alex said persuasively. 'By teaming up to skate in pairs we'll learn new things we could never do as individuals. We could be the new Torvill and Dean.'

Katie had to smile at his ambition and his enthusiasm. From anyone else, it would have sounded ridiculous, but from Alex Michaelson, it sounded plausible. Logical, even. Some people called him arrogant, but Katie thought that anyone with his prodigious talent could afford to be so confident.

'You can do the triple axel. You're fearless on the ice, you're the best, you're …' He bit his lip with a grin. 'Beautiful. I think you and I would make the most amazing match, Katie.'

She looked down at the table with a smile and blushed, warmth spreading through her cheeks and a twist of pleasure knotting her stomach at his compliments. She knew they would make a striking pair – with their pale skin and dark hair, both very rhythmic on the ice with strong technical skills. She understood why he had asked her and felt a thrill at the flattery of his suggestion – he was after all the best male skater the UK had seen for many years. Katie had always been in awe of him, especially when they bumped into each other at various competitions and she had been too shy to talk to him properly and too busy with her preparations with Ivan and her dad to approach him. Although Alex was just two years older than her at twenty years old, she had always thought of him as much more experienced than her. Now she was sitting here with him and he considered her his equal, enough to ask her to partner with him. Katie's stomach knotted with excitement. It was the first time in weeks that she had felt anything other than hopeless, all-consuming grief.

'Are you talking to anyone else about this?' she asked, glancing up at him shyly, hoping the warmth in her cheeks had subsided.

Sergei shook his head. 'No. You are the first choice. The only choice.'

She sipped her tea, which was insipid and cool, and tried not to look too pleased.

Sergei clasped his hands neatly in front of him on the table. 'Another thing you should think about. We train in Guildford – it's not far from you, so you wouldn't have to move. I will be your coach, and Alex and I have a programme and a plan for the next four years leading up to the next Winter Olympics. We are ready to work.'

Alex nodded eagerly as Sergei carried on. 'We have plenty of sponsorship and there will be more if you two team up, after all, you both won gold at the recent Olympics. It will be an easy sell to sponsors. You won't have to worry about anything – it will all be done for you.'

A wave of relief washed over Katie. She wouldn't have to worry about money. She would have a coach and a plan again. She could focus on her skating and she wouldn't be alone every single day. Suddenly, she felt as though the path before her, which had been obscured by fear and debt and loneliness, was now lit up – with the possibility of another Olympic gold glowing in the distance. Alex was offering her a brilliant, shining opportunity, a new career path, and most importantly, the support and friendship she so desperately needed right now when, at eighteen, she found herself entirely alone and deeply afraid of the future. A nagging voice in her head told her to walk away and give this huge decision some thought, but Katie didn't want to think, didn't want to take her time, didn't want to feel as though it was her on her own anymore. It felt like she was drowning and Alex was throwing her a rope, and she reached out to seize it.

She put her mug down on the table as Alex stared at her, his eyes blazing hopefully.

'I'll do it.'

Chapter Eight

Jamie loved his mum's Sunday roasts. It was a family tradition for them all to get together on Sundays, no matter how crazy things were. It was an anchor he held to, the smell of gravy and home and the sense of being truly nourished not just physically, but emotionally too. Cassandra had never cooked roast dinners and hadn't wanted to go to his family's every weekend – a long-running source of friction in their marriage. At least he didn't have to worry about that any more.

Family felt more important to him now than it had ever done. When he was at home with them, ensconced in their cheerful domesticity, he felt less lonely. They didn't think of him as Jamie the screw-up, the one who lost the World Cup, the cheater. With them, he had the freedom to just be Jamie – brother, son, uncle. He was grateful for all the regular occasions throughout the year, the birthdays, the anniversaries, Easter, Christmas, Sunday lunches, when he got to enjoy that feeling of being loved regardless of his mistakes.

The sky was a dull grey outside when he pulled up on his parents' driveway, the gravel pleasingly crunchy underfoot and shining from the recent rain. He pushed open the front door, wiping his feet, and Alice and Isabelle came running to greet him.

'Uncle Jamie!' they cried out, ploughing into his legs. He laughed, swinging them both up under his arms and carried them, squealing, into the kitchen at the back of the house. The warmth of the cooking enveloped him, taking away the damp chill from outside. He set the girls down and they promptly ran off again to play.

His mum was behind the counter, stirring cornflour into a small cup, a soft sprinkle of white falling onto the kitchen worktop as she drew the spoon from the packet.

'Hi, Mum.' He stepped forward to kiss her on the cheek, which was ruddy from the heat of the oven.

'Hello love,' she said. 'You did so well last night, we were all so proud of you.'

Maddie came and leaned on the counter, head on her hands, as their dad methodically carved pink moist slices of gammon. 'I was on a night shift at the hospital but I watched it this morning, and bro, you did great,' she said, tucking a strand of blonde hair behind one ear.

'I couldn't quite believe it was you out there on the ice,' his dad added, passing Jamie a tender slice of meat to try.

Maddie laughed. 'You almost looked graceful!'

Jamie grinned and shook his head, nibbling the ham. 'Liar! I was all over the place.'

'Dad this is perfect,' he said, nodding with approval at the gammon.

Jamie helped to scoop piles of food onto freshly warmed plates, as Maddie went to fetch Alice and Isabelle. The plates were passed around with eager expectation as everyone took their usual places at the table.

'No Harriet today?' Jamie asked, glancing at Maddie. She made a disappointed face.

'Nope, she has a big case she's working on, so she's at home drowning in papers,' she said.

Jamie felt a flicker of disappointment that he wouldn't get to see her. Maddie first came out to him when she was sixteen, and he had wondered what it would be like for his sister to bring girlfriends home, and whether or not it would be awkward and weird. As it turns out, he and Harriet got on like a house on fire. The first time he had met her, he had turned to Maddie and told her never to let Harriet go. Fortunately, she had taken her little brother's advice – not that he was any kind of relationship expert, as time had proven.

'What are you going to be skating to next week?' Susan asked excitedly, trying to help Alice cut her potatoes into smaller chunks.

'Not sure yet,' Jamie said, smothering his plate in gravy. 'Katie will let me know at practice tomorrow.'

'It would be so nice if she and Alex could get back together,' said Maddie dreamily. 'They were such a beautiful couple.'

'Just imagine if they could skate together again,' said Susan, wistfully. 'They were so promising together. Like the new Torvill and Dean.'

Jamie smiled grimly. 'I don't think that's going to happen.'

'Why?' Susan leaned forward, hoping for some insider information.

'Just that Katie still seems pretty mad at him.'

'After all this time?' asked his dad, shaking his head. 'That's no way to live. Gotta forgive and forget, and move on.'

Maddie and Susan nodded in agreement, their heads bobbing in unison.

'I feel sorry for the guy. I think he still really likes her,' said Jamie, thinking of the way Alex's face had crumpled when she turned her back on him after he was announced as the third judge.

'Such a shame,' Maddie sighed, 'although it looks as though Theo and his partner are getting pretty close, right J? So, there's got to be one romance at least!'

Jamie shrugged but before he could reply, Alice and Isabelle started to squabble, diverting the attention of the table.

As he ate, Jamie hoped the awkwardness between Alex and Katie could be resolved soon so they could focus on the show. It seemed that all anyone could talk about was whether or not she and Alex would get back together, and he was starting to feel overshadowed by their personal issues. It was just his luck to be assigned to skate with Katie – as great as she was on the ice, he was starting to think he would prefer someone with less drama encircling them. He sighed and carried on eating, hoping his family wouldn't mention Alex and Katie again.

Katie scrolled restlessly through Twitter. She knew she shouldn't, but she was desperately curious to see what people were saying about the show. She couldn't quite stop her finger from continuing to scroll past comment after comment, GIF after GIF.

At least it was one way to stave off the boredom. Katie found Sundays terribly dull. She sipped from her mug of hot chocolate and winced at the thin sugariness. It wasn't like the hot chocolates her dad used to make her on Sunday afternoons. His were always thick and creamy, a perfect blend of milk and chocolate, with cream gently melting on the top, studded with tiny marshmallows. No matter how hard she tried, she could never quite make them like he used to.

She skipped over the tweets that were about Alex's comments to her on the show. She didn't want to know what other people thought about them and what the public wanted to see from them both. She had made the mistake years before of giving social media way too much power over her decisions. Now she had an account under a fake name to occasionally check things that interested her.

She didn't bother with Facebook and Instagram any more. They were a waste of time when she had no friends or family, plus it seemed that everywhere she looked, Alex was there, plastered all over her timeline, in her photo albums, tagged in memories that she would rather forget. She couldn't seem to get away from him.

She poked angrily at the stale mini marshmallow bobbing around in her hot chocolate, and turned off her phone.

'I didn't see you after the show,' Jamie said, lacing up his skates as they prepared for another intensive practice session before the second live show. 'It's a shame you didn't get to say goodbye to Angela.'

Katie looked down at the floor. 'I was a bit worn out,' she said, carefully.

Jamie leaned on one knee and faced her. 'It was a good night. You missed out.'

She nodded, clearly in no mood for chatting, and Jamie sighed inwardly at her stony silence. 'So, how do you think we did on Saturday? What are we working on next?' he said.

'You did well on Saturday night. It's not easy performing on ice for the first time,' she said. She smiled at him and he got the sense it was genuine, as for once the smile migrated to her eyes. 'That said, we can definitely improve. This week we need to add in some backwards skating, more complex footwork, and at least one spin. I still feel like it's too early for you to try proper lifts yet.'

He nodded, relieved. He knew he wasn't steady enough on the ice yet to try lifting Katie, as petite as she was, and he wouldn't want to be responsible for injuring her, especially not with her particular history of disastrous accidents.

'All the athletes are doing a group routine this week too,' he said, nervously.

She nodded. 'I know. I'll help you prepare, don't worry.'

'It's a lot to learn in one week,' he said, running a hand through his thick blond hair. It was still damp from that morning's shower and the slight wave in it was more pronounced than usual. His anxiety must have been obvious as Katie's expression softened a little.

'Look, I know I've been a little distracted by … well, other things,' she said, hesitantly. 'But we'll work really hard this week and I know you can do it.'

'Thanks,' Jamie said, relieved at her encouraging words. 'I hope I can.'

Katie glided over to where Jamie had tumbled onto the ice and lay, panting, flat on his back.

'Are you okay?' she said, her forehead furrowed with worry.

'I'm fine,' he groaned. 'I don't know how many more times I can take falling over in one day.' He slammed his fist down on the ice in frustration.

Katie offered him her hand as he sat up and he grabbed her

arm, his fingers wrapping completely around her forearm, and struggled to his feet. She could see the latest fall had shaken him and there was a tremor in both his voice and his legs as he got up from the ice.

'Listen, even the best skaters in the world fall and keep falling, all through their careers. It's just something that happens. The measure of how good you are is not how many times you fall, it's how many times you can get back up again,' she said, remembering what her dad used to say to her when she would cry with frustration at not being able to land the triple axel, and fell again and again during practice sessions.

'Very wise,' Jamie said, nodding unconvincingly, and stretching his back with a wince.

'It was something my dad used to say,' she said.

'Used to?' Jamie asked, as they skated to the barriers and leaned on them for a moment so he could take a rest.

'He passed away,' Katie said. 'Six years ago, from a heart attack.' She grimaced at just the words, let alone the terrible memories they evoked.

'Hey, I'm sorry. That's terrible,' said Jamie. 'I don't know what I'd do without my dad. He's always been there for me, even when things got messy,' he said thoughtfully, looking at her. 'You must miss him a lot?'

Katie leaned on her arm over the barriers. 'I do. He ferried me around for years, enabling me to do this career. He put everything he had into my skating, his whole heart and soul, all his money, all his time and energy.' She paused, looking out at the empty seats, not meeting Jamie's gaze. 'It's a shame it was all for nothing.'

Jamie raised his eyebrows. 'You're an Olympic gold medallist and a World Champion. I wouldn't call that nothing,' he said, gently.

Katie shook her head, her eyes still not meeting his. 'I just didn't think I would be doing shows like this in my twenties. I still feel like I had so much left to give.'

She looked at her skates so Jamie wouldn't see the tears that threatened her eyes.

'Listen, I know what it's like to have a career that ends before you're ready to let it go,' he said sadly. 'I understand how it feels to constantly wonder about the opportunities that you lost and how things might have been.'

Katie was surprised at how well Jamie knew what she was feeling. 'I know it sounds crazy, but it's like a kind of grief. You base your whole life around one thing, then it's gone and there's nothing that can fill that void,' she said.

'I get that,' said Jamie, nodding. 'But if it's any consolation, you managed to get me into week two. It's no gold medal, but I think that's a pretty big achievement considering how I skate.' He smiled and Katie laughed at him, turning towards him this time, grateful for his ability to lighten the mood.

He straightened up. 'I'm ready to carry on falling now.'

Katie followed him back to the centre of the ice, and thought that when Jamie wasn't hung-over, he seemed like such a nice guy, and he clearly loved his family a lot. It was such a shame, she thought, that underneath his nice-guy façade he was a cheat and a love rat.

Then

Jamie felt the pleasurable fog of alcohol numb his brain, the heat and the noise from the bar enveloping him like a comfortable blanket. The boys were in high spirits, the drinks were free, and he had nothing to do tomorrow except sleep off his hangover.

He squinted at his watch, the numbers fuzzy and jumping before his eyes: 3 a.m. He knew there was no point in going home. That opportunity had passed hours ago when he had kept on downing drink after drink, shot after shot. He would have to stay at the hotel. He was sure they would have a room for him, or he would just crash with one of his teammates. He hoped that Cassandra wouldn't mind. He hadn't had a good night out for a while and he needed to let off some steam.

He heard a loud, shrill giggle from one of the women who had joined them, one of a number of pretty young girls who were invited to come over by some of the team. Jamie grinned and resisted the urge to roll his eyes as the girls preened and tittered, flicking their hair and flirting hopefully. Some of the younger lads were always looking to score, both on and off the pitch. They weren't married, like he was, or if they were they didn't seem to care as much about their vows as Jamie did.

He didn't mind a bit of harmless flirting, but Cass was always in his heart, and even though they had their fights and he knew he wasn't the perfect husband, he couldn't ever imagine cheating on her.

He felt a hand on his arm and looked around to see a stunning brunette. She grinned at him.

'Hi Jamie,' she said, a little breathlessly, her eyes wide. Jamie couldn't help but notice how striking her eyes were; a pale aquamarine that glittered against her tanned skin. Her chocolate brown hair cascaded down her back, glossy and smooth. Her amazing curves were wrapped tightly in a fuchsia dress that skimmed her thighs and did little to hide her generous cleavage.

'Hi,' he said. He smiled at her, although his face was feeling numb from the alcohol. 'You are?'

'Cleo,' she said, shuffling a little closer to him. He studiously kept his eyes on her face. Jamie could see Harry casting admiring glances at her, but she had turned her back to him and was focusing her gleaming white smile on Jamie, the deep raspberry shade of her lip gloss shining in the dim light of the bar.

'It's so nice to meet you,' she said softly. 'I'm such a huge fan.'

'Thanks,' Jamie said, running his hands through his hair self-consciously. He was starting to feel woozy and the warm air of the bar suddenly felt cloying rather than comfortable. He took another gulp of whiskey and blinked hard. The floor was beginning to sway and the noises of the bar became an incoherent jumble of voices and laughter and glasses clinking. Jamie knew he was reaching the end of his tolerance, and should probably leave, but still he stayed, listening to Cleo's admiring chatter and her giggles, determined not to flake out early and be called an old man by his younger teammates. Even though he was only twenty-eight.

As dawn approached, Jamie found himself stumbling through thick carpeted hallways to a door he didn't recognise and opening it with a key card he didn't remember paying for. He didn't care. All that mattered to his weary head was the king-sized bed calling his name. He dived onto it and closed his eyes, waiting for the world to stop spinning as he passed out, too drunk and too tired to care where he was or who it was that gently climbed underneath the duvet with him.

The afternoon light felt like an attack on Jamie's head as he woke up. He scrunched his eyes against the intrusive sunshine streaming in through the curtains he had forgotten to close. His head ached, his throat was sore, and his stomach churned. He groaned and made his way to the bathroom with stumbling legs, splashing his face with cold water and gasping at the sting of it on his skin. He rinsed his mouth with mouthwash and gagged over the sink, swallowing hard and telling himself not to be sick. He glugged some water straight from the tap and stood still, breathing deeply, hoping his nausea would subside. As he did, he noticed a small tube by the sink: a deep raspberry lip gloss. He frowned at it in confusion. Could the previous guest have left it? Or perhaps he was in one of his mate's rooms and it was from someone they had hooked up with the night before?

Jamie rubbed his fingers over his eyes and went back to the bed, flopping onto it, and wondering whose room he was in. A blurry recollection of someone else there with him last night emerged from the fog of his hangover, but he couldn't quite remember who, and the memory faded along with the realisation that he was desperately hungry. He picked up the phone to order some food, and grabbed his mobile to check his messages. There was a slew of texts from Cass and he winced when he saw them, realising that he hadn't told her he wasn't coming home. What an idiot, he thought, berating himself as he texted her back, running through in his head where he could stop on the way home to buy her flowers as an apology. As much as Jamie enjoyed his nights out with the boys, he always looked forward to seeing Cass again the next day. He hoped she wouldn't be too pissed off with him.

His phone beeped and he expected it to be from Cass, but instead it was a message from a number he didn't recognise.

Thanks for last night. It was followed by a winking emoji.

Jamie frowned at it. He had all his teammates' numbers on his phone, so he wasn't sure who this unknown messenger could be.

He texted back. *Sorry, who is this?*

The reply beeped in immediately. *Cleo* – followed by a heart and a kiss.

Jamie stared at his phone, and the image of a woman with aquamarine eyes and raspberry lip gloss emerged from his blurry hung-over memories of last night. He jumped off the bed and grabbed the lip gloss from the bathroom. It was the same shade as Cleo had worn last night. He was sure of it.

His heart beating quickly, he looked down at what he was wearing. He still had on the same clothes as last night. Nothing had been taken off, not a button undone, even his socks were still on. He took a fistful of his shirt material and lifted it to his nose, breathing in deeply. He smelt only his cologne, and no trace of a woman's perfume. He turned quickly and checked the bin in the bathroom, looking for any evidence that he and Cleo had had sex, and found nothing.

He sat back on the bed and held his phone with trembling hands, shaking his head. Despite what Cleo was insinuating, he knew in his heart that he hadn't cheated. He'd been in no fit state to do anything last night except sleep. He doubted he could have got it up if his life depended on it. And he couldn't, he wouldn't, he was sure. He had let his guard down, perhaps, but he wouldn't cheat on Cass, his brilliant, beautiful wife.

His phone beeped with a few more messages from Cleo, and he quickly blocked her number, not wanting any more to do with her. She would go away and leave him alone, he hoped.

Right now, all he wanted was to get home to Cass and forget about last night.

Cassandra sat in front of him, her lips pressed together in a thin line, her eyes red and puffy from crying. She looked pale and wan without her make-up, her long blonde hair swept up into a messy bun on top of her head. She twisted her hands together.

'I'm here to grab a few things, Jamie. Don't try to stop me,' she said stiffly.

'Cass please, please just give me a few minutes to explain,' Jamie begged, staring at her pleadingly, his hair wild and his face unshaven.

A few days had passed and he was hoping that her return to the home they shared meant that she was in the mood to listen to him. He had spent the last seventy-two hours in a daze, wandering around his silent and empty home they had bought five years ago and furnished and decorated together. He wanted to fill the spare bedrooms with kids, although Cassandra still said she wasn't keen on the idea of having children. He had been hoping this would be the year she changed her mind.

'Nothing happened,' he said as firmly as he could, staring at her earnestly.

Her jaw clenched. 'Then why were those photos of you in the hotel room splashed all over the front pages, J? Why is that *woman*'—she spat out the word—'saying that you and her had sex, that you slept together?' Her brown eyes flashed hot and angry at him.

He held up his hands. 'I did go out drinking with the guys that night and we were all wasted, but I swear I passed out on that hotel bed and I had no idea she was there with me. She saw the opportunity to take those photos of me and sell her story for money.'

He went to her and kneeled before her, clasping her hands in his. Her fingers were like ice and he covered them with his hands and looked up into her eyes, flinching at the hatred he saw burning in them.

'Cass, you have to trust me. I know it looks bad, but I never touched her even though she was in the room with me. I swear on my life, on my parents' lives.'

She looked down, tears extinguishing the fire in her eyes. 'Jamie, this isn't the first time this has happened. There was that other woman a few years ago who said she hooked up with you in the club, remember? You said she was lying too, but now this …' The tears ran down her cheeks and dripped from her jaw onto the neckline of her dress, leaving damp splotches on the silk. 'And the drinking – I've asked you not to go out so much, but you never listen to me.'

Jamie hung his head. He hadn't listened to her. He had made stupid decisions, taken risks and left himself open to bad press and speculation.

'I'll change,' he said hopefully. 'I'll go out less, spend more time with you.'

She shook her head. 'The image of you and that woman together in that hotel room …' She twisted her mouth in an expression of disgust and jealousy. 'I can't bear it. I could hardly stand it the last time and now …' She trailed off as she began to sob, her shoulders shaking. Jamie tried to comfort her, but she pushed him away and looked him square in the eye.

'I can't do this any more. I want a divorce.'

Chapter Nine

'That was a great session today – you did really well,' Katie said, and she meant it. Jamie's fitness levels were improving and she could sense that he was feeling more motivated by being voted through to week two, maybe even starting to enjoy himself a little.

For her part, she had put Alex and the show out of her mind and decided to treat Jamie like a coaching client, and that had improved her focus. The fact that Jamie was turning up on time and trying his best helped them both.

They strolled out to the car park together at the end of their session. Spring had arrived and the sky was a pale bright blue, the smattering of frost on the ground that morning had crept away, only seen by those who had risen exceptionally early. The crisp air danced around Katie's hair and wisps of it waved over her forehead, which she tried unsuccessfully to tuck behind one ear.

'See you tomorrow,' she said. 'And good luck with your group practice later today.'

'Thanks,' he said, giving her a wave and heading to his car.

She watched him go for a moment, then hefted her bag over her shoulder, pushed her hands deep into her pockets and started walking to the bus stop.

She checked the electronic board to see when her bus would arrive. Only thirteen minutes to go. Katie leant against the freezing glass of the shelter, and closed her eyes for a second. An older lady shuffled up to the bus stop and sat down, huffing and fiddling with her scarf. A mother with a child in a pushchair joined them, giving Katie a sideways glance. Katie sensed her looking and opened her eyes. The mother quickly glanced away and busied herself with the child, who was deep into a packet of orange-coloured snacks that had scattered small puffs of lurid colouring over the child's cheeks and hands. Katie tried not to grimace.

She was surprised to hear her name and saw Jamie pull into the bus stop, hazards flashing, calling her name from the open window.

'Katie! Do you need a lift home?'

Katie hopped over to the car, leaning down to see Jamie behind the wheel. 'Erm no, I'm okay. I'm happy to wait for the bus,' she said, embarrassed by his act of charity.

'Don't be ridiculous, get in.' He waved at her with a warm smile. She hesitantly pulled the door open and slid onto the leather seat, shoving some papers onto her lap that were in her way so she didn't sit on them. The mother at the bus stop was staring at them both as they pulled away, and suddenly she turned and shouted out after them, 'Good luck on Saturday!'

Katie was startled but Jamie laughed. 'Good to know we have some fans,' he said, chuckling.

'Can you punch your postcode into the satnav for me?' Jamie asked, nodding at the screen in his car. Katie tapped in the postcode and the route came up.

'I guess your car is still in the garage then?' he asked.

Katie sighed. 'Sadly no. It wasn't fixable, so I had to get rid of it.'

'What's Kick Start?' she changed the subject, seeing the brightly coloured logo across the papers on her lap.

'It's a project in London that works with young lads from difficult backgrounds,' he said. 'I'm a volunteer there.'

'Wow, that's so nice.' Katie was impressed.

Jamie shook his head. 'Nah, it's fun for me too, you know? I get to mess about with the boys, teach them stuff, go on day trips. No big deal.'

'You don't have any kids of your own?' asked Katie, wracking her brains to think if he had mentioned any.

'Nope. Just my two nieces, Alice and Isabelle,' he said with a smile.

Katie remembered that he had mentioned them before, but she hadn't been paying much attention, and she flushed with embarrassment at her lack of social skills.

'Anyway, I'm off to Kick Start for a quick volunteer meeting, then I'll be going to group rehearsal later this afternoon. What have you got planned?' he asked her, focusing on the road, methodically changing gears.

'Nothing really,' she murmured, and suddenly felt ashamed and saddened about all the empty hours she spent alone in her crummy flat, doing nothing. She had never had anything else to do besides skate. Her life seemed very empty in comparison to Jamie's, with his close family, friends, volunteering.

'No boyfriend to hang out with?' he asked quickly.

'Nope,' she said, and turned her head to look out of the window at the suburbs sliding by.

They listened to the radio until Jamie pulled up outside her building. 'Thanks so much for the lift,' she said.

'Anytime, seriously,' Jamie said. Katie slid out of the car and she headed to the front door as he drove away to his meeting.

Practising the group routine was more fun than Jamie had expected. Everyone was in high spirits as they swooshed around the studio to a high-tempo medley of pop hits. The show's choreographer, Jacob, had drafted in Deborah and Tate from the judging panel to give some pointers, and Jamie did his best to keep up and follow their instructions. Alex was notably absent, but Jamie had seen him giving interviews on TV that morning and guessed that Alex was just too busy to make the session.

While they took a quick breather and gathered at the edges of the rink to drink and check phones, Theo skated over to Deborah and Jacob. Jamie didn't like to eavesdrop, but all the participants could hear Theo's determined voice as he gesticulated energetically with his hands.

'Listen, I think the more confident skaters should have

bigger roles.' He gave Deborah a charming smile, but she was unimpressed and stood impassive as stone, entirely unmoved by his pleas.

'Everyone gets equal attention in this routine, Theo,' she said firmly, the studio lights gleaming off her silver hair. Jacob nodded in agreement.

Theo's mouth pressed into a thin line and he frowned as Jacob reiterated what Deborah said.

Vicky nudged Jamie. He glanced at her as they both stared towards Theo.

'He's a bit up his own arse, isn't he?' she said, her voice hoarse from a recent cold. She rubbed the tip of her nose, tinged pink around the nostrils, and grinned at Jamie. Her greying blonde hair was swept back off her face, the shorter greys at the front frizzing around her forehead, dried out from years of being immersed in chlorinated swimming pools. Jamie grinned as they listened to Theo arguing.

Lara glided up to them, downing a Lucozade. She leaned casually on Jamie's arm. 'You're looking good out there, Jamie,' she said, ignoring Vicky, who raised her eyebrows incredulously and turned away to check her phone.

Jamie smiled down at Lara, whose tanned cheeks were warm with the exertion of the routine. 'Nowhere near as good as you or Theo,' he said. She giggled and patted him on the arm. 'Oh no, you're doing great,' she said, widening her eyes, and Jamie got the feeling she was trying to flirt with him, but they were called back to continue the rehearsal before their conversation could carry on.

Tate glided gracefully over to the group and stood next to Jacob, tucking his hands behind his back.

'Tate, would you please demonstrate some *basic* movements for the group and how to look more graceful,' Jacob said, his voice heavy with sarcasm. He had made no secret of the fact that he found the group to be lacking in skill on the ice and didn't hold back on criticising them, apart from Lara, whom he seemed to adore. Despite his obvious disdain for their skating efforts, the group didn't let it dampen their spirits, and largely ignored his cutting remarks, which only served to infuriate him more.

Jo was standing next to Jamie and she met his eye and giggled. She was a powerful snowboarder, much more comfortable in snowsuits than sequins. Dancing didn't suit her either, though her balance and fearlessness were impressive. She also had an amazing capacity for downing Jaeger Bombs, as demonstrated at last week's drinks. Jo shrugged off Jacob's critiques and Jamie was glad the group wasn't taking things too seriously. Apart from Theo.

After the rehearsal ended, Rory slid up to Jamie as they skated off the rink together.

'How's it going?' he asked. 'You look like you're making real progress. I guess Katie is a good teacher?'

Jamie nodded as they walked off the rink and he leaned down to untie his laces. 'She's pretty good really. Needs a lot of patience with me though – I keep falling.'

Rory laughed, husky from a lifetime of cigarettes and shouting at football matches. 'Tell me about it. I spend more time on my arse than upright.'

Jamie laughed with him, shaking his head. 'How are you getting on with Anna?'

Rory smiled. 'She's a nice lass. I feel a bit sorry for her, being paired with an old codger like me though.'

'Age is just a number, gents,' Lara said, winking at Jamie as she walked past them to the changing areas.

'Right you are, love,' Rory boomed after her.

A high-pitched giggle travelled through the still air of the studio and Rory and Jamie turned their heads, catching a glimpse of Maria and Theo sharing a close conversation in a dark corner.

Rory raised an eyebrow. 'I was wondering who might be the first to strike up something,' he said.

Jamie stared at them for a moment, then turned back to Rory. 'They did have a lot of chemistry in their performance the other night,' he said. 'The papers were all speculating about it.'

'What do you reckon as to this whole Alex and Katie situation then?' Rory asked him curiously. 'Seems like he's still half in love with her.'

Jamie shrugged. 'I really don't know about that. I'm not getting in the middle – it's too complicated,' he said.

'Wise choice. Anyway, better dash.' Rory turned and lumbered towards the changing rooms, his long legs striding out quickly. Jamie went to get changed and glanced behind him as Theo and Maria wrapped their arms around each other in a goodbye hug that lingered longer than it needed to.

'Are the rumours true, Theo – about you and Maria?' Lara leaned across to Theo, her face shadowed by the dim light in the hotel bar.

Lara, Theo, Jo and Jamie were ensconced in a large corner booth, tucked away from prying eyes, as midnight approached the night before the second live show. The bar was still busy, with clusters of groups and couples at the tables, soft murmurs filling the air as waiters whisked drink orders around the room with brisk efficiency. A storm crackled outside, the rain pounding fiercely onto the large windows that looked out onto a damp and windswept golf course.

'Well,' Theo raised an eyebrow and grinned. 'Guess who's waiting for me in my room right now?'

Jo's jaw dropped and Lara clapped a hand over her mouth. 'What?! Are you two really together?'

'Seriously?' Jamie asked, leaning his elbows on the table.

Theo nodded and held a finger to his lips. 'Don't tell anyone though,' he said, winking at Lara.

Jo snorted. 'It doesn't sound like it's a well-kept secret, Theo.' She swirled her vodka and Coke, the ice clinking gently against the glass.

'How long have you guys been hooking up?' Jamie asked curiously.

Theo leaned back into the booth, smiling triumphantly. 'Since practically the first week of training. Can't keep our hands off each other.'

Lara giggled, brushing a golden strand of hair from her forehead. 'I knew it,' she said, nodding. 'It's so obvious, the chemistry you two have.'

Theo looked smug as Jo slid out of the booth. 'I've gotta go you guys. I'm shattered and we've got the show tomorrow,' she said.

'Have a good night, Jo,' Jamie said, smiling up at her as she gave the group a wave and headed off through the bar, the bright white soles of her Converse trainers squeaking slightly against the dark wooden floors that gleamed in the half-light.

'I'd better make a move too – can't keep Maria waiting.' Theo laughed and slapped Jamie on the back as he left.

Jamie yawned and stretched his arms above his head as Lara moved to close the gap between them now the other two had left. She smiled at him and sipped her wine, her bright pink lipstick leaving marks on the rim of the glass. She extended one tanned hand to grab a napkin.

Jamie was about to make a move himself, but Lara began talking and he felt it would be rude to leave, especially as she had a full glass to finish. He signalled to the waiter to bring him another rum and Coke and leaned back, resting his hands on his knees.

Lara chattered excitedly about her routine for the second show and Jamie nodded along, trying to feign enthusiasm, but his energy was waning fast, even with the sugar and alcohol. His mind started to wander and he thought about what the other budget hotel was like where the pro skaters were staying, where Katie was tonight, and where Maria was supposed to be if she wasn't with Theo.

'Jamie? Are you listening?' Lara was frowning at him, and he gave her a sheepish grin.

'Sorry,' he said. 'I'm feeling shattered and wasn't concentrating.' He ran a hand through his hair. 'I ought to go soon and get some rest before tomorrow.'

Lara looked disappointed. 'Sure, no problem.' She tipped the remains of her glass into her mouth and swallowed the rest of the wine, wincing slightly at the mouthful of tepid alcohol.

She followed Jamie to the lobby, walking down the quiet corridors, lined with paintings in heavy gilt frames. Jamie jabbed at the button for the lift in reception and the mirrored doors opened with a soft hush.

'Which floor?' Jamie asked as his finger hovered over the buttons.

'Six,' Lara replied, leaning back against the carpeted walls of the lift.

'Me too,' said Jamie.

As the doors gently closed and the lift began to rise, Lara took a quick step towards him and pressed her mouth onto his, taking Jamie completely by surprise. Lara ran her hands down his chest and stomach and kissed him again, more insistently, and he responded instinctively as her tongue met his and her fingers brushed his crotch. A flush of heat rose in him and he slid his hands down over her white silk top, breathing in the scent of her perfume and enjoying the taste of wine that lingered in her mouth.

His mind, fuzzy from tiredness, suddenly focused on visions of Cassandra, and news headlines of hotel hook-ups. Love rat. Cheater. Unfaithful. Cassandra's face blurred and morphed into the woman's who sold the photos. He broke the kiss and took a step back, his mind and his body reeling with lust and confusion.

Lara's blonde hair was tousled around her face, her lips parted and warm, and she shot him a quizzical look. 'What's wrong?' she asked, as the lift doors opened on the sixth floor.

Jamie shook his head and stepped out of the lift. She followed and crossed her arms.

'Lara, I'm sorry. I'm not looking for anything to happen and I don't think this is a good idea,' he said, his mind still flashing back to those hotel images that had ruined his marriage. He had been wrongly stereotyped as a cheat and a love rat ever since, and he didn't want anything to happen that might seem to bolster that reputation.

'How come? You seemed pretty keen just a moment ago,' she said, running a hand up and down his arm, and standing so close to him that he could feel the warmth of her body emanating towards him.

'I'm sorry,' he said, at a loss for what to say as she scanned his face.

'Okay,' she said, finally, looking crestfallen. 'It would have been fun.' She turned and walked towards her room, glancing over her shoulder at him invitingly.

Jamie watched her go and turned to his own room, stopping short as he saw Maria leaning against the door to Theo's room, giving him a wicked smile.

She flipped her long pale hair over her shoulder and arched an eyebrow. 'Tut tut, Jamie. I didn't realise that you and Lara …' She trailed off, grinning.

He shook his head. 'Nothing happened,' he said, wondering why he felt so defensive. 'What are you doing hanging out in the corridor anyway?' he said.

'I popped to Jo's room for something,' she said, turning to open the door with her card key. 'Don't worry, Jamie. Your secret is safe with me.'

'There's no secret!' he said urgently. She closed the door behind her and left him alone in the corridor.

The plates clattered noisily at the breakfast buffet as the guests helped themselves. Katie wrinkled her nose at the sausages and bacon laying wet and greasy under the heated lamps, small incubators of cholesterol and fat, and turned to the cereal and yoghurt instead.

The pale brightness of the strip lighting lit the faces of the guests with a haggard glow, the diners looking washed out and tired as they wolfed down their early morning buffets. Katie walked between the plastic tables to find a spare one, when she heard her name being called.

She turned to see Andy Gilkov and Eric Bowen waving at her. Her heart sank. She was in no mood for small talk, but she didn't want to seem rude so she walked over and reluctantly took a seat at their table.

'Morning, sunshine,' Andy said, the bright southern twang in his voice giving away his American roots. She smiled weakly at him. 'Morning,' she replied, unpeeling her banana.

Eric gulped a mouthful of coffee. 'Sleep well in this budget hell-hole?' he asked, a wide grin on his pale features, his mousy-brown hair tousled from sleep. Eric was surprisingly awkward and clumsy-looking for an ice dancer, with disproportionately long limbs and large hands, but on the ice, he was as smooth and graceful as a gazelle. Katie had always thought of him as rather clownish but knew that underneath his quirky sense of humour he had a kind spirit – she had seen his patience with Vicky on the ice, gently coaching her and boosting her confidence when she fell again and again.

'I slept okay,' she said, pouring out the tea from the small pot on the table. 'What about you?' she asked.

Eric grimaced. 'Awful. There's no soundproofing and the couple in the room next to me were having extremely loud sex at 3 a.m.'

Katie raised her eyebrows as Andy chuckled.

'Poor guy,' Andy said. His nut-brown eyes sparkled in his face, his skin warmly tanned courtesy of the Florida sunshine he was accustomed to. 'It's a shame we didn't get to stay in the fancy hotel with the others,' he added.

Eric threw his hands in the air. 'It's so unfair!' he exclaimed.

'All of us professional skaters are in this cheap horrible hotel and all the sports stars are in the luxury one down the road – downright divisive that is. Don't you think it's ruddy awful, Katie?'

Katie shrugged. She wasn't keen on the hotel they were in, but she knew the judges were also staying in the luxury hotel before and after each show every week, and she was grateful that she wasn't in the same hotel as Alex. She would rather be in the cheapest, dingiest hotel around if it meant she could put some distance between herself and him.

'Of course,' Andy drawled, 'not *all* of us professional skaters are staying here …' He trailed off.

'Meaning?' Eric asked indignantly.

'I've been told that Maria's been staying there, courtesy of Mr Theo Jarvis,' Andy said, grinning, his teeth perfectly whitened despite drinking black coffee about eight times a day.

Katie concentrated on chewing her mouthful of muesli, uninterested in the gossip. At the moment she wanted to get through each week, avoid Alex, and help Jamie get better on the ice, though she couldn't help but feel a slight pang of envy that Maria and Theo had such chemistry between them.

Eric looked delighted at this piece of news. 'I knew those two were together,' he said. 'How did you find out, Andy?'

'Maria and I are good friends. She tells me lots of interesting tales. Apparently, she and Theo aren't the only ones hooking up around here,' Andy said, knowingly. 'Your Jamie is having a bit of a thing with the lovely Lara,' he continued, looking at Katie.

She looked up from her cereal in surprise. 'What?'

Andy nodded, delighted to have got her attention. 'Maria texted me that she saw them last night. She said there was definitely something going on.'

A small bubble of irritation rose in Katie's throat. She didn't care who Jamie hooked up with, of course, but she needed his mind to be on the show and not distracted. She plopped her spoon back into the bowl and pushed her chair back quickly. 'I'm pretty much done with breakfast,' she said. 'I'll see you guys at the studio in a bit.'

Then

Jamie slumped over the kitchen counter, resting his head on his hands. The thick stubble on his chin was spiky against his fingers, and he hadn't showered in days. His dad silently passed him a cup of black coffee and eyed up the mountain of takeaway boxes littering the counter.

'Thanks Dad,' Jamie muttered, gazing out of the windows at the gloomy grey skies which reflected his mood.

Phil bustled around, sweeping the takeaway boxes into a black bin bag, and wiping a cloth over the counter.

'You don't need to do that,' Jamie said, shaking his head.

Phil gave him a stern look. 'It's a pigsty in here.'

Jamie shrugged. 'Who cares? It's not like I have a wife living with me any more.'

Phil's gaze softened with sympathy. 'I'm sorry, Jamie. I know this is hard …'

Jamie snorted angrily and slammed his fist down on the counter, ignoring the pain that reverberated down his wrist. 'Hard? It's hell, Dad. I could accept Cass asking for a divorce if I had actually done anything wrong, but the story about that Cleo woman wasn't true, and nor was the one before that.'

Phil stared at him, his expression unreadable.

'You do believe me, don't you, Dad?' Jamie asked, and hated the pleading note in his voice, hated that the untrue stories made his wife leave him and his own family doubt him. 'I swear that nothing happened with either of those women. They were just opportunists who wanted to make some cash by selling their lies, at the expense of my marriage,' he said bitterly.

'I believe you, J, you know I do,' Phil said softly. He came up to him and put a hand on Jamie's shoulder, giving it a firm squeeze. 'I know you're going through hell, but you have to take care of yourself – you're an athlete. You can't eat crap all day and stay up all night – you've got the World Cup next year. And I really think you should shower,' he added, with a gentle smile.

Jamie looked at him and nodded, knowing his dad was right, wishing his head wasn't so jumbled and his heart wasn't aching so badly he could hardly breathe.

'I'll try to pull myself together,' he mumbled.

'You can do it,' Phil said encouragingly. Jamie nodded, but he was filled with doubt.

Chapter Ten

Anna was watching from the viewing room as the group of athletes completed their routine to end the show for this week. She sighed in annoyance as the screens showed Rory fluff one of his turns. She bit her lip to stop the irritation registering on her face. She had hoped that this programme would raise her profile and get her some better work, but being paired with Rory was worse than not taking part at all. He was the joke contestant, the one who would get all the YouTube views but for all the wrong reasons. She should have been paired with Jamie or Theo, if life were fair.

Maria caught her eye from across the room and gave her a tight smile, looking smug at Theo's performance that evening. Anna scowled at her, hoping she would fall on her face during her next routine. She turned away from the screens and glanced around the room, bored and restless. Eric was trying to flirt with Carmen, but she had her arms crossed and looked unimpressed as he waved his arms around, spilling drops of Sprite on both the sofa and his trousers. Andy grinned at her from across the room, rolling his eyes at Eric's clumsiness. Anna gave him a small smile back and was about to head over to sit with him when the athletes trooped in noisily, still panting heavily from the exertion of completing their second routine of the night. Maria made a big show of wrapping her long limbs around Theo and shrieking as he gave her a bear hug that lifted her off the ground.

The air swelled with chatter and laughter, but Anna slipped out of the viewing room, unwilling to make small talk with Rory under Maria's smug gaze. She wandered down to the ice where the audience was shifting from their seats for a break.

Alex saw her and waved, sauntering over. He looked like a model, his long limbs in a designer blue suit, perfectly tailored, his hair brushed off his face. If only she had had the chance to skate with him, just once, thought Anna wistfully, but she knew that Alex was way out of her league in every way.

'Hi Anna,' said Alex as he approached. 'Good show so far, right?'

She gave him a huge smile and coquettishly flicked her hair. 'Wonderful. Skating with Rory is such a dream. I only hope we can stay in for a little while longer,' she murmured longingly, looking down at the floor and turning her eyes up to meet Alex's beautiful gaze. Her heart pounded a little harder as their eyes met. What she wouldn't give for just one date …

'It's a shame you haven't been paired with someone a little more suited to you,' he said, thoughtfully. 'You're such a lovely dancer.'

Warmth rushed through every part of Anna's body at his words, and her legs felt slightly weak.

'You know, I think you and Rory really deserve a chance to stay in the competition,' he said. 'Rory's such a great guy, and this could be really good for both of you.'

Anna's mind started shrieking at her excitedly, but she kept a straight face. 'But what can we do?' she shrugged casually while her palms started to sweat. 'He isn't the best skater.'

'Maybe not,' said Alex, 'but the judges' comments make a huge difference. And where one judge leads, the others often follow …'

Anna couldn't quite believe that Alex was offering to throw his support behind her and Rory. It could make a difference to the public votes. Perhaps she did stand a chance with him after all, she thought as she gazed at his eyes, drinking in every feature of his chiselled face.

'Of course,' said Alex, his eyes not moving from hers. 'It would be quite a big favour.'

'I'd be happy to do anything you wanted in return …' stammered Anna, her face turning hot. She would be very happy to sleep with Alex if the opportunity arose, even in a transactional sense. She bet he would be amazing in bed.

Alex put his hand to his chin, as if thinking. 'Well, there is something you could help me with.'

Anna smiled. 'Anything.' Her stomach trembled with anticipation.

'I'd love to have some time alone with Katie,' he said, watching her carefully.

Anna felt as if she had swallowed a bucket of iced water and her stomach constricted with envy. Katie – of course. She should have known.

'You know, just to talk to her properly,' he continued, smoothly.

She nodded, her mouth dry, not trusting herself to form any words just yet.

'Of course, it's kind of tricky for me to arrange, given that she won't speak to me,' he was saying. 'And I'm not sure I can ask Jamie – we're not exactly mates. It wouldn't feel …' He paused. 'Appropriate for me to approach him.'

Anna patted him on the arm and leaned in confidentially, close enough to smell the scent of his aftershave. It took all her self-control not to lean in and nuzzle into his neck. 'Leave it with me,' she murmured, breathing him in. And cursing Katie inwardly.

'We're going out for drinks for Derek. Are you coming?' Jamie asked Katie as she emerged from her dressing room.

To his surprise, she nodded and smiled up at him.

'You did really well tonight Jamie,' she said, tapping his arm.

'Hey, well, I have a great teacher,' he said, giving her a grin.

She shook her head. 'That was all down to you this week. You've worked really hard, and I think you managed to surprise some people in the group routine too.'

Jamie felt a warm glow of satisfaction. He was no Theo Jarvis, but he knew he hadn't made a fool of himself, and his parents and sister watching at home could cheer him on without embarrassment. He had caused his parents a lot of pain and aggravation with a slew of bad headlines before, and it was heartening to think of them feeling proud of him once again.

He had enjoyed this week a lot more than he expected. Katie had been kinder, more patient and more relaxed, and he had felt increasingly steadier on his feet. He was surprisingly pleased that she had decided to join them for drinks that night.

'We've got a space booked at a bar nearby,' he said, and she followed him as they walked with the others out into the cool night air.

The bar was boiling hot and crowded, thrumming with people. The bass of the music throbbed right through them and a babble of voices hung over their heads like a cloud, unintelligible and oppressive. A few people from the show had already arrived and were in the private area reserved for them – tucked away in an alcove, with deep purple velvet benches along the white stone walls. Bottles of wine, beer and prosecco were scattered around tiny metallic tables and Jamie grabbed a beer, grateful for the cool condensation in the heat of his hand. Katie had melted away into the throng already, strolling casually over towards Theo. Jamie watched, amused, as she gazed up at Theo with admiring eyes.

Jamie started chatting to Carmen, who made no secret of her distress at her and Derek being voted off, although Derek was as calm and jovial as ever, seemingly unbothered by his time on the show coming to an abrupt end.

Jamie glanced back over at Katie, where she looked completely bored as Theo droned on. Jamie chuckled inwardly – she had finally discovered how incredibly self-centred Theo could be. Katie caught his gaze and mouthed "help" while Theo talked on, oblivious to her boredom. Jamie laughed and walked towards her when Anna sidled up to him and gently touched his elbow just before he got to Katie.

'I noticed you finished your beer,' she said, handing him

another bottle and taking him by surprise. 'Thanks,' he said, forgetting about trying to help Katie escape from Theo. 'How's things with Rory going?'

Anna smiled insincerely. 'Oh, just fine. He's a dear.'

They chatted about the show, Anna laughing a little too hard at his jokes. He could sense that she wanted to talk to him about something else but was biding her time, and it was making him feel on edge. There was something a little too desperate in the way she was trying to keep his attention. He couldn't help but glance over the top of her head just in time to see Alex walk up to Katie and Theo. Jamie could see Katie instantly tense up, her fingertips turning white as they tightened around her empty wine glass.

'You two look like you're having a very in-depth conversation,' Alex said, folding his arms and giving Theo a pointed look. Jamie felt bad about watching but he was too curious to turn away, even though Anna was still trying to talk to him.

'I have to go and get another drink,' said Theo.

'Hi Katie,' said Alex, turning his smile back on and taking a step towards her, leaning his head down slightly. 'You skated beautifully tonight. It was a joy to see.' Alex spoke loudly, and Jamie was pretty sure he wasn't the only one in the room listening to their conversation.

Jamie watched as Katie's expression changed to her best ice queen look but Alex didn't seem to care, leaning towards her and then whispering something in her ear. Her face was expressionless, though Jamie could have sworn she flinched.

'It's such a shame about those two,' sighed Anna, still at Jamie's side despite his distraction. 'I know them both really well from the competition circuit. I've never met a couple more right for each other than Katie and Alex,' she said wistfully.

Jamie turned to look at her. 'But she really seems to hate the guy now,' he said, unable to reconcile the images he had seen of them together when they were a pair with the coldness he saw between them now.

Anna shook her head. 'She was telling me earlier that she really misses him. In fact, she's still in love with him.' She sighed.

Jamie raised his eyebrows, baffled at how he could have misunderstood Katie so badly. 'Really? Nothing about her behaviour suggests she likes him at all.'

'You don't know Katie like I do,' Anna said, matter-of-factly. 'She's an expert at covering up how she really feels. She's still mad about the accident, but I know that deep down she still loves him.'

Jamie sipped his beer and studied them closely. Katie's gaze remained steadily fixed on her empty glass while Alex tried to engage her in conversation with the hopeful eagerness of a puppy wanting a treat. He couldn't see what Anna was talking about but then again, he had never been that good at understanding women, even his own wife. 'You really think so, Anna?'

Anna nodded. 'They need some time to properly talk about things, you know, in private, without loads of people around them, watching and gossiping. I know Alex is desperate to apologise properly, to see if she'd like to be together again.'

Alex had been caught by Deborah Mercer at this point and she was hauling him away to talk to someone else. He was glaring at her darkly, but she didn't seem to notice, and Katie had drifted away to get herself another drink.

'See?' Anna said, inclining her head at them. 'He can't get a moment alone with her.'

She turned to Jamie and twirled a strand of shiny chestnut hair around her finger, her eyes gleaming. 'I have an idea. What if you arranged to meet Katie for a team catch-up and then Alex turned up instead?'

Jamie frowned. 'I don't want to get in the middle of this,' he said, uncertainty pooling in his gut. What Anna was suggesting felt too underhand, too intrusive for his liking.

Anna grabbed his arm and said pleadingly, 'C'mon Jamie,

help them out. You and I could play matchmaker.' She gave him a dazzling smile.

Jamie drained his beer and tapped his finger on the bottle anxiously. 'I'm really not sure that's a good idea,' he said, finally.

'Think about it?' she asked, rubbing his arm gently. She saw Katie heading towards them and quickly walked away, giving him a flirty wink as she did so.

Jamie felt awkward as Katie came up to him, Anna's words ringing in his ears. He felt like he had intruded on a secret and wished Anna hadn't told him about how Katie felt about Alex. It was none of his business, after all.

Glancing over to Anna, Katie asked Jamie, 'What did she want with you?' She looked at him curiously as she brushed away a strand of hair, which curled slightly in the damp heat of the bar.

'Just comparing notes about the show tonight,' Jamie said, trying to sound casual and knowing that he was a terrible liar.

'It seems you're very popular with all the ladies at the moment,' Katie said, with a knowing look.

'How do you mean?' Jamie asked, confused.

'You and Lara?' she said, looking at where Lara stood laughing with Andy, her golden hair tossed back, one hand on her hip.

Katie stepped closer and lowered her voice. 'Listen, Jamie, do you think it's a good idea to get involved with someone from the show? I mean, all the gossip and stuff could be a real distraction, plus she is our competition ...' She trailed off. Jamie swallowed hard, feeling annoyed at her hypocrisy when most of the gossip so far had been about her and Alex, and she was the one who was distracted.

'I don't know what you've read or heard, or from who, but there's nothing going on with Lara and me,' Jamie said firmly. He gave her a hard look.

'Oh,' she said, looking taken aback at his glare.

'Did you have a nice chat with Alex?' he asked her, pointedly, and she bit her lower lip and looked at her feet. 'After all, if we're going to talk about rumours, how about all the ones saying Alex is still in love with you?' Jamie asked her directly, emboldened by alcohol.

Katie looked troubled and shook her head. 'Just gossip, rumours without foundation. Like the ones about you and Lara,' she said. It was dark in the bar, but he could have sworn she blushed. Maybe Anna was right after all, he thought, and she was trying really hard to hide how she felt about Alex and didn't want to admit it after all this time.

Jamie was about to respond when Eric bounded over and interrupted them. Katie walked off before Jamie had a chance to ask her anything else and he didn't see her again for the rest of the evening.

Jamie sat at the kitchen counter. Cass had chosen everything in the house and every smooth and shiny surface seemed to reflect a memory of her back at him. He munched on a bowl of cereal and browsed the news on his phone. Rumours were flying about Theo and Maria's relationship, especially as they did nothing to hide their chemistry during the show. Jamie was taken aback to see a photo of Alex and Katie chatting at the bar last night splashed over the news and social media as well. He guessed someone had taken a furtive snap and sold it to the papers. He scrolled through the headlines related to the show, hoping there wouldn't be too much criticism of his performance.

"Are Relations Thawing Between Katie and Alex?" The headline from the *Mail* caught Jamie's eye. His finger hovered over it, and he hesitated for a second. He felt slightly guilty reading gossip about Katie, as if he were prying, but he opened up the article about the ill-fated couple anyway.

"Alex and Katie were both at the top of their game when they combined forces to become the new power couple in pairs

skating, the likes of which hadn't been seen since the legendary Torvill and Dean. She was the beautiful Olympic ice princess and he was the most successful and good-looking male skater in the country, so it was no surprise when the sparks flew both on and off the ice for the couple. Shortly after, speculation started that their partnership was more than professional, and Alex made it official by posting this picture of the couple on his social media."

Jamie looked at the photo of Katie staring into the camera at a breakfast table, her eyes wide as if she had been caught by surprise, a faint smile on her lips. He carried on reading.

"From then on, the golden couple could do no wrong. They were feted for their daredevil throws and lifts, their balletic grace, their bold choreography, and their flawless technique. It seemed like a match made in heaven, until that fateful day of the accident which ended Katie's skating career and their relationship."

There was another series of pictures of Katie and Alex in happier days, social media posts from Alex with loving captions and heart emojis, smiling selfies. There was a picture of them after winning third at the World Championships, Katie in a beautiful black dress and Alex with his arms around her, celebrating their success. Jamie couldn't reconcile the pictures with what he knew of them, the way that Katie tensed up at even the mention of Alex's name, the way that Alex looked so heartbroken every time he saw her.

Jamie read on about how Alex had spoken of his regret about the accident, and how he would always love Katie and hoped she would forgive him one day and bring him in from the cold. Jamie sighed. He knew what it was like to have a partner you loved who wouldn't forgive you when you'd made a mistake. He knew the pain of loving someone who couldn't trust you and who chose not to believe you.

He took a sip of coffee. Maybe there was a chance for Katie and Alex to be happy again, he thought to himself, looking over the photos of their days together. Jamie put his coffee down with a decisive clink and pulled out his phone to text Anna: *Hey, Katie will be at Slough ice rink on Monday at 6.30 a.m. I'll be "running late". Let Alex know if he wants a chance to talk to her.*

Jamie pressed send before he had a chance to change his mind. He knew it was a sneaky thing to do, and not something he was entirely comfortable with, but maybe Anna was right and they needed a nudge in the right direction.

Then

Alex was like an unstoppable force on the ice. Every training session with him had an intensity to it – a drive and an urgency fuelled by his desire for perfection. Katie could see how he had reached the top levels of the sport. There were no excuses and no off-days for him, and there couldn't be for Katie either. Sergei was hard on them too, much tougher than Ivan had been. Katie didn't care – it was a welcome distraction from the yawning gap in her life that her dad had left. With Alex and Sergei driving her forward there was no time to think and off the ice she was simply too tired to sit and ponder the family life she missed.

Switching to pairs skating opened a whole new world of lifts and throws, a new variety of challenges and techniques to learn that excited both Katie and Alex. She knew that fear was her enemy – she had to be totally fearless and completely trusting when her body was in Alex's hands and he held her over the ice, himself only balanced on two razor-thin blades. When the lifts went well, Katie soared. She felt invincible.

They finished one session late on a Saturday and were both looking forward to a rest the next day. They came off the ice panting and dripping with sweat, Alex mopping his face with a towel. He grinned at her as she flopped down in a chair, groaning.

'Our triple twist lift is really coming along,' he said, looking pleased. She nodded, downing water and wiping sweat from the back of her neck.

'Shame about this though,' she said laughing, pointing to a huge bruise on her upper arm that she got in their practice a few days ago, now a violent mixture of purples and yellowing edges that marred her pale skin.

'Sorry about that,' he said, trying to look contrite and failing. She laughed. 'Well, at least I haven't broken your nose yet,' she said.

'It worries me that you're saying "yet",' he said, shoving his towel into his bag. 'Stay away from the face, Katie.' He wagged his finger at her and raised an eyebrow. She giggled while he fished out his phone.

'I think people are excited to see us perform at our first big competition next week,' he said, scrolling through his Twitter feed. 'It's a lot of pressure.'

Katie nodded, peering at the screen, her hand on his shoulder as she leaned over him. 'I know. There's been more hype than I thought there would be.'

The news that the two champions were joining forces to skate together had made a few headlines. There was a sense of expectation on them to do something really special with their combined talents. Even though they'd been training intensely together for over a year, Katie felt more jittery than usual about the upcoming performance at the Bavarian Open competition, their first international performance as a pair.

There was so much more than just the technical elements to get right. They'd met with their choreographer, Juliette, to discuss how they interpreted the music they'd selected. She and Alex had to spend a lot of time in practice sessions trying to look longingly into each other's eyes, even when they were tired and sweating and in pain. In every minute of the piece, they were keeping time and focusing on setting up the next move, so combining that with romantic acting was a new challenge for both of them.

'Wanna get something to eat?' Alex asked her.

She shook her head. 'Thanks, Alex but I'm so tired. I just want to go home, shower and crash.'

He smiled. 'No problem. I'll see you Monday, sweet cheeks.' He gave her a theatrical wink and she sputtered with laughter.

'Sweet cheeks – that's a new one,' she said giggling.

He laughed with her. 'Just trying to keep up the romance.'

'Save it for the ice, Alex,' she said, grabbing her bag and ruffling his damp hair as she walked past him.

Katie knew that she had truly made the right decision to skate with Alex the moment they started their routine at the Bavarian Open. Everything was in sync and they skated beautifully – in time with the music and each other, anticipating each other's moves, completely in a world of their own. They were magical together. Katie was amazed at how good Alex was at acting – the way he looked at her and held her during the routine, she could almost believe that he was actually in love with her.

After the competition, they watched a video of their performance with Sergei, so he could point out any mistakes, not that there were many. They were both still on a high from the performance and couldn't take anything seriously. Alex looked over at her and made faces while Sergei was speaking, and Katie had to bite her lip hard to stop herself from giggling.

Sergei noticed and stopped the tape. 'Why are you laughing? You think it is fun and games?' he said, frowning and glaring at them both.

Katie tried to look chastised but a sideways glance from Alex sent them off into helpless laughter, both of them slightly delirious from the exhaustion of months of preparing and the rush of relief that it had all gone well. Sergei threw up his hands in exasperation and pushed back his chair.

'I will leave you two to calm down,' he said annoyed, and walked off towards the hotel bar, shaking his head and muttering under his breath about their childishness as he did so.

Katie leaned back in her chair and wiped her eyes. 'We shouldn't antagonise him,' she said, grinning so hard at Alex that her cheeks ached. He looked at her, eyes gleaming with tears of laughter, and he pushed his chair closer to hers and threw an arm around her shoulder.

'Don't listen to Sergei,' he said, leaning in so his mouth was close to her hair. 'We did great. To rank fourth when we're so new to pairs skating is amazing.'

She nodded. 'It was brilliant. We could really go for gold next season, Alex,' she said, her expression suddenly serious as she swivelled her head to look up at him, finding his face closer to hers than she expected. She pulled back slightly.

He nodded firmly, his eyes tracing her features. 'You read my mind.'

He paused for a moment and they both fell silent, the noise of the hotel café swirling around them.

'I'm going to go and rest for a bit,' Katie said, breaking the stillness that had settled on them.

'See you later?' Alex looked up at her as she stood to leave, his expression hopeful.

'Sure, you know where to find me,' she said, and headed off, grateful for the restful blandness of her room, the muted colours and the warmth lulling her quickly to sleep as the adrenaline from the day wore off.

Hours had passed when she finally woke, heavy from sleep but shaking herself awake to eat something. The daylight outside had seeped away leaving only a gleam on the horizon. She was considering what to do for dinner when there was a tentative knock on the door. She opened it to find Alex, the smell of soap and shampoo drifting from him. His hair was still wet and a towel hung around his neck.

'Wanna hang out and order room service for dinner?' he asked, leaning on the frame.

'Sure, I actually just woke up,' Katie said, as he followed her into the room and threw himself onto her bed, stretching out his long legs.

She perched beside him and grabbed the room service menu. 'What are you in the mood for?' she asked.

A slow smile spread across his face and he leaned back on her pillows, hands behind his head, one eyebrow raised. 'Well ...'

Katie flushed – a bright wave of red rising over her cheeks. 'Um, I meant what do you want to eat?' she asked, waving the menu at him and hoping he wouldn't try flirting with her any more. She never quite knew what to say or do when he did that.

'Oh right, food,' he said, grinning at her embarrassment. 'I'd murder some fish and chips,' he said, and she nodded, turning to phone for the food while he scrolled through the news on his mobile.

'Lots of good headlines from today,' he said. He indicated at his phone and flicked through the stories as she sat beside him, having to lean against him to see the screen.

"Champs Romance?" one headline asked suggestively, with an image from their routine where they had their arms wrapped around each other and were looking into each other's eyes.

She laughed. 'I wish they would focus on the skating rather than the speculation,' she said. Alex shrugged, looking a little peeved. 'It's nice that they're interested in us though. So much of sport is about personality these days. Having a little drama and romance thrown in helps.' He glanced at her.

'Do you want to watch a film?' she asked, changing the subject.

'Sure, what's on?' he asked, still thumbing through his phone.

They watched a romcom in companionable silence. Eventually, Katie couldn't keep her eyes open any longer and politely nudged Alex off the bed to leave. She got the feeling that he did so reluctantly.

Chapter Eleven

When Jamie arrived at the rink, he could see Katie standing by the barriers, her back ramrod straight, her arms folded rigidly across her chest, jaw clenched.

Shit, he thought, as he approached her nervously to start their practice session. Things clearly hadn't gone well, and there was no sign of Alex.

'Morning,' he said warily.

She whipped her head around at him and her arms went straight to her sides, her hands balled into tight fists.

'How *dare* you,' she hissed at him through clenched teeth. 'How dare you tell Alex when and where to find me. You had no right!' Her voice raised with every word until she was screeching the last syllable at him.

Jamie winced and raised his hands. 'Okay calm down,' he began and for some reason, this seemed to anger her even more.

'Calm down?! Don't tell me to calm down!' she yelled.

'I mean, please let me explain,' he said, stuttering under her furious gaze.

The way she glared at him reminded him of Cassandra when she found out about the cheating claims in the paper. Katie crossed her arms back over her chest, breathing heavily, her eyes wide and lips pressed together to stifle whatever choice words she was probably saving up for him.

'It's just that Anna said you still had feelings for Alex, and he was so desperate to have a chance to talk to you properly, and I, I wanted to help that's all,' he babbled, the words jumbling together.

'Anna said I still have feelings for Alex?' She gave a short harsh laugh. 'What the hell would she know about the way I feel, about anything?' She looked at Jamie incredulously.

'Okay you're right, I'm sorry, clearly she, I, was completely wrong,' he said. 'It's just that Alex seemed so sad and so keen to talk to you, to put things right—'

She shook her head at him and cut him off, spitting out her words. 'You literally have no idea what you're talking about!'

Jamie ran his hands through his hair, half wanting to tear it out in frustration. Why did he have to get caught in the middle of this mess?

Katie looked at him and raised her eyebrows. 'Wait, please tell me you don't actually feel *sorry* for him, do you?' she said, with a disgusted expression.

Jamie grimaced at the question. 'I mean, c'mon Katie, he's spent years saying that he's sorry for what happened, and from what I can see you won't even give him the time of day.' He thought of Cass refusing to believe a word he said and how awful it had been, how it had ripped his heart from within him, leaving a hollow in his chest that he still carried with him even now.

'Maybe if you hear him out, it could be good for both of you,' Jamie suggested, hopefully. 'You know, make peace. Let bygones be bygones.'

Katie glared at him. 'He. Ruined. My. Life,' she said, emphasising every word.

Jamie shook his head. 'I know, and it's awful but are you going to punish him forever? I mean, you seemed so perfect together. It seems a shame to throw that all away.'

To his surprise, tears fell from her eyes when she blinked, though whether they were tears of rage, regret or sorrow he couldn't tell. She drew a breath and angrily brushed the tears away, blotting her eyes roughly with her sleeve.

'What are you basing this on? On what Alex has told you?' she asked.

'I haven't spoken to Alex about this, only Anna,' Jamie said, as Katie shook her head at him in exasperation. 'But anyone could see looking back over your relationship that you were made for each other,' he added quickly, knowing it was none of his business but blurting it out anyway, trying to make her understand why he had interfered.

Katie stepped closer to him, and in a low taunting voice, said: 'And anyone could see looking back over your marriage that you cheated on your wife, right Jamie?' And she jutted her chin out in defiance, staring up directly into his eyes.

He was taken aback. 'None of those stories were true. It was all bullshit,' he said, staring down hard at her, a wave of tight anger spreading across his chest.

She opened her mouth to reply, when a child's voice called out. 'Uncle Jamie!'

Katie stepped back from him in surprise and they both looked around. Jamie groaned inwardly. His sister had brought his two nieces down to the rink to see him practice, as they were on an inset day from school. Her timing literally could not be worse.

Katie stared at him and he shrugged helplessly, walking away from her to greet Alice and Isabelle who were running down the gap between the seats towards him. Opening his arms wide, he scooped them both up in a bear hug.

'Hi, I hope you don't mind us dropping by to say hello!' Maddie called out cheerily.

Jamie hoped she hadn't heard the argument they had been in the middle of moments ago. He glanced at Katie, who plastered on a wide fake smile and extended her hand. 'Hi, I'm Katie.'

'I'm Maddie, Jamie's older sister,' Maddie said, and shook Katie's hand. 'It's so nice to meet you, Katie! We've all been so excited to see Jamie skating with you.'

'It's been, er, a wonderful experience so far,' Katie said, a bit too enthusiastically as she and Jamie looked at each other awkwardly, and Jamie was sure Maddie could sense from their strained expressions that something was off.

Katie shifted uncomfortably. Her cheeks were hurting from the fake smile and she wasn't sure Maddie was buying their false enthusiasm. Despite the awkwardness of the situation, she was grateful for the interruption. Although she was furious with Jamie, she hated confrontation, and having the girls there was taking the raw edge off her anger.

'Uncle Jamie, please can you skate for us?' Alice asked hopefully.

'Maybe another time, sweetheart,' Maddie said, giving her brother a look that Katie couldn't interpret.

The girls both pouted. Katie felt bad to be the cause of their disappointment, so she knelt beside them.

'Would you like to skate with us?' she asked, smiling a genuine smile this time, brushing a bright blonde lock of hair gently off Isabelle's forehead, thinking how nice it would be to have a niece, or a sister, or anyone she could call family.

The girls both smiled and nodded eagerly, looking at their mother with pleading eyes.

Maddie hesitated. 'Are you sure?'

Katie nodded, looking at Jamie cautiously. 'Just ten minutes or so. We'll treat it as our warm-up.'

Jamie looked relieved and gave her a nod. 'Okay girls, let's get some skates for you.' Jamie took them by the hand as they squealed excitedly, and he walked them to the skate hire.

'You skate so beautifully,' said Maddie to Katie, while they waited.

'Thank you,' Katie murmured, still feeling tense and awkward.

'Jamie raves about you. He said you're such a good teacher.'

Katie laughed. 'I somehow doubt that.'

Maddie shook her head. 'Not at all. I think he's really enjoying being on the show.' Casting a glance around to check Jamie wasn't in earshot, she lowered her voice slightly. 'It's such a relief for us in the family to see him motivated again, especially after the divorce and being kicked off the team ... It's been a tough few years.'

Katie felt uncomfortable at Maddie confiding in her so freely, but she nodded. 'I'm glad he's finding it to be a good experience,' she said, somewhat stiffly, her mind scrambling to change the subject. 'Your girls are adorable,' she said, watching them tie up their skates with Jamie.

Maddie smiled proudly. 'Thank you. I agree of course but I'm biased.'

'Jamie seems very good with them,' Katie observed.

'Oh, they adore him, and vice versa. He would be such a good dad.' Maddie sighed.

Katie stared at the girls, her anger at the argument dulled by the stirrings of a deeper sense of longing, something she often experienced when her younger students were picked up by their parents. She found it hard to fight the jealousy when their children ran to greet them with such abandon, such needy and unconditional love.

Katie thought that she would like to have kids but since Alex, all she'd had were a few awkward dates, some that had ended in fumbling and unsatisfactory sex that had left her feeling even more lonely the next day. Skint, with no friends or family, she felt that life was passing her by and she didn't know how to stop it from melting away.

Jamie returned, girls in tow, chattering excitedly.

'Off we go then,' Katie said, and led the way to the ice, holding Alice tightly by the hands as she gently helped her onto the slippery surface, as Jamie held onto Isabelle.

Soon the girls were shrieking with joy as Katie and Jamie pulled them around the ice, and they watched in awe as Jamie showed off his backwards skating. Katie couldn't help laughing with them as he made funny faces and pretended to fall. She was still mad at him and felt annoyed with herself for laughing, but she couldn't help it. The girls' enjoyment was infectious.

Maddie had been enjoying a few moments to herself with a coffee by the side of the rink, laughing along with them.

'Come on girls, it's time we got going,' she called out eventually. The girls moaned disappointedly.

'Sorry ladies, but Katie and I have to practise for the show on Saturday so we do really well and people vote for us,' Jamie said, depositing them back with Maddie. He made to get off the ice, but Maddie stopped him. 'I'll take the skates back – you two have to crack on.' Maddie and the girls waved goodbye to Katie and she watched them go, feeling gloomy at the prospect of having to face up to her argument with Jamie now they were gone.

Jamie slid back onto the ice, and they looked sheepishly at each other.

'Listen, Katie,' Jamie said, awkwardly, rubbing the back of his neck. 'I'm sorry about Alex. I shouldn't have done that.'

She nodded quickly, desperate to move on and forget about it. 'Apology accepted. *Please* can we not talk about Alex any more? We need to focus on our own skating, okay?' she said, and Jamie nodded in agreement.

She sighed inwardly as they prepared to start their practice. Like it or not, they were stuck together for their time on the show.

Then

'Nailed it!' Katie shrieked in delight as she high-fived Alex. Sergei looked on, nodding with a pleased expression on his face – the most exuberant reaction she had seen from him yet.

They had completed a clean run-through of their new programme for the first time, all the elements flawless and flowing from one to the other, a culmination of months of early starts, late finishes, pain and pleasure, exhaustion and exhilaration.

Alex wrapped her in a hug, squeezing her so close that Katie could hardly breathe.

'You are fearless,' he said admiringly. 'That was brilliant.'

She broke free from the embrace, spread her arms and twirled in a circle. 'I can't wait to get on that podium!' she cheered.

Alex laughed. 'Come and have a drink with me to celebrate!' he said, grabbing her by the hand and pulling her off the ice. 'We've earned it.'

'All right, all right,' she said, pulling back her hand and grinning up at him. 'But I'm not going anywhere till I've showered and changed.'

Alex smiled and rolled his eyes. 'Fine. Meet me at my place at seven.'

Katie waved goodbye to Sergei and practically ran to the car park, smiling as she drove home singing at the top of her lungs to whatever songs she could make out on the car's old radio, which crackled and fuzzed with static.

Her heart was still thrumming from the excitement of their routine, the adrenaline high making her feel shaky and light-headed. The programme was fast and daring, the lifts were exhilarating. As a singles skater, she had largely been grounded, but with Alex, she could truly fly. Despite the fact that they hadn't been skating together for long, they both knew there was medal potential in the programme if they could complete it cleanly, just like they had managed in today's practice.

Katie couldn't stop smiling as she showered and threw on a pair of skinny jeans and a pale blue jumper, breathing in the pleasing scent of fabric softener and shampoo. She headed to Alex's flat, jamming her thumb on the buzzer, keen to talk more about how their routine was shaping up.

Alex's voice crackled over the intercom, buzzing her in. 'Hey, come on up.'

She had only been to his flat in Guildford a handful of times, and she was slightly envious. It was a new build, with shiny appliances and new flooring, tastefully decorated. She wasn't one to pry about finances, but from Alex's comments, she knew that his family were sufficiently well off to have paid all his training and travel fees and buy him a flat close to the rink to stay in, even though his family lived in Godalming, which wasn't far away. It was a far cry from how Katie's dad had struggled to pay her expenses.

Alex met her at the door and she followed him into the lounge, sinking into the soft brown leather sofa and leaning back with her arms behind her head. She stretched out her legs and tilted her head right back so she could see Alex in the open-plan kitchen behind her.

He grabbed two glasses and filled them from a bottle that he had already opened, bringing them over and sitting beside her.

'Cheers!' he said, raising his glass to her own.

They clinked glasses and Katie took a few sips. She rarely drank alcohol – she had never liked the taste or the way it made her feel, but she didn't want to be rude.

'Dinner will be ready in about twenty minutes,' Alex said, stretching his long legs out in front of him, clad in black jeans with rips at the thighs. He was pure muscle, hard and toned all over. His T-shirt rode up slightly to reveal a smattering of dark hair running down from his stomach to underneath his waistband. Katie found herself staring momentarily and quickly looked away embarrassed, but Alex hadn't noticed.

'You cooked? Alex that's so nice,' she said appreciatively. She thought they would be going out to the pub and wasn't expecting him putting in the effort of cooking for her.

He gave her a lazy lopsided smile. 'Anything for the best skating partner I could hope for,' he said, his eyes gently gleaming in the light of the lamp that stood beside him.

Katie saved most of her wine to have with dinner, but Alex insisted on topping up her glass even though it was still half full. They chatted about their routine, comparing competitors between mouthfuls of pasta. Alex was scathing about the other male skaters they would be competing against, and Katie couldn't help but laugh at his comments, even though they often verged on the mean side.

After dinner, Katie started to feel exhausted. She could feel the heat in her cheeks and knew she must look terribly flushed thanks to the wine, the heavy meal and the warmth of the room. Alex's flat was always so warm, one of the benefits of new-build apartments.

'Alex, I shouldn't stay too late, I'm so tired,' she said, her head lolling back on the couch. She looked at him through half-closed eyes and yawned.

Alex started laughing. 'You're such a lightweight. You're drunk? You've only had two glasses,' he said, a big grin on his face as he looked across at her.

'I'll have to get a taxi home,' she murmured.

Katie could feel sleep taking over. The sofa felt so irresistibly buttery soft underneath her cheek, her fingers gently stroking the velvet throw that lay crumpled across the cushions. She tried to keep her eyes open, but they felt weighed down. Her head floated and throbbed at the same time. A fuzzy blackness enveloped her that she was powerless to resist.

Katie could feel an ashen taste in her mouth and a throbbing in her temples as she tentatively opened her eyes the following morning. Squinting against the morning light, she cursed its intrusive brightness. Saliva rushed into her mouth as she sensed the nausea in her stomach.

Her eyes focused on the green duvet and … she frowned. That wasn't right – her duvet was purple. She opened her eyes fully and turned over to see Alex smiling at her from the other side of the bed, hair ruffled.

'Morning beautiful,' he murmured lovingly, still sleepy.

Katie stared blankly at him and realised that he was completely naked. And so was she.

'Are you okay in there?' Alex rapped on the bathroom door as Katie sat on the loo, her heart pounding, holding onto the cold porcelain of the sink with one hand. She tried to breathe deeply to quell the churning in her stomach and the nervous panic she could feel rising in her throat.

'Yes!' she called out, and turned the taps on full. Steam started to fog the mirror above the sink as she put her head in her hands.

She couldn't believe she'd slept with him and couldn't even remember what had happened between them, although little snatches of last night kept surfacing like shipwrecks from a fog – his lips hot and insistent upon hers, hands pulling on clothing, his weight upon her. She cringed with embarrassment at having allowed herself to cross her professional boundaries.

She knew this could damage their partnership and affect their skating; it had happened to others before them. She rested her forehead on the coolness of the sink and sighed deeply. Apart from the professional damage this could do, she didn't want to be in a relationship right now, with Alex or anyone. As talented and undeniably beautiful as he was, it didn't feel like the right time, and he didn't feel like the right guy. She was going to have to find a way to tell him.

Alex was busy putting the final preparations on the table as she emerged from the bedroom, showered and dressed in the clothes she had come in last night. He smiled at her as she walked in, handing her a strong sweet coffee that she sipped gratefully, even though she usually stuck to tea. She looked around in dismay at all the effort he had gone to while she had been in the bathroom.

On the table there was fresh orange juice, warm croissants, jams, butter, fruit, and yoghurt. In the middle was a vase of fresh flowers he must have gone out and bought while she lingered in the shower, their perfume scenting the morning air over the warm aromas of the coffee and pastries. The sun was streaming in the windows, lighting up the whole room. If she hadn't felt so awkward and physically wretched this domestic gesture would have been a delightful thing to behold.

'Sit down, help yourself,' he said, eagerly offering her a

croissant. She took it and spread the butter and jam on it, the butter sliding gently down her fingers. It smelled delicious and despite her nausea, she was desperate to eat. Her head still throbbed dully at her temples, but the caffeine and carbs were already having their effect, calming her stomach and soothing her nerves. She closed her eyes and chewed slowly.

'Hey,' Alex said, and she looked up to see him quickly taking a shot of her on his mobile phone.

'Gorgeous,' he said, pleased, reviewing the picture.

She smiled weakly. 'Thanks, but I must look like such a mess.'

He shook his head and took a sip of his coffee, his eyes regarding hers across the table, like he was trying to absorb every detail of her. She chewed slowly on her croissant as he smiled at her like a lovesick puppy. His hair was uncombed and he had thrown on a crumpled black T-shirt but he still managed to look gorgeous, the tufts of his hair sticking up only making him seem more youthful, more innocent.

Katie kept wanting to speak, to talk about what had happened, but her brain scrabbled for words and she couldn't think of anything that would be helpful or appropriate, so she kept her mouth full and stayed silent.

'What do you want to do today?' he asked, when she had finished eating. 'It's a beautiful day. We could go for a walk? Or do you want to hang out here …?' He left the question open-ended, raising one eyebrow suggestively at her.

Katie's stomach tensed and she rubbed her fingertips over her denim-clad knees, her hands suddenly clammy.

'Um, actually Alex I have a bit of a headache. I'd quite like to go home and sleep,' she murmured, trying to ignore the look of disappointment that swept across his face.

'Really? You could sleep here,' he said, hopefully, his eyes flicking to the bedroom where not long before this conversation they had both been naked in bed together. He grinned at her and she flushed, wondering what he remembered of last night, what details he could recall of what they did together.

'I'd quite like to get changed,' she said, biting her lip, looking down at the flakes of pastry left on her plate, hoping that he would let her go without her having to make any more excuses.

'Of course,' he nodded. 'Maybe I'll come over later and we could watch a movie?'

'Text me later and I'll see how I feel,' she said, trying not to sound too dismissive. Right now, she wanted to be alone in her own bed and sleep and not think about how awkward this whole situation was.

Alex insisted on seeing her down to her car and wrapped his arms around her before she got in, giving her a tight hug and kissing the top of her head. She didn't raise her face to his in case he wanted to kiss her on the lips. She was relieved when she left his embrace to slide into the car and drive away from the flat.

Her mind was spinning in time with her stomach as she drove home. A dark shadow of a thought lingered in her mind that she had been too drunk to remember what happened, which meant that Alex had taken advantage of her. She shook her head fiercely, trying to dislodge the ugly thought. Alex was her partner and her friend, and clearly had feelings for her. She didn't want to think he was capable of such a thing. No, Katie thought, it was a drunken mistake, nothing more sinister than that.

It was only when she got home and checked her phone for the first time since last night that she saw all the social media notifications. There were thousands of likes and comments on Alex's post: the picture of her at breakfast, smiling, looking tired but her face and hair lit up by the morning sun, with his string of heart and kissing emojis underneath.

Their "relationship" had already gone public.

Chapter Twelve

'Hi Jamie.' Katie spoke quickly as he picked up the phone.

'Hey, what's up?' he said, hoping she hadn't called to continue the argument they'd had earlier in the day. He still felt bad about getting in the middle of her and Alex, and was grateful that Maddie had come along with the girls and warded off Katie's ire.

'Listen, I've been thinking that we need to get you doing some more lifts this week. Theo is already doing more complex ones, so we need to catch up.'

Jamie nodded. 'Sure, okay,' he said, relieved that she was phoning about the show.

'Can you meet me at the pool tomorrow instead of the rink?' she asked. 'It's helpful to try them out in water first, you know, like that scene in *Dirty Dancing*.'

Jamie laughed. 'Sure, sounds fine, but we don't need to go to the public pool – I've got one in my house,' he said.

'Wow, that's great. Give me your address and I'll come over tomorrow at nine if that's okay?' she said, scribbling down the address Jamie gave her.

Jamie hurried to the door as Katie punched in the code to the gate that he had given her. She was dead on time despite taking the bus in rush hour. He watched as she paused and stood in awe on his driveway for a moment. Jamie knew the house was impressive – a bright white cube punctuated by large windows, with a sweeping driveway in front. The house was all hard angles and shiny surfaces, gleaming in the sunlight, completely unique. Cassandra had chosen it and loved it.

Katie crunched up the drive to where he stood waiting for her at the front door.

'Morning,' she said, as Jamie stepped aside to let her in. 'Your house is amazing.'

Jamie nodded sheepishly. He was rather embarrassed at its audacious size, and while he was playing and being sponsored the bills weren't an issue, but the house was now a financial sinkhole that he couldn't really afford any more. It also held so many memories of Cass – she was the one who had fallen in love with its modernist details and oversized windows. He was thinking about moving.

'You look like you're ready to swim,' Katie said, smiling at him. He had pulled on his swim shorts and a T-shirt and was thrilled to find how loose they were. He'd been steadily tightening up since starting the programme and he'd now found the motivation to add weights into his daily routine and started running again. The hard edges of his jawline had returned from the fleshy softness that had been gradually gathering at his throat, and his abs were newly uncovered, the layer of fat around his midriff melting away with every training session. He was starting to feel like himself again.

'Do you want a drink or anything first?'

She shook her head. 'I wouldn't mind a tour though,' she said.

They padded down the hallway to the kitchen. Katie stopped in front of his wedding photos lining the hall.

'I really ought to take them down,' Jamie said, not wanting to stand there looking at the happy memories he had marred with his stupidity three years ago.

'She is so beautiful,' Katie said, looking longingly at the couture wedding gown that Cassandra had had made especially for her. She was resplendent in white, a tiara of glittering diamonds shining out from her hair.

Jamie smiled sadly. 'We were together for over eight years,' he said, wishing he could take the photos down but never quite able to remove them and leave empty walls behind to taunt him.

'Shame she believed the papers over me,' he sighed, shrugging and turning away.

'I'm sorry,' Katie said. Jamie wasn't sure she really believed him, but she sounded sincere.

She followed him into the kitchen, with huge folding doors overlooking an enormous garden which had seen better days. 'I'm not much of a gardener,' he said, gesturing at the unkempt lawn. 'You sure you don't want anything to eat or drink?' he asked.

'No thanks,' she replied, shaking her head and checking her watch. 'Maybe we should get started?'

He nodded and she followed him down a flight of stairs to the basement, where he had a pool and indoor gym. Katie gaped at it. 'This is ... something else,' she said, sounding amazed at the luxuriousness of it.

'I'm very lucky,' he said.

He indicated to a bathroom on the side where she could change into her swimming costume while he slid into the pool. He was doing a few lengths to warm up when she emerged and lowered herself quickly into the warm water. She swam up to him.

'I'm not much of a swimmer,' she said with a grin. 'I can glide on top of the water when it's frozen but dunk me in a pool and I flounder.'

Jamie grinned at her. 'I can't promise to save you if you start drowning,' he said, laughing.

'I'll bear that in mind,' she said with a smile. 'Right, let's practise lifting.'

She taught him about weight distribution and balancing her weight against his need to stay upright on the ice. Fortunately, Jamie found he could easily lift her weight out of the water. The key challenge would be staying balanced on razor-thin blades while holding Katie aloft in the air and spinning around, and at the same time making it look effortless, even graceful.

The warm water was a comforting support around them, so he could get used to the lifts and not be afraid that she would get hurt if he made a mistake. Jamie had to admit he felt nervous about lifting her on the ice, given her past accident. He would hate to be responsible for injuring her.

Jamie was completely focused on what she was telling him, keen to make sure he didn't drop her or grab her in the wrong places, until she wrapped her legs around his torso and he had to hold her close, her wet hair drifting over his shoulder, his face buried in her neck. Her arms threaded around his shoulder blades and he could feel the swell of her breasts pressed up against him.

A thrill of desire ran right through his body that he hadn't felt for a while, even when he'd had the chance after the divorce to hook up with other women. His encounter with Lara at the hotel hadn't left him reeling like this. He swallowed hard and tried to ignore it.

'Good,' Katie said, breaking the lift, pleased with his progress but seemingly unaffected by their proximity.

His focus completely thrown, he fluffed the next lift entirely so she fell crashing into the water with a shriek and a laugh.

'What happened there?' she said, emerging from the water, wiping her eyes and blinking against the chlorine.

'Nothing, sorry,' he said and forced his mind to focus on the techniques and not her soft wet skin and her limbs entwined around his.

After their session, she showered and changed, and he went to the kitchen to prepare some lunch. They tucked hungrily into chicken wraps while sat at the kitchen counter, staring at the rain that had started pouring outside, chasing away the bright sunshine of earlier.

Jamie chased a stray piece of chicken around his plate. 'I was wondering if you feel nervous about the lifts,' he asked hesitantly. He had been thinking that she might be anxious about falling again, especially being lifted by an amateur like him.

She chewed slowly and swallowed, taking her time to reply.

'A little,' she replied eventually. 'But I know you can do the lifts and you won't let me fall,' she said. Jamie felt pleased with the compliment of her trust, and it helped his confidence to know that she herself wasn't afraid.

'I'll do my best.' He smiled at her.

Katie tucked a strand of damp hair behind her ear and nodded towards the photos of his family around the kitchen. 'Are you very close to your parents?' she asked, spying a photo of him in his rugby uniform, covered in mud, with his mum and dad either side of him.

'Yep. They've really supported me all through my career, ferried me to practice sessions on freezing rainy days when I'm sure they would have preferred to stay at home,' he said, with a smile.

He looked down at his plate. 'They were on my side when the cheating rumours happened too. They never doubted that I was telling the truth.' He glanced back up, her cool eyes watching him warily. He wondered if she believed him too, not that it really mattered all that much, but the thought of her thinking that he was a love rat bothered him.

'They sound like nice parents to have,' she said, softly, a shadow crossing her face.

'What about you?' Jamie asked, cautiously. 'You told me that your dad passed away a few years ago? That must be tough.'

Katie nodded. 'My dad was amazing. He drove my career from the get-go. He took me skating when I was four because I saw someone on TV doing it and told him I wanted to try.' She smiled sadly. 'He gave up everything to take me to competitions and pay for my coaching, my costumes, the fees. He gave everything he had from my mother's payout.'

Jamie looked at her questioningly, confused.

'My mother died in hospital from a severe haemorrhage after she gave birth. They were found to be negligent and my father won a settlement, out of court,' she explained, seeing his confused expression.

'That's terrible,' Jamie said, shaking his head. 'I'm so sorry.'

He felt a flash of gratitude for his family, the infallible support he knew he sometimes took for granted. They had had their difficulties of course, but they had stood by him when he had made all those mistakes, when he had let the entire country down and it had seemed like everyone hated him. He couldn't imagine how Katie had felt after the accident when her parents hadn't been there to help her recover, not just physically, but also emotionally, from the end of her career and her relationship with Alex too, all at once.

'Do you have any other family?' he asked.

She shook her head. 'Nope. I have a great aunt in Australia, I think, but I've never met her.'

He chewed his chicken wrap, thinking about how life would feel if his family weren't around.

'Sounds lonely,' he said finally, glancing at her.

She paused and met his eyes. 'It can be,' she said, and he felt for the first time that the ice between them was a little bit thinner than it had been before.

Then

Katie winced as she heard her landlord's voice bleating over the voicemail. She knew her rent was due and she was fast running out of money. She didn't understand why – Sergei had promised everything would be taken care of but clearly it hadn't been.

She took a deep breath, knowing that she would have to talk to him about it after their practice today. She and Alex were gearing up for the skating season with ambitious choreography and the training was intensive, Katie spending long nights afterwards with Alex at his apartment. Sometimes she wanted time to herself but Alex always begged her to stay, wrapping his arms around her and refusing to let her out of the bed, and she always relented, touched by his neediness and flattered by his hunger for her that she could never quite seem to satisfy.

She felt worried about talking to Sergei all the way through their training session, embarrassed and awkward about raising the issue of money. Before her dad died, he had handled all those tricky questions on her behalf and Katie had never been interested in paying attention to financial matters, though she wished she had been, as now she felt completely unsure of herself when it came to managing money.

'Sergei, can I have a word?' she asked timidly, after their session had finished.

He nodded curtly, folding his hands together expectantly.

'Um, my rent is overdue,' she said, sheepishly fiddling with a strand of hair.

Alex looked up quickly from where he sat untying his skates. 'What's that?' he asked.

She glanced at him. 'Just asking about my rent,' she said, running a hand over her arm and wishing she could go.

Sergei shot Alex a look that she couldn't decipher, and he walked up to her and wrapped his arms around her, kissing the top of her head, then tilting her face up to his. 'Sergei and I were going over the figures the other day and, well, we're not sure that paying for your separate flat each month is a good use of money, especially as it's so run down,' he said, matter-of-factly.

She frowned at him while Sergei scuttled away quietly, unnoticed.

'What do you mean?' she said, confused. 'I thought we were getting sponsorship money and we had applied for that funding too? You did both promise me that finances would be taken care of.'

Alex nodded, smoothing his hand over her hair. 'Sure we did, and we sorted everything out about your dad's problems didn't we?'

She nodded and opened her mouth to speak but he interrupted her before she had a chance to begin.

'The money, our money, will go further and can be used more effectively if we're not paying for your extra rent as well. Then we can put it all towards training and travel and equipment, and specialist coaching if we need it,' he said, soothingly.

He smiled when he saw worry crease her forehead. 'But what am I going to do about my rent?' she asked helplessly, wishing she had been more involved, suddenly disliking the sense of dependency she felt on Alex and Sergei.

'Well, you should move in with me,' he said, running his hands down her back, holding her closer.

Katie was taken aback at the suggestion. They had only been dating for a few weeks and she was still getting used to the idea of being in a relationship with him.

'Alex, that's so nice of you to offer, but it's so fast, don't you think?' She stuttered the words out disjointedly, not wanting to disappoint him.

His face, predictably, fell. 'But I'm so crazy about you. I want to be with you all the time ...' he said, looking searchingly into her eyes. 'Don't you feel the same?'

'Sure, I just—'

'Then what's the problem?' he interrupted. 'My flat is close to the rink, so you won't have to drive every morning. You're always complaining how much you hate your flat and saying how much you love mine.' He stared at her so intently that she wanted to look away. 'And saying how much you love me,' he added.

Inwardly, she winced a little. After several nights together he had whispered to her about how he was falling in love with her while she still lay entwined underneath him, hot and damp after yet another lengthy sex session. She had murmured the words hesitantly back, knowing that he expected her to, feeling awkward and unsure and yet thrilled with how happy it made him.

Katie couldn't understand what was missing. He was strikingly beautiful, wealthy, talented, and yet she couldn't shake that feeling of unease that something wasn't quite falling into place in her heart the way it seemed to in his. Maybe she needed time. And he was right, she loathed her flat, where she was lonely all the time, constantly reminded of her dad's death, and where the neighbours' arguments came throbbing through the walls at night.

She smiled at him. 'Of course, you're right. It's a great idea, Alex.'

He beamed at her, his smile lighting his entire face, setting his hazel eyes aglow, and she hoped that she was making the right decision.

Katie and Alex held hands atop the podium and lifted their medals high, beaming, waving to the crowd. Katie felt like her chest could burst with joy and she gripped Alex's hand tightly, her delight at coming third at the World Championships matched only by the surge of affection she felt for him, the one to whom she owed this victory. They had honed their programme after coming fourth at the European Championships two months ago, and their hard work had paid off, the medals around their necks testament to painstaking hours of training to perfect the jumps, throws and spins necessary to make it to the podium.

Alex looked at her and mouthed "I love you" and she grinned back, basking in glory once again.

A wave of sadness crossed her heart as she thought of how proud her dad would have been to see her there with Alex, the path to Olympic victory wide open before them, and beloved by the crowd for their romance – helped in no small part by Alex's savvy social media posts about their love affair. Katie hoped her dad could somehow see her, wherever he was now, and know that she was truly happy. She felt no envy or sadness about not competing as an individual any more. It wasn't possible to do both pairs and individual skating, the training demands for just one discipline were all consuming. Alex had been right; as a pair they could do lifts and throws that no skater could do on their own, and Katie loved the challenge and the thrill of it.

They had decided to stay in Canada for a few days after the competition to relax and had booked into a fancy hotel suite where they could enjoy the spa, room service, and time to reflect on their performance. Sergei agreed that they both needed a break.

The hotel reception was cool and calm, the sleek marble tiling reflecting the low voices of guests passing through the lobby or gathering in small groups for dinner or drinks. Katie waited patiently by a faux Grecian fountain, the incessant murmur of the water a comforting lull over the voices of visitors. She closed her eyes gently and smiled, contentedly running over the perfect evening they had enjoyed together at an exquisite restaurant. Her body still ached but she was looking forward to the rest of the evening alone with Alex in their room, their four-poster bed waiting for them. She hoped that he had managed to retrieve his jacket he had left behind in the taxi, and that he wouldn't take too long.

'Hey, congratulations Katie.' Tristan Lomax approached her from across the lobby, bounding over eagerly, a big grin on his boyishly handsome face. He had come sixth in Worlds with his partner this year and Katie knew he would be disappointed that he wasn't taking a medal home.

'Thank you,' she said, as he came up to her and gave her a hug and a kiss on the cheek.

'You and Alex, what a combination. Everyone is going to be gunning for you two now. You're the ones to watch,' he said, his warm brown eyes gleaming.

She laughed. 'Well, we've still got the Russians and the Japanese to beat Tristan, so we're not resting on our laurels yet.'

'Yeah but you two are the most popular,' he said, leaning in close. 'And the best looking out there,' he added, and winked at her.

She smiled and shook her head, knowing Tristan was a terrible flirt, but not really minding. She knew she looked nice that night – she was wearing her favourite black dress that cinched in her waist and had an elaborate beaded neckline that glimmered against her pale skin. Alex had bought it for her as a gift for their six-month anniversary. She never really went shopping for herself – partly because she found it boring and partly because since she and Alex had opened the joint account and she had lost the card, she never had any money on her anyway. She didn't mind – Alex was great at being in charge of all the bills and he gave her whatever she needed.

'Where's Angelica?' she asked, looking over Tristan's shoulder to see if his skating partner was nearby.

'She's out with Richard,' Tristan said, referring to their coach and Angelica's fiancée.

'So, you're on your own tonight?'

'We'll see,' he said, and winked at her again and she giggled.

Tristan stuck his hands in his pockets and sauntered off with a cheery wave and she turned to see Alex walking towards her across the lobby. She waved at him and he walked over with an odd look on his face.

'Having a nice chat with Tristan?' he asked, mutedly.

'He was just saying good night,' she said. 'Ready to go up? I'm glad you got your jacket back.'

She looped her arm in his and they headed towards the lifts, but she could tell that something was off. Alex's curt replies were monosyllabic and he barely said a word on the way to their room. Katie wondered what was wrong as her heels dragged on the thick hallway carpeting and she walked slightly slower than Alex, trailing behind him as he strode on.

When they got to the room, she threw herself on the bed, curling up contentedly under the thick duvet, but Alex stood at the window and stared out, his arms crossed and a sullen expression on his face.

'Alex what's wrong?' she asked, thinking that maybe he argued with the taxi driver.

He turned and looked at her, his face white and unreadable like marble. 'I don't like being made a fool of, Katie.'

'I don't understand what you mean,' she said, confused, looking up at him trying to work out what the problem was.

He walked over slowly and stood at the end of the bed, leaning down over her and grasping her legs with his hands.

'You were flirting with Tristan,' he said in a low voice, with a look on his face she had never seen before, a tautness to his mouth that ran all the way up to his eyes and down into the sinews of his neck. He gripped her legs tightly and she flinched as he squeezed them just a bit too hard for comfort.

'I wasn't, Alex, I swear, he came over to say hello and he was being friendly,' she said, pleadingly, wanting his gaze to soften.

'I don't want you talking with other men like that. Ever,' he said, his voice level and cold, leaving no room for questions or anything other than obedience.

'I won't, Alex, I promise,' she said, feeling a damp chill of sweat gathering under her arms and down her back.

'And if you're thinking about switching partners …' he started to say.

'Alex!' she interrupted, shocked. 'As if I would!'

He glared at her and she kneeled up and grabbed him by the shoulders, looking at him in the eyes, wanting to press her mouth to his to make the tension in his face melt away and reveal the loving, passionate Alex that had been with her only moments before. 'I don't want to skate with anyone else,' she said. 'Please believe me.'

Something in him seemed to slacken then, and he leaned forward into her and put his arms around her back. 'Promise me,' he murmured into her hair.

'Promise,' she said, and felt bad for having ruined their evening.

Chapter Thirteen

'Careful!' Katie shouted as Jamie missed the timing for the lift and wobbled dangerously. He managed to stabilise himself enough to put her down without both of them falling on the ice.

'Argh sorry,' he said, for the tenth time that practice, grimacing.

She squeezed his shoulder. 'It's okay, don't worry. Take five.' She breathed deeply and tried not to let him see her nervousness, as it would make things more difficult for him. She kept telling herself that Jamie wasn't Alex, and that history wouldn't repeat itself. She knew that Jamie didn't want to hurt her.

He skated around slowly, trying to shake off the failure, his jaw clenched with frustration.

'You may not believe me,' Katie said, coming alongside him, 'but it is getting better. Honestly.'

He glanced at her and shook his head, rubbing the back of his neck. 'Doesn't feel like it,' he said grumpily.

'You want a break?'

'Nope. Let's try again.'

Katie admired his determination. They had been working harder than ever this week, spending hours on the ice as his stamina had improved. She could see that he was tired and annoyed at himself for making mistakes, but both of them were born competitors and couldn't stand to be left behind by the other contestants, especially Theo and Lara, who were shaping up to be the clear front runners.

They tried again. Jamie's timing was slightly off and when he lifted her his arms failed to lock in place properly. He put her down as gently as he could and sighed, grinding his teeth.

'I don't get it. It's like I can't get you up in the air properly,' he said, running a hand through his hair, damp with perspiration. He looked exasperated. 'I mean, it's not like you weigh a lot.'

Katie looked up at him sharply. 'You think I'm too heavy for you?' she said, heat flashing across her cheeks, her hands automatically running over her stomach to feel if her clothes were a little tighter that week.

'What? No, don't be ridiculous. You're tiny.' Jamie stopped skating and looked at her in surprise.

'I weigh more than when I was competing,' she said, her hands tugging anxiously at her waistline, pinching tiny mounds of flesh between her fingertips.

She had been so careful with her diet, especially being back on the ice for the show. She didn't think she had put on weight, but Jamie did seem to be struggling to lift her. She glanced at him and he shook his head vehemently.

'Katie seriously, this isn't about you. I can't get the timing right so the momentum isn't there.'

She nodded, feeling doubtful.

'Let's go again,' he said, and she followed him back to their starting position, swallowing hard as a sudden burst of anxiety washed over her.

Then

'I disagree,' Katie said, putting her hands on her hips and pursing her lips as she and Alex stood in the middle of the ice, toe to toe.

Alex threw up his hands with exasperation. 'Listen to me, I know what I'm talking about. I don't think the triple toe loop works there. It should be earlier – it goes better with the rhythm.'

Katie shook her head determinedly, her mouth set in a firm line. 'But then we have to move the quad throw and you know I need more energy for that one, so I need to do it earlier in the programme.' She met Alex's gaze defiantly. 'I don't see why we have to change the choreography now.'

Sergei called out to them from the side. 'Why are you discussing and not skating?'

They skated over to ask his opinion and he listened to them both before, inevitably, siding with Alex. Katie sighed and bit her lip with annoyance that, despite working with a top choreographer, they were going to change the programme they had agreed upon.

Alex looked pleased. 'Good. The triple toe comes earlier then.'

She nodded, knowing there was no point in continuing to press her case for keeping the original choreography. They skated back and she tried to ignore her disappointment at being overruled yet again. Alex always thought he knew best, and as much as she respected his opinion, she felt that her input was swiftly being silenced.

As they carried on practising Katie struggled to land the quad throw, and the more they tried, the more tired she became, eventually falling three times in a row. The third time she knew she had to stop as the nagging pain in her hip became increasingly uncomfortable, further bruised and weakened from the hard falls.

'Alex, I'm not happy with this,' she said, pleadingly, pushing herself wearily to her feet after the last fall. She hesitated for a moment, as she rarely insisted on her own way. 'Please reconsider.'

Alex shook his head. 'I'm right about this,' he said, crossing his arms.

A flash of anger sparked in her chest, balling up into an energy she couldn't contain as she opened her mouth to reply. 'No, you're not, Alex!' she said, her hands clenched at her sides. She shuddered at the confrontation, but she carried on regardless. 'This is no good. And I won't keep pushing myself and get injured – you and I both know better than that.'

Alex stood still and silent before her. 'I'm wrong?' he said, eventually, raising his eyebrows. She hated the fact that he looked so incredulous, a small smile playing on his lips as he looked at her so hot and flushed with anger before him while he stood calm and languid.

She nodded tersely, unwilling to speak any further.

'I've been skating longer than you, Katie, been in more competitions, won more medals, and you think you know better?' he said, in a low voice, standing close to her so her face was turned up towards his.

Anger constricted her throat, making her voice shaky. 'Yes, you're wrong about this,' Katie said, in a whisper.

He looked at her calmly and stepped back slightly. 'Fine. We do it your way.'

'Really?' she said, surprised that he had given in, relief flooding into her muscles like warm air.

He nodded, without speaking, and she felt the delight of getting her own way, just for once.

Alex hadn't mentioned their confrontation about the programme order since they had argued about it a week ago, and the training sessions were running smoothly. Katie was relieved that he hadn't continued to argue the issue, knowing that she would have caved in if he had decided to be more forceful about it. She had never liked confrontation.

But as one element was resolved, another problem reared its head, and Katie noticed Alex seemed to be struggling with the lifts one session. After four failed lifts, she decided to ask him what was wrong. Alex didn't like acknowledging failure, but she was concerned there was some pain or injury he wasn't telling her about.

'What's wrong Alex?' she asked gently.

He shook his head tensely. 'Let's call it a day.'

She followed him off the ice, shrugging at Sergei when he looked at her questioningly, and they left the rink, their usual companionable chatter replaced by a stony silence. Back in the flat, Katie suggested getting a takeaway, and Alex shrugged and sat looking gloomy on the sofa, idling through the channels. She knew he was upset but decided not to push the issue and called for a pizza. They watched TV in silence, and when the pizza arrived, she popped the box between them on the sofa and grabbed a slice, leaning back to savour it and hoping that Alex would snap out of his mood soon.

Alex reached out to take a slice and chewed it slowly. Suddenly, he pointed the remote at the TV, jabbed at the mute button, and swivelled round to her.

'Katie, we need to talk,' he said, looking uneasy.

She nodded and put her slice down, hoping that he would tell her what the problem was.

'I'm having trouble with the lifts,' he started.

She nodded. 'What's going on?'

He looked at her shiftily, not quite meeting her eyes. 'There's no easy way to say this, but … I think you've put on weight.'

Katie stared at him in silence, a breath catching in her throat. She opened her mouth to speak but he interrupted.

'I don't want to hurt your feelings, but I noticed it last week and I think you need to be more careful about what you eat, darling.' He finally met her gaze, looking at her warily to gauge her reaction.

Tears pricked at Katie's eyes and she tried to speak in a level tone, though her voice wobbled when she tried to respond.

'I didn't think I was getting fatter, I mean, all my clothes still fit fine. I don't feel any different,' she murmured.

'C'mon, Katie. I have my hands over you all day and all night long. You don't think I'd notice?' He leaned forward and gently tilted her head up to meet his eyes. 'All those banana milkshakes you love. And you do have a weakness for junk food too.' He gestured at the pizza box.

'So do you,' Katie said, feeling petty for pointing it out.

'Yeah but sweetheart, I'm not getting, well, you know,' he said, and patted her stomach.

She flinched at the gesture, which he did gently and lovingly, but it might as well have been a punch to the gut for the way it made her feel.

'Listen please don't worry,' he said earnestly, grabbing her hands and running his thumbs over them. 'I'll help you. I'll set up a meal plan tomorrow, okay? I'm good at nutritional stuff.'

'All right,' she said unhappily, turning back to the TV and picking up another slice, but Alex gently took it from her. 'Maybe just the one slice tonight, okay?'

She nodded and went to the kitchen to grab an apple instead while Alex carried on munching his pizza, his low mood seemingly lifted now that he had got the awkward truth off his chest.

The meal plan had been in place for two weeks and Katie hated it. She hated the tasteless meals of steamed fish and vegetables, the powdery slimming shakes which she had to gag down – she even hated the paper printout of the plan itself, hanging jauntily on the fridge door, taunting her.

Their bathroom scales were broken and she had suggested they buy new ones to help them keep track of the plan's impact, but Alex shook his head. He would know from the lifts, he told her. And it seemed he was right – their lifts had improved dramatically and his lust for her was even more insatiable than usual, which she put down to him finding her more attractive now she was losing weight.

On the second Friday after she went on the plan, Katie was hoping she could treat herself to a banana milkshake. She had always had them with her dad on Fridays – they would stop by the Shake Shack not far from the rink and he would order her a thick banana milkshake with cream on the top.

After Friday practice ended, Alex was talking with Sergei and Katie walked up, ready to go. 'We'll be a few minutes,' Alex said over his shoulder. She guessed they were having a chat about money or sponsorship, which she was never involved in.

'I'm going to go to the Shake Shack,' she said. 'Want anything?'

Alex swivelled around and indicated to Sergei he would be back in a moment. He took her arm and pulled her to one side. 'Katie, you know the banana milkshakes aren't on the meal plan, right?'

She nodded. 'But Alex, it's been two weeks, surely I can have *one*?'

He shook his head. 'I don't think you should. You need to be a bit more disciplined, Katie.'

She was stung by his words. 'I am,' she snapped. 'I just want *one* milkshake, that's all.'

Alex's face darkened at her irritated tone. 'Fine,' he shot back, and strode to Sergei, his back turned towards her.

She headed to the Shake Shack and ordered her favourite, still annoyed with Alex, and wishing that her dad was there too. Sometimes it would have been nice to have someone fighting in her corner, she thought sadly.

Katie sat in a booth, swirling the cream around the top of her glass in slow circles, remembering how many times she and her dad had sat there together. Warm tears dropped onto her cheeks and she brushed them away roughly, gulping down her shake. Somehow it didn't make her feel any happier, the taste marred by Alex's disapproval and wistful memories of her dad.

Alex was muted with her on the drive home, but they ate their dinner together and talked over their programme, trying to identify some of the elements where they could add on a few points. He was quieter than usual, but still pulled her eagerly into bed that evening. He didn't mention the banana milkshake and Katie was relieved that he didn't seem to want to make a point of it not being part of the meal plan.

The next day she woke up late and stretched out, wriggling her toes and yawning. She felt for Alex next to her, but he had already got up, and the flat was silent. She checked her phone and was surprised to see that it was already gone 9 a.m.

She padded into the kitchen to make tea. Alex wasn't there, nor was he in the bathroom. She thought that he must have gone out, although she couldn't think where he might have gone as she was sure neither of them had made plans for that day.

Katie opened the fridge to look for milk, glaring at the meal plan wafting in her face, only to find there was no milk. In fact, there wasn't anything in the fridge except ketchup. When was the last time they shopped? She thought carefully – she was sure they had food in the flat last night, although she couldn't really remember. Alex was always in charge of the food and grocery shopping, and Katie realised that he must be out buying some food. She grabbed her phone and sent him a text.

Where are you? We're out of milk.

She swung open the cupboard to get her special, low sugar, no-flavour muesli. She was starving and a handful of that would get her through till Alex returned, but the muesli box was empty. She guessed she must have finished it yesterday, although she could have sworn there had been at least some left in the packet.

She texted him again. *And muesli …*

She sipped a mug of tea without milk and waited, but he didn't reply, so she threw on some clothes and decided to head to the corner shop to get a few things, thankful that she had a bit of money in her purse.

She headed for the front door, but as she grabbed the handle, she realised it had been locked from the outside. Frowning, she scrabbled in her bag with her free hand, looking for her keys to unlock the door, but she couldn't find them. Her fingers clasped inside her purse, rummaging past tissues, lip balm, and old receipts, but the keys weren't in their usual pocket. She dumped the entire bag out on the kitchen counter. No keys. She ran through her coat pockets, her jeans, and looked around the living room, but she couldn't find them anywhere.

Katie realised with a sinking stomach that she was locked

in the flat with no way of getting out. She strode over to the kitchen and threw open the rest of the cupboards. There was almost nothing edible in the entire flat. She sat on the sofa, close to tears, and grabbed her mobile to ring Alex. He didn't answer.

Where are you? There's no food and I'm locked in! She typed out the message, feeling foolish even as she wrote it, thinking that any minute she would hear his key in the door and he would laugh at her for being so silly.

She stared blankly at the TV, sipping her now-cool tea, her stomach rumbling insistently. After an hour she started to get really worried, a cold fear pulsing in the pit of her stomach. Maybe he had been in an accident? She pushed that thought out of her head and waited, hands trembling around another cup of black tea, a bitter taste starting to rise in her mouth and her head starting to ache.

Her fingers scrolled shakily through her phone to see who she could call, but she knew Sergei was away in Manchester this weekend and she had no friends, no family, she didn't even know the neighbour's names. The extent of her isolation brought tears to her eyes as she realised she was entirely dependent on Alex for love and company. And what if he was now lying dead somewhere, run over by a car or mugged and injured?

They were upgrading their Wi-Fi and her internet wasn't working, though even if it were, she wasn't sure who she would contact. She sat and waited, the hours passing, fear growing in her heart with the minutes that ticked by.

By the time Alex came home at seven she was weeping on the kitchen floor, woozy from lack of food, and convinced he was dead. When she heard his key turning in the lock she leapt to her feet and dashed to him, wrapping her arms around him, holding him tight, breathing in him.

'Alex!' she shrieked. 'Are you okay? I was so worried!' Her tears smeared a wet patch on his shoulder.

He looked at her, bemused, as he tried to untangle himself from her clasp. 'What happened to you?'

'I've been locked in all day with no food and you weren't answering your phone and I thought you were ...' She sobbed, her hands wringing at his T-shirt, unwilling to let go.

He held her close and chuckled, an amused expression on his face. 'You silly thing. Don't you remember I told you that I was going to be out all day today?'

She stared at him through tear-blurred eyes and shook her head, sniffing.

'I mentioned it to you last night, but I didn't think you were listening,' he said, smiling and shaking his head at her. 'I made plans to meet up with a few friends.'

'Who?' she muttered, a queasy embarrassment spreading through her stomach.

'Paul and Josh,' he said, and raised his eyebrows. 'Wow, you really didn't listen last night, did you?'

'I guess not,' she said sadly, wracking her brains to try and remember him telling her that he would be going to see his old school friends.

'And you've been locked in all day?' he asked, looking at her with pity. She nodded.

'My phone died this morning,' he said. 'I had no idea.' He gently smoothed away the tears on her cheeks with his thumbs.

'What happened to all the food?' she asked.

'Oh well, I figured you were done with the meal plan, so you know, I threw it away and thought you would go shopping. For once,' he said, looking at her carefully.

She frowned. 'Why did you think that?'

'Well Katie,' he said, smiling at her sweetly. 'You clearly want to follow your own rules about what you do or don't eat – you made that clear yesterday. So, I figured you wouldn't want any of the healthy stuff I bought for you and you would go out and buy your own.'

'Of course,' he continued, 'I didn't know that you would lose your keys and be stuck with no food all day. How silly.'

Katie blushed at her own foolishness, weeping and wailing about food and accidents like a child, like someone incapable of looking after themselves. She felt small and stupid.

'Alex, I never said I didn't want to follow your meal plan. I wanted one treat, that's all,' she said morosely, wiping her damp cheeks and sitting on the sofa with him.

Alex nodded. 'Oh right, I clearly misunderstood. I was so hurt when you seemed to be rejecting all the hard work I'd put into your meal plan so we could skate better. I really genuinely thought you were chucking the plan out of the window.'

'I'm sorry I hurt you,' she murmured, putting a hand on his arm. 'I didn't even enjoy the shake that much. I won't have any more, Alex, really. Your meal plan is great. Of course I want to carry on with it.'

Alex looked delighted, a big boyish smile spreading across his face. 'Thanks, sweetheart.' He checked his watch. 'It's a bit late to go shopping, but fortunately I happen to have some food in my bag,' he said, triumphantly fishing out a cereal bar and an apple and handing them to Katie like a prize she had won.

She grabbed them gratefully, glad he was okay, and happy that she had something to eat. Alex called over to her as she headed to the kitchen to slice the apple. 'Hey, your keys are right here!' She turned to see him dangling them from one finger, grinning.

'Where were they?' she gasped.

'Just down the back of the sofa cushions,' he said, switching on the TV and putting his feet up on the coffee table.

Katie frowned as she chopped up the apple. She was so sure she had checked there, but clearly hadn't done so thoroughly enough. What an idiot she was.

Chapter Fourteen

'Yes!' Jamie shouted in triumph as he completed the routine for the second time with no falls, wobbles or stumbles.

Katie clapped him delightedly. 'Well done! That was so good!'

Jamie swooped round the ice and grabbed her in a bear hug, wrapping his arms right around her and lifting her off her feet. It was only a momentary squeeze before he quickly put her down, feeling embarrassed about being so tactile with her. He was used to holding her close during the lifts, but they were all about the technical execution – timing, momentum, balance – rather than affection. He hoped he hadn't offended her with his impromptu hug, but she looked pleased and flushed a rosy pink as she looked at her skates.

'I know how hard you've worked this week, and it really shows,' she said, looking a little flustered. 'You could really be a dark horse contender.'

He grinned proudly at the improvement he had made. 'I hope so.'

They skated to the side of the rink to finish their session. 'Hey what are your plans for tonight?' Jamie asked.

'Um, the usual,' Katie said. 'Dinner, TV. You?'

Jamie hesitated. His parents were celebrating his dad's birthday and they had asked him to invite Katie, but he wasn't sure she'd say yes and he didn't want to put her on the spot.

'It's my dad's birthday and my family are having a special dinner,' he said, after a pause.

'That sounds nice.' She smiled at him and began to pull off her skates, stretching out her toes. 'Have a great time and I'll see you tomorrow for the dress rehearsal.'

She packed up her things quickly while he dithered with his skates and she walked out of the rink. Jamie couldn't understand why he felt so nervous about asking her to come along. He felt just like he did as an awkward teenager, trying to play it cool while wiping sweaty palms on his jeans and hoping the girl he liked wouldn't say no. This was ridiculous, he decided, and marched after Katie.

'Hey, Katie, hold on!'

She turned around and waited for him expectantly with raised eyebrows. 'Everything okay?'

'Do you want to come?' he asked, knowing he spoke too quickly, the words rushing out with a nervous urgency.

'To your dad's dinner?'

'Yeah. I know my family would love to have you there,' he said, sticking his hands in his pockets in an attempt to be nonchalant, hoping she would say yes.

Katie paused for a moment and he thought she might be trying to think of an excuse.

'I'd love to,' she said warmly, to his surprise.

Jamie grinned. 'Great. Come over about 7 p.m.?'

She typed the address into her phone and waved goodbye as he headed for his car. It felt like he'd asked her on a date, though, of course, it was just a family dinner, he told himself.

Later that evening Katie showered and changed and was dithering over what to wear, sat in her underwear in the midst of piles of clothes strewn over her bed.

'This is stupid,' she said to herself, wagging her finger at her reflection in the wardrobe mirror. 'What does it matter what I wear? It's just a casual family dinner.'

She grabbed a dark blue dress with a delicate blossom print that accentuated her eyes and her slim waist. She perched in front of the mirror to do her make-up, knowing that she was making more of an effort than was usual for her. She left her hair loose, swinging below her shoulders in dark waves. She didn't have time to do anything with it as the cab was already outside to take her to Jamie's parents' house in Surbiton, and she perched nervously in the back seat, watching the suburbs roll by in the dark.

When she arrived, she hesitated before knocking nervously on the door, feeling slightly tempted to run back down the driveway and hide behind the wall. Her last big family dinner was with Alex's parents and it had been awkward and stilted and uncomfortable. She hoped Jamie's family were a bit more normal.

Maddie opened the door. 'Katie! Come in!' Maddie pulled her into a hug as Katie stepped through the door. She looked stunning in a green wrap dress that brought out her emerald eyes, the same shade as Jamie's.

Katie followed Maddie through to the kitchen at the back of the house, where clusters of people stood chatting and laughing warmly, sipping glasses of wine.

She could see Jamie deep in conversation with a raven-haired woman by the back doors. His sandy hair fell over his forehead. He was wearing a dark green shirt and black jeans that accentuated the powerful muscles in both his arms and his legs. Katie cast another look at him, trying not to stare, as Jamie's dad appeared at her elbow.

'Katie, it's so lovely to have you here. I'm Phil.' He shook her hand, his skin rough and calloused but his grip gentle. He was slightly stooped with tanned skin and pale blue eyes, and surprisingly slight for someone with a son as tall and built as Jamie.

'It's lovely to meet you,' Katie said, slightly flustered that she had been staring so obviously at his son from across the room. 'Happy birthday,' she said, handing him the bottle of wine she was clutching.

'That's so sweet,' he said and turned to hand it to his wife. 'Susan, look what Katie bought.' He put the wine before Susan on the counter, where she was busy stirring something that smelled delicious in a large saucepan.

Susan looked up and smiled warmly at Katie, looking

delighted. 'I'm so pleased you could make it.' She hurried around the counter and extended her hand eagerly, grasping Katie's. 'I'm such a big fan, Katie,' she said, her eyes wide.

'Thank you,' Katie said, feeling slightly embarrassed.

Jamie must have heard his mum say her name and he looked around quickly. He grinned at Katie, excused himself from his conversation, and bounded over eagerly. 'Hey, thanks for coming,' he said, leaning in awkwardly to kiss her on the cheek. Katie went slightly pink as he did so, but she was sure it was just because the room was so warm.

'Let me introduce you to people,' he said, taking her around the room and introducing Katie to Phil's sisters, Patricia and Margot.

He approached the dark-haired woman who he had been talking to earlier, pulling Katie along.

'I've saved the best till last,' he said delightedly. 'Katie, this is Harriet, Maddie's wife and the fiercest lawyer you will ever meet.'

Harriet laughed and looked at Jamie with affection. She put out her hand to shake Katie's, her crimson nails shining. She was exquisitely dressed in black with a large silver statement necklace, her midnight hair smooth and shining, with bright red lips to match her nails. Katie would have felt intimidated if it weren't for how friendly her eyes were.

'It's lovely to meet you, Katie. Jamie's told me so much about you,' Harriet said. Her accent was cut-glass but her tone was warm and genuine. Jamie and Maddie excused themselves to help Susan, so Harriet and Katie turned towards the open doors, where a light breeze was carrying in cool air.

'What type of law do you practise?' Katie asked.

'Mainly contract, some intellectual property, copyright, defamation. I also do quite a lot of pro bono work for a women's shelter. It's never dull.'

Katie wrinkled her forehead, trying to remember something she had read in the papers. 'Wait, are you Harriet Laine?'

Harriet laughed. 'My reputation clearly precedes me.'

Katie was impressed. Harriet was a well-known lawyer who had recently worked with celebrities on invasion of privacy and defamation cases, including a very famous actress whose reputation had been tarnished by untrue rumours about an affair.

'I read about your win with Katerina Murphy,' Katie said admiringly.

Harriet nodded. 'She's a very dedicated and talented actress. It's such a shame that people wanted to blacken her name.' She glanced at Katie curiously. 'Of course, you've had your fair share of rumour and speculation about you and your relationship with Alex.'

Katie sipped her wine and nodded, not really keen to comment further on that last point. Harriet sensed her reticence and changed the subject to what Alice was working on at school. Occasionally Katie glanced over to where Jamie was busy helping his mum, and more than once she thought that he was looking over at her as she chatted with Harriet. She guessed he was just checking she wasn't left on her own and bored.

Katie enjoyed the dinner, listening to family anecdotes about Phil, laughing at how the family gently poked fun at him, and enjoying the delicious home-cooked food that was so much better than she could do herself.

'Katie, we're all excited to see you and Jamie perform again,' said Susan, leaning over the table. 'We can't wait to see what Jamie's learnt this week.'

Katie grinned and looked at Jamie. 'He's really come along – I think you'll be amazed.' Jamie smiled proudly at her praise.

Susan clapped her hands. 'We're so proud to see him trying something new and so hard like ice skating,' she said. 'Though of course for you this must be child's play,' she added.

Katie shook her head. 'It has some … unique challenges, skating in a show like this,' she said.

'It's a miracle you can skate again,' said Phil, sawing enthusiastically at his lamb. 'What was it they put in your ankle?'

Jamie shot her a concerned look, but she didn't want to be rude, as much as she didn't like talking about the accident.

'Titanium rods,' she said. 'They seem to be holding up well.'

'Dreadful business,' murmured Phil. 'Still, the wonders they can do with medical technology now, eh?'

Katie nodded, hoping the conversation was over.

'Oh, it's a delight to see you back on the ice,' said Susan, dreamily. 'It's a shame you and Alex …'

She trailed off when Jamie drew a finger across his throat and glared at her. Katie looked down at her plate and pretended she hadn't heard the last part or seen Jamie's urgent gesture, and focused on carefully cutting through a large roast potato.

Maddie, sensing her discomfort, diverted the group with a birthday toast, and Katie put her best fake smile on to disguise her upset at how the conversation had included Alex. No matter where she went or what she did, Alex's name always seemed to follow her.

After dinner, she excused herself and went to the toilet. She was wandering back to the dining room when a colourful wall of posters caught her eye through an open doorway. It led to a trophy room, the door standing proudly open to display all of Jamie's sporting accolades. She looked around at them with interest.

She was staring at one of the posters of him, when he was still in the national team, posing proudly in his England shirt, when he found her. She smiled at him as he came in.

'A Jamie shrine,' she said, raising an eyebrow, and he laughed.

'I've told them to clear this room out, or at least shut the door,' he said, shaking his head. 'It's embarrassing.'

'Not at all,' she said, continuing to look at the trophies. 'They're so proud of you.'

'I suppose so,' he said.

She stood in front of the team picture taken at the World Cup that he eventually would be blamed for losing. He came and stood beside her.

'Shame it all went so wrong,' he said. 'Just when you think you're at the top of your career – bam,' he said, smacking his palm down on the shelf. 'Everything can change in one second.'

She nodded. 'I know what you mean. It just takes a second. Timing's off, your focus isn't right, the balance is wrong … and that's it.'

'And you're not ready for it, you're never prepared for when it will end,' he added, and sighed.

They looked at each other with sympathy, each knowing the grief of losing something that formed part of their identities for so long, something that had required so much sacrifice.

'I know how it feels – to not be prepared to lose it all, and how … *lost* you feel after it's gone. Your whole life, all your dreams, your entire career,' Katie said. She wished with all her heart that she could go back and reverse her decision to skate with Alex. She had been so young and so terribly vulnerable then, and she wished she could tell her eighteen year old self to walk away so she could have carried on her solo career and won gold again. She would give anything for that feeling of being the absolute best at something she loved. Instead, she ended up broken – in more ways than one.

Jamie ran grasping fingers through his hair, gently tugging at it as he hung his head. 'At least yours was an accident. I have only myself to blame,' he said.

Then

Jamie couldn't sleep. His nerves were frayed and his mind was racing, darting from one thought to another on a relentless treadmill of fear.

He was sure he was slowly going mad in the dark of the

hotel room. The World Cup final was tomorrow and the pressure of expectation was crushing his chest. He couldn't breathe. Normally he was able to switch off before a big match, but everything was different this time. He felt like a jigsaw with all the pieces slightly out of place – nothing fitted any more.

He knew he shouldn't have phoned Cassie this evening. She'd sounded so cold and distant and irritated when she'd picked up the phone, providing curt answers in clipped tones. She had always been there with him before the big matches, helping him to unwind and stay relaxed. Now she was off somewhere with someone else, starting a new life without him. He missed her, a deep physical ache inside that felt as though his heart had turned to acid and was corroding his guts, and he had foolishly hoped that she might talk to him for a few minutes to help him steady his nerves, to help him feel whole again.

Jamie lay underneath the hotel sheets, sweating, his stomach tense. He still couldn't believe Cassandra had finally walked out on him, all because of a stupid press story that wasn't true. He knew she was hurting but why couldn't she choose to believe him over that Cleo girl? He couldn't stop his mind picking over the fragments of the past few months as the divorce was finalised, replaying the worst memories in high definition, like scenes in a film he would rather forget.

Jamie sat up and switched the light on, breathing hard and pulling at his hair as he looked at the red dial of the bedside clock. It was already 1 a.m. and he had to sleep before tomorrow. In desperation, he decided to grab something from the mini bar, anything to take the edge off and get him some rest.

He yanked open the tiny fridge and winced when he saw the paltry selection. He sat before it silently for a moment and knew he would have to head to the bar if he wanted a proper drink.

Jamie closed his eyes and felt a dull ache behind them, his mind rambling and his thoughts fuzzy from lack of sleep. He wasn't supposed to go to the bar – not now, not before the match. It was unacceptable. He pressed his fingers to his eyes and sat until his legs became stiff, his body tense and shivering.

He stood up decisively and threw on his tracksuit bottoms and a sweatshirt. Screw the rules. He would have one or two and then come straight back up.

Phil slammed the paper down in front of Jamie at the kitchen table.

'This looks really bad J,' he said, leaning over him, his eyes stern. Jamie studied the front page of *The Sun* and shuddered as he looked at the large photo of him in the hotel bar the night before the game. The black and white image from the CCTV was blurry but it was obviously him leaning over the bar counter, several empty drinks in front of him. The judgement of the media and the public was swift and brutal – he was to blame for losing the World Cup because of his drinking session the night before.

Jamie put his head in his hands. 'Shit.' He couldn't meet his dad's eyes and see the disappointment written across his face.

Jamie's phone had been ringing insistently every minute this morning until he had turned it off, knowing in his heart what was coming. His fears were confirmed when his dad arrived with the newspapers and was accosted by journalists at the front gate. Paparazzi were waiting eagerly outside his house, and the hatred was ramping up on social media.

Jamie knew this was going to be very bad.

Katie and Jamie joined the family in the kitchen to sing happy birthday to Phil, who was delighted by his gardening-themed cake.

'Where did you two disappear off to?' Susan sidled up to Jamie after the cake had been portioned out.

'She found the shrine, Mum,' Jamie said, laughing. Susan smiled and followed her son's eyes to where Katie sat, playing with Alice and Isabelle.

She looked at him for a moment. 'You're not …?' She left the question hanging and nodded in Katie's direction, her eyebrows raised.

'What?'

'You know, more than skating partners?' she asked, curiously.

Jamie grinned at her. 'No, of course not.'

Susan sighed with relief and Jamie looked at her, confused. 'Well, you sound pleased.'

'No darling, it's just that I think a lot of people are keen to see her and Alex back together and you don't want to get in the middle of that, do you? It would be like …' She waved her hand around, trying to think of an example. 'Like you breaking up Harry and Meghan.'

Jamie snorted. 'You don't need to worry, there's nothing romantic between us.' He paused. 'But I'm not sure she'll get back with Alex, although that won't be anything to do with me, I can assure you.'

Susan nodded. 'We'll see.' She leaned in and lowered her voice. 'But I have a feeling those two are meant to be together,' she said.

Jamie wanted to remind her that she'd said the same thing about him and Cass, but he let it go. Besides, it was none of his business whom Katie wanted to be with or not. He watched her playing with his nieces, and found himself thinking about the possibility … He dismissed it. He was eight years older than her and divorced, with a reputation for being a love rat on top of that – she wasn't interested in him, he could tell.

And if Katie wanted to get back together with Alex, that was her business, he thought.

'I had a lovely time tonight,' Katie said, gratefully, as she slid into the car and buckled her seat belt. 'Thanks for offering to give me a lift home as well,' she said to Jamie, who started the engine and reversed out of the drive.

'Sure, it's no problem at all,' he said, looking backwards over his shoulder, guiding the car out into the road.

'How are you feeling about this week's performance?' she asked as he flicked through the radio channels.

'Pretty good,' he nodded. 'I think we know the routine pretty well, and I finally nailed those lifts.'

Katie leaned back into the leather seat. 'You'll do great. Plus, I think you're quite popular with the public.'

Jamie shook his head. 'I can't think why.'

'There's lots of positive stuff about you on Twitter after each show. And I saw your morning TV interview the other day and you came across really well.'

'It'll take time to mend the damage I did,' he said. 'But people do forgive and forget. I mean, remember when David Beckham was sent off in the World Cup and everyone hated him? People are fickle, hate-figures change.'

Katie sighed and ran her fingers up and down the leather seat. 'I wish their perception of me would change a bit. I think I'll always be the uptight ice queen who's a bitch for not forgiving Alex.'

Jamie shrugged. 'That's just the story they're running with now. Give them a new story and they'll forget pretty quick.'

'You're very lucky to have your family around you. They're so supportive,' she said, envy adding a slight edge to her voice.

'I am lucky. I wouldn't have got through the really bad times without them ...' He trailed off and focused on the road.

'I wish my dad was still around. I relied so much on his protection,' Katie said sadly, staring out of the window.

'Protection from what?' Jamie asked, curious at her choice of words.

'He always kept me safe from the usual pitfalls of sporting fame, you know, the media, drink, drugs, going out and making a fool of myself, ill-advised relationships ...' She was quiet for a moment, and only the rumble of the engine broke the silence between them. 'When he died, I had no one to fight for me or advise me, and I made choices I regretted,' she added eventually.

'Alex?' Jamie asked.

'*Hmmm.*'

'But you and Alex won big together, you don't regret that, surely?' Jamie asked, incredulously.

Katie shrugged. 'We only came third at World Championships,' she muttered, and Jamie raised his eyebrows incredulously.

'*Only* third?' he asked with a smile, but she didn't reply. They drove in silence for a while.

'Something that kind of confuses me,' Jamie said, breaking the silence, 'is why I never saw you doing many interviews or sponsorship deals, even when you were so popular after your gold medal.'

'My dad was really funny about all that fame stuff,' she replied, her eyes still turned towards the window. 'He always said I should focus on the skating and not get caught up in TV or social media, and he never wanted me to take sponsorship deals.'

'Seems a bit strange to me.'

'He was very proud and very old fashioned,' Katie said, feeling defensive. 'He was so protective too – I guess he was worried I would get distracted or get involved in things that weren't of value. Plus, he died so soon after I won gold and then I was in no fit state to do anything like that.'

'That must have been awful,' Jamie said. 'Kind of a shame though,' he continued, 'not to capitalise on the popularity when you had it.'

'Tell me about it,' Katie agreed. 'Then perhaps I would have had more income and wouldn't have become so trapped.'

Jamie raised his eyebrows. 'Trapped?'

Katie took a breath and nibbled on her lower lip, feeling that she had said far too much. Eventually, she gave a small shake of her head. 'I mean, you know, stuck in a rut with no money and having to do this TV show.'

'Right,' Jamie said, sounding unconvinced.

He pulled up in front of her flat. 'Thanks for the lift,' she said, opening the door. She walked quickly towards the block of flats, a light rain misting on her hair, the orange glow from the street lights reflecting off her like a halo.

She had enjoyed the evening more than she had expected. Jamie's family were so kind and welcoming, and she hadn't felt part of a family in a long time. And Jamie was turning out to be more of a friend than she had thought possible. Not that she was interested in him romantically, especially as it was clear that he was still hung up on Cassandra, she thought.

She turned around as she reached the front door and was surprised to see him waiting till she reached the entrance. He waved and pulled away, and she felt an unexpected surge of disappointment to see him go.

Chapter Fifteen

The studio hummed and clattered with nervous energy, people darting here and there to finalise the preparations for the show, the smell of fake tan and hairspray cloying in the air. Katie had finished in hair and make-up and was looking for Anna. Her eyes scanned over the rinkside set, seeing Jo anxiously tying and retying her skates, Maria posing with Theo, but no Anna.

She walked backstage, passing frazzled runners with clipboards and technicians in sweat-soaked black T-shirts, making final lighting and sound adjustments. Katie finally found Anna by the refreshments table, where she was grabbing a Diet Coke, dressed in a frilly white dress that frothed around her like bubbles. Katie strode up to her.

'I know that you convinced Jamie to tell Alex where he could meet me alone,' she said, folding her arms.

Anna turned to her and gave her a sweet smile, her pale pink lip gloss reflecting the studio lights. 'I was doing Alex a favour. Give the poor guy a break, Katie,' she said, and rolled her eyes.

'Stay out of my business!' Katie hissed angrily at her.

A few of the assistants looked over with interest. Katie glanced at them and stepped back, forcing herself to smile and look calm.

'Don't interfere. Please,' Katie asked, as nicely as she could speak through gritted teeth.

Anna raised an eyebrow and looked unimpressed. 'Honestly Katie, I don't know what your problem is,' she said, running a manicured nail along the ring pull of the can she was holding.

Anna looked around to see who was listening, and leaned towards Katie, lowering her voice. 'Alex is still crazy about you.'

'Alex is crazy. Full stop,' Katie said stiffly.

'What I wouldn't give for him to look at me the way he

looks at you,' Anna said longingly, taking a long sip of her Coke and running her tongue over her lips.

Katie shook her head, feeling her throat tighten. 'Anna, mark my words, stay away from Alex,' she muttered.

'Why? You don't want him, but you don't want anyone else to have him either?' Anna spoke indignantly, raising her voice slightly.

Katie threw up her hands in exasperation. 'No! It's just that he's …'

'I'm what?'

Katie and Anna whipped round to see Alex grinning at them, his jet-black hair falling over his forehead, his shirt slightly open.

Katie shuddered and though her brain tried to find something clever to say, it came up with nothing. She looked at the floor. Anna gave her a sideways glance then looped her arm through Katie's.

'Oh nothing, we're just having a gossip,' said Anna brightly, winking at Alex flirtatiously.

'About me?' Alex put his hands on his chest. 'I'm flattered. Only good things I hope.' He winked back, while Anna beamed at him and Katie looked down to stare stonily at the floor. There was an awkward silence and she could sense Alex looking at her, as though waiting for her to reply. She refused to meet his gaze and eventually he sighed and strolled away, waving to some of the crew members.

Anna extracted her arm from Katie's and watched him leave wistfully. Katie followed her gaze.

'Be careful, Anna,' she said softly, and walked away to find Jamie, leaving Anna behind shaking her head in bemusement.

Jamie didn't expect to find himself leading that week. A couple of stumbles by Theo and Lara failing to complete one of her lifts meant that technically he was the best, though his style was rougher and less polished than either of the other two.

Rory Henderson was doing surprisingly well too, in spite of his clumsiness on the ice.

Getting voted through to the fourth live show was not something he had planned for. As Faith announced the result, Jamie and Katie embraced excitedly and she whispered, 'Well done!' in his ear. He held her tightly and was reluctant to let her go, but she broke off the embrace quickly as they turned to leave the ice, the applause of the audience clattering around them.

They watched the rest of the results from backstage and Jamie was disappointed when Jo was voted off. He had always found her to be a lot of fun to hang around with.

'Shame she's going,' Katie murmured in a low voice to him. Jamie nodded. He was sad about Jo, but he couldn't help but feel delighted at their performance that night and still felt the buzz running through his veins, a giddy high, fogging his head. He knew it was more than excitement at getting the highest score, more than the thrill of doing the routine well and having the audience cheering along. It was also to do with the rush of pleasure he felt at how he and Katie were working as a team, her body responding to his, knowing what each one of them would do in the routine and how they supported each other to do it. She trusted him and he could feel it, and that was a thrill greater than being at the top of the scoreboard.

He glanced at her sideways as they watched the final dance, her hair styled into curls tumbling down her back over her shimmering 1920's-style dress. Jamie wondered if she might want to go for a drink that evening to celebrate. He turned his head quickly to ask her, knowing no one would hear over the backstage din and the applause for Jo, but he was interrupted by an announcement from Faith.

'Now here's a new twist for you at home and for our participants,' Faith chattered excitedly to the cameras. The participants backstage listened, smiling nervously at each other as the cameras zoomed in on them. Jamie caught Katie's eye and shot her a confused look. She shook her head and looked bemused – apparently, she had no idea what the twist would be either.

Faith continued. 'Next week we'll be having an additional special skating performance from a couple chosen by you, the public. On your screen in a minute, you'll see the numbers of all our professional skaters and our athletic participants ... Is there a combination you'd most like to see skate together next week? If so, make sure you vote for them!' Faith beamed into the TV screens as the audience cheered.

'What if they vote for Rory and Theo to skate together?' Vicky laughed, and the participants backstage started excitedly imagining different combinations.

'And the selection doesn't just include our skaters and athletes. It also includes'—Faith swept her arm wide and the camera followed her—'our panel of judges too!'

Alex, Tate and Deborah waved to the camera, and their names appeared on the screen with numbers beside them for the public vote.

'Get voting now because you only have fifteen minutes to decide which pair will skate together next week!'

Jamie looked at Katie, but she didn't turn to him. Her eyes were on Alex as he laughed and chatted with the other judges. She looked as though she might cry, a red flush spreading across the bottom of her neck, her teeth biting hard into her lower lip. He hoped for her sake the public wouldn't vote for her and Alex to skate together.

'Donald, Katie is on her way in to see you and she is pissed off,' Hannah hissed down the phone as Katie stormed towards Donald's office, the eyes of everyone following her as she strode past their desks.

He hung up on Hannah and she grabbed a few papers off her desk and headed to his office. Katie got there before her and barged in without knocking, and Hannah sidled into the room behind her.

'Katie, such a pleasure to see you,' Donald said calmly. He pointed at one of the chairs in front of his desk. 'Please do take a seat.' Hannah edged around to the side of Donald's desk. Katie glanced at her then turned her attention back to Donald.

She folded her arms, her lips thin, her cheeks flushed a mottled red.

'I won't do it,' she said, refusing to sit down and hovering over Donald's desk, breathing quickly.

'Do what my dear?' Donald asked, his voice smooth like oil on water and Hannah tried not to smile as they both knew perfectly well why Katie was there.

'Skate with Alex!' Katie yelled loudly enough that people in the office who were trying to listen could hear her easily. 'I won't skate with him. You *cannot* make me do it.' She'd lowered her voice and spoke firmly.

'Now, Katie, I understand you're a little upset. Can I offer you a drink?'

Katie glared at him. 'No. I don't want a drink.'

Donald folded his hands over his chest and leaned back in his chair, sighing gently. 'Well, this is a pickle.' Hannah chewed the inside of her gum and tried not to smile at his calmness.

'You can't make me skate with him,' Katie repeated.

'Actually sweetheart, it's in your contract for the show that you'll skate with whomsoever you are paired. That means anyone – including Alex,' Donald said, and Hannah swiftly handed him a copy of the contract with the relevant clause highlighted, glad she had come prepared. He waved the contract in the air with his large hand, and gave Hannah a slight nod of approval.

Hannah looked at Katie and raised an eyebrow. 'Plus, Katie, the public voted for you and Alex by a landslide.'

Katie scowled at her and Hannah was frustrated by her rudeness. She had to restrain herself from frowning back at her.

'Ipso facto.' Donald laid the contract on his desk, smoothed it out, and tapped it with a meaty finger. 'You will skate with Alex or be in breach of contract, and you know what that means.' He rubbed his thumb and his forefinger together.

Hannah nodded in agreement, feeling satisfied that there was no way out of this for Katie. She was so ungrateful, thought Hannah. She had been given the chance to skate on TV, up her profile, get paid, and had Alex itching to get back with her again. What more could she want?

Katie stared at them silently, blinking furiously, and Hannah thought she might actually cry.

Hannah studied her carefully and couldn't for the life of her work out why she was being so hysterical about it all.

'Please,' Katie said, changing tack. 'I can't do it. You must understand. Can't you find a way to spin this so I don't have to?' She looked at Donald and then Hannah with a pleading expression.

Donald shook his head firmly and Hannah tried not to smirk when she thought of the ratings bonanza awaiting them. Katie was a fool to think they would pass on the opportunity to get her and Alex reunited on the ice again.

'I'm so *so* sorry, Katie,' Hannah said, trying to look sympathetic. 'I know this is *very* hard for you, but the public voted and we can't see a way out of that – can you?'

Katie curled her hands into fists and chewed on her lip, a red flush creeping up her neck.

'What happens next, Hannah?' Donald asked, turning to her and ignoring Katie's obvious distress.

'You and Alex will need to have several rehearsal sessions this week,' Hannah said. 'He will be in touch to arrange the times later this morning.' She pressed her lips together and gave Katie a tight smile.

Katie nodded, and looked defeated. She walked out of the office without another word to Hannah or Donald.

Hannah grinned at Donald and gave him a thumbs-up as she walked back to her desk. She watched Katie enter the lift and felt slightly guilty at the way she had manipulated the show and the vote to make sure Donald got his way. Still, at least she was in line for a promotion, she thought. She turned back to her computer. Reading the headlines about Alex and Katie's reunion, she smiled at the media frenzy they had created.

'Katie, are you okay?' Jamie asked, watching Katie fiddle with her laces with trembling hands.

'I'm fine,' she said tightly, not looking at him and focusing on the laces.

Jamie shrugged and laced his own skates as they sat side by side in silence. He was still surprised he hadn't been booted out yet, but the public vote for Katie to skate a special performance with Alex had thrown them both off guard and cast a shadow on their triumph. He knew she wasn't okay. There were rumours of a showdown with the producers that hadn't gone her way, and she looked pale with dark smudges under her eyes this morning. Jamie wondered if she had slept since the show.

'Ready to skate?' she said, standing up abruptly.

'Sure.' Jamie followed her to the ice so they could start learning their next routine. Their casual exuberance from the last week had gone and Katie's guard was back up, her thoughts elsewhere. She walked him through the new routine without passion, on autopilot.

Jamie was disheartened at her lack of enthusiasm and wished she could put Alex out of her mind, just for a few hours. The Katie of last week, the one he'd been thinking about almost constantly, had been replaced by the ice queen again, their new friendship cast out into the cold every time Alex came into the picture.

'You can talk to me, you know, if something's on your mind,' Jamie offered cautiously after they finished their rehearsal.

She gave him a weak smile. 'Thanks.'

'You're staying?' he asked, as he took his skates off, but she left hers on.

She nodded. 'I'm meeting Alex here in a little while, so I'll hang around and stay warmed up.'

He nodded. 'I hope it goes well.'

'It'll be fine,' she said, wanly, looking tired.

Jamie hesitated for a second then leaned in and gave her a hug. She was startled by the sudden embrace but slid her arms around him for a second and leaned her forehead onto his shoulder before pulling away.

He gave her a lopsided smile, feeling disappointed that she had pulled away so quickly. 'Have a good one,' he said, casually, and walked away.

Katie watched Jamie walk away and wanted to call out for him to stay. The sensation of his embrace lingered in her mind and she wished she had stayed in his arms and held onto him. She blinked back tears and checked her phone, hoping Alex had sent her a message to cancel their practice. Of course, he hadn't, but the producers had sent their recommended song list through for her and Alex's performance. She took a breath and opened the email, wincing when she saw their suggestions.

- "I Miss You" – Clean Bandit
- "Lovesong" – Adele
- "A Thousand Years" – Christina Perri
- "I Will Always Love You" – Whitney Houston
- "Endless Love" – Mariah Carey and Luther Vandross

Katie groaned inwardly as she looked through the list. And the final suggestion, the cherry on the cake at the end of the list, was the song they had been skating to at the Olympics when everything had gone wrong.

Katie threw her phone against the barriers, a crack splitting the screen where the email still glowed at her, and waited for Alex to arrive.

Then

The skate had been a disaster. To go from third place at the World Championships to seventh at the Warsaw Cup a few months later was deeply disappointing.

Both Katie and Alex had returned home feeling worn out, injured and dejected. Katie's shoulder was killing her from the death spiral, and Alex had an injury in one foot that caused him to fall on the triple lutz, something he hadn't done since he learned the jump years ago.

They decided to take time off to rest and prepare for the Olympics, and Katie was thankful they had already qualified for their spot, regardless of this latest result. Alex hadn't been himself since the competition and Katie tried to stay quiet and stay out of his way as much as she could, leaving him to wallow. He had barely spoken to her for the two days since they had arrived back and she decided to make him a Thai green curry that evening. It was his favourite and she hoped it might cheer him up a little, even though she could only have a tiny portion thanks to the meal plan that continued without end in sight.

She was padding around the kitchen in her socks, trying to follow the recipe without making too much noise. Alex was sitting on the sofa, scowling at his laptop, scrolling through Twitter and the headlines, searching out the commentary on their performance, and watching it over and over again on YouTube.

'Alex?' Katie said, tentatively, after he had watched the video for a fourth time, muttering darkly to himself. She sat down on the sofa and put a hand on his knee.

'Don't torture yourself,' she said gently. 'We'll regroup, forget about it, and move on.'

He stared at her blankly and then jabbed a finger at the screen.

'Look at this,' he said, and he reran the shaky elements of

the programme for her. His fall on the triple lutz, her stumble after the death spiral, the bad landing on the throw salchow. She watched silently, having already seen it many times both on screen and in her head.

'What do you see?' he asked her, looking at her intently.

She shrugged, uncertain what he wanted her to say. 'I don't know, we've been over this like fifty times already. Some skates are bad. You've got to learn to move on from them,' she said, hoping he would stop and get back to his usual self soon.

She walked back to the kitchen to carry on with the cooking. He followed her and stood in front of the counter, his hands spread wide, leaning on his arms and looking down at her.

'You know, Katie, it's only since I started skating with you that I've ever had a bad skate.' He watched her carefully as he spoke, the accusation hanging in the air like poisonous fumes.

Katie put down the knife she had been using, stung by his words.

'You think it's my fault?' she gasped.

He nodded silently, his jaw tense and his hands curled into fists on the black countertop. There was a dangerous look in his eyes that sent a cold shiver of fear into her stomach.

'That's so unfair,' she said, her voice trembling as a knot formed in her throat. 'We're a team. There's no blame, there can't be,' she said, stammering over the words, feeling the force of his anger emanating from his hot gaze upon her.

'You've become sloppy,' he said. 'Your landings are soft. Your timing is off. And you distract me.'

'Actually, Alex,' she said, wiping away a tear angrily, 'it was *your* landing that was off with the lutz – that's why *you* fell and I didn't.' Her chest tightened with anger at how petulant Alex was being. She hated confrontation and hated telling him he had made a mistake, but he had gone too far.

She glared at him then turned her back and walked to the fridge to grab some limes, slamming the door shut with annoyance.

She didn't hear Alex come up behind her, but she felt the force of his hands at her back as he shoved her into the cold hard edges of the countertop. Her socks slid hopelessly on the tiled floor beneath her. Gravity clutched at her and everything went dark as her temple came into contact with the ground, her eyes level with Alex's feet standing over her.

'You poor ice skaters, you're always covered in bruises,' the seamstress said, as she pinned Katie's dress for alterations. She gently folded over layers of emerald green, inserting pins to make it cling to Katie's shrinking frame.

Katie self-consciously touched the large purple bruise on her arm, wincing at the tender injured flesh.

'Injuries are part of the sport,' Katie said softly. Especially when your partner grabs you in just the wrong way, she added morosely in her head.

The seamstress smiled and carried on pinning and Katie stared mutely at herself in the mirror. She was at her thinnest now yet Alex didn't want her to stop the meal plan. He insisted it was to make sure he could lift her without injuring either of them and she didn't want to doubt his words, but she knew it was about more than that. Alex always had to be in control.

The vivid bruise stood out starkly on her skin, one of a growing collection that were additional to the normal bumps and grazes. Alex always apologised and there were always excuses – getting carried away with the choreography, or the momentum was slightly off, or he had gripped her too hard so she wouldn't fall, and so on. The reasons he gave, of course, never related to when she disagreed with him, dared to correct him or tried to stand her ground, although the timing of his injurious errors was always coincidental to those rare occasions.

'Turn please,' the seamstress gently moved her so she could pin the other side. Katie turned obediently, facing away from the mirror.

As she stared at the wall, she calculated the months till the Olympics. The long and short programmes were progressing, this was their shot. As long as she kept her mouth shut and did what Alex wanted, it would probably be okay, she thought hopefully.

'How much will the alterations cost?' she asked. The seamstress scribbled down some numbers on a notebook and ripped off the bill for her to see.

Katie glanced at them. 'I'll have to give the bill to Alex to pay,' she said.

The seamstress grinned at her. 'He's in charge of the purse strings, is he?'

Katie nodded. Alex was in charge of everything from bills to bank accounts. To be fair, he never denied her anything when she asked for it and showered her with gifts on a regular basis. He could be so sweet and passionate with her, especially when they were curled up together at night and he put his arms around her, murmuring into her neck how much he loved her, kissing her ear to make her giggle. In those moments she felt safe and loved and grateful for him.

She folded the bill and put it into her bag. He was stressed out more than usual as the Olympics approached, she thought, thanking the seamstress. Maybe she needed to try harder to do what he wanted and then Loving Alex would appear more often in place of Angry Alex. She left the studio determined to make more of an effort and hoping that it would be enough.

"Olympic success here we come!"

Alex's selfie of them together at practice already had thousands of likes on Instagram. Katie leaned back against the pillows in their bed and flicked back through his feed as he brushed his teeth.

As she scrolled down there were dozens of smiling photos, heart emojis, affectionate nicknames. This was Alex's soppy side, his best side, all laid out for the public to fawn over. She scrolled down wistfully. The vibrant photos of happy memories contrasted violently with the other side of Alex that wasn't on his feed. Angry Alex who was too rough, Perfectionist Alex that demanded that she too was perfect, Controlling Alex who was in charge of her money, her meals, her time and her body, both on and off the ice.

Katie was starting to feel like a puppet. "Yes Alex, no Alex" she would nod and obey, bowing constantly to his demands on the ice, in the kitchen, in the bedroom. She had tried so hard to appease him, but it never seemed to be enough.

Only three months till the Olympics, she thought, turning off her phone as Alex slid into bed beside her and looked at her expectantly, both of them knowing that she would do whatever he demanded.

Alex groaned with frustration and Sergei shook his head disappointedly as Katie sat on the ice in tears after her fourth fall that practice session.

'Please, Alex,' she said, pushing herself up stiffly. 'Can we move on from this element right now? I'm completely psyched out with it and I don't want to get injured.'

'I think if you try it a few more times you'll get it,' said Alex tersely. 'How did you ever win before with that attitude?'

Katie bit her lip. She knew she could do the routine, but she found herself stiffening up and holding back, losing momentum and unable to focus. The more she tried, the worse it became. Her energy levels were low too, her muscles trembling and her lungs unable to draw enough breath to sustain her.

'I need a break, Alex, please – five minutes,' she said and skated away from him and off the ice without waiting for an answer. He watched her go then began throwing himself into practising spins, which he executed perfectly, while she limped off the ice and grabbed her water bottle.

She took a few deep draughts of water and watched Alex skating for a few minutes with a mixture of awe and envy.

He was able to channel even negative emotions into his performances – any anger, anxiety or tension seemed to give him greater strength, greater dynamism. It was a rare gift and Katie wished she had it too.

As the Olympics approached, she could tell that Alex was nervous, and he was increasingly taking it out on her on the ice. A couple of the lifts and throws had gone badly awry in the past two weeks, adding something new to their performances she hadn't felt before: fear.

Katie stood silently, watching him, taking in the perfect turns and spins. He was beautiful on and off the ice, but with a jolt, she realised she was dreading going back in the rink with him. She wasn't sure she was even in love with him any more either.

Alex came to a smooth stop and bounded off the ice towards her. He took her face in his hands, bent down and gave her a rough and insistent kiss on the mouth, leaning his forehead against hers with his eyes closed.

'I'm sorry I got annoyed,' he whispered to her. 'I'll try to stay calm, I swear.'

He drew back and looked her in the eyes, kissing the tip of her nose. 'I love you,' he said, looking at her intently.

She smiled weakly at him and took his hand to go back to the ice, trying to ignore the dread that grew in the pit of her stomach.

Chapter Sixteen

Jamie arrived for his next practice a few minutes early and went down to the ice, where Alex and Katie were finishing off their rehearsal session.

He sat down to watch with a mixture of curiosity and jealousy, keen to see what they were working on and at the same time feeling inadequate and envious. The routine was truly breathtaking and Jamie couldn't mistake the look of absolute adoration on Alex's face as he held Katie, nor the look of love on Katie's face as she wrapped her legs around his torso and they put their faces close to each other, almost but not quite kissing.

As they finished practising and slid to a halt on the ice, Katie looked up and saw Jamie. She waved, looking embarrassed. Alex followed her gaze and grinned across the ice at Jamie, and jealousy stabbed at him as Alex leaned down and whispered in Katie's ear, his arms still wrapped around her, holding her closely. Her face was turned away from Jamie so he couldn't see her reaction, but it looked like a lovers' reunion to him. He tried to ignore the gnawing feeling of disappointment in his gut as he saw them together, knowing there was something there that he just couldn't get in the way of.

Alex passed him on his way out. 'You guys look good out there,' Jamie remarked.

Alex nodded. 'Thanks. It's like we were never apart.' He walked off, looking pleased with himself, and Jamie wanted to hurl one of his skates at his head.

Instead, he laced them up and joined Katie on the ice. She seemed jittery and anxious, and Jamie assumed that was because something was going on with her and Alex and he had caught them in the throes of a reconciliation.

'Nice routine,' Jamie said as he approached her.

'Um, thanks,' she said, unenthusiastically.

Jamie wanted to ask her outright if she and Alex had reunited, but sensing her reticence to talk about it, he kept his mouth shut and they continued their own rehearsal. Her encouragement was muted and he kept making simple mistakes, his feelings of inadequacy growing in comparison to Alex's superior talent.

'So, tomorrow's the final session before the show,' Katie said, as he offered to drive her home and she slid into his car, both of them worn out and aching.

'Yep. Do you think we might have a chance this week too?' Jamie asked hopefully, annoyed at himself for wanting her praise.

'I think so.' She nodded, staring into the distance.

'Are you looking forward to skating with Alex?' Jamie asked, gripping the steering wheel harder so the blood was squeezed from his knuckles.

She glanced at him. 'Mmmm,' she said. He decided not to press the issue. After all, it was none of his business, though the desire to know for sure what was going on bothered him like an itch he couldn't scratch.

They drove the rest of the way in silence, Katie chewing on her lower lip and staring out of the window.

'See you tomorrow!' Jamie waved. He watched her walk away from the car towards her front door, hoping with every step that she might look back at him. She didn't. Her mind, and her heart, were clearly very much elsewhere.

Jamie knew he shouldn't intrude, but he was curious to see more of Katie and Alex's routine, as he had only caught the very end of their rehearsal yesterday. He turned up early to the rink, his breath clouding the cold morning air, wondering why he was really there, wondering what good it would do to have his suspicions confirmed and see them together as he knew they would be.

His phone vibrated in his pocket as he walked towards the

rink, and he quickly answered it, seeing his sister's name flash up on the screen.

'Hey Maddie, everything okay?' he said, worried to get such an early call from her, and relieved when it was just about Isabelle's birthday plans. Jamie held the phone to his ear as she wittered on, eager to get inside, trying to find a moment to end the conversation. He walked around the outside of the rink a little way, the chill of the air settling on his hair and making his hand holding the phone start to throb with cold.

He stopped and looked in the large side windows to the rink – now partially hidden by overgrown bushes covered in a fine film of dew that hadn't quite made the transition to frost. Maddie kept talking as he watched Alex and Katie through the grey veil of dust on the window.

The routine was still beautiful but every time they stopped to work on a specific part or discuss something their whole body language changed. Alex crossed his arms and leaned over Katie, his jaw tense, the charming expression he usually wore replaced by a scowl that made Katie seem to shrink before him. The loving gestures and looks that she used during the routine were gone, and in their place, Jamie saw an expression on her face he had never seen before – fear.

Their discussion was becoming more intense, Katie gesticulating pointedly and Alex's shoulders tensing, until he swiftly shoved Katie down onto the ice where she crumpled under the force of his hands.

'Maddie, I have to go,' Jamie said urgently, and hung up the call, turning to run to the entrance. By the time he got down to the rink, Alex had stormed out of the side exit and Jamie found Katie sitting in a heap on the ice.

Jamie knelt beside her and she glanced up at him, dry-eyed and in despair. It was obvious from the expression on his face that he had seen the altercation.

He sat down beside her without saying a word and put an arm over her shoulder. They sat in silence for a while, the cold of the ice seeping through their clothes. Eventually, Jamie turned to her.

'It isn't just because of the accident that you don't want to be around Alex, is it?' he asked.

'Oh Jamie,' she sighed, shaking her head. 'Don't you get it? It wasn't an accident at all.'

Then

The athletes' village was alive with intense excitement. Katie could feel it running through the air like electricity as she and Alex arrived. Alex was feeding off it, she could tell. He was wired up, pumped, ready to go. She tried to match his enthusiasm as he grabbed her hand and pulled her along with him to their room.

The Olympics was like the summit day for Everest after all the base camps and acclimatisation training. It was the peak and the pinnacle, what they had been working towards for several years now. Katie had loved her first Olympics when she was seventeen. It was the most exciting thing she had ever done. Her dad and Ivan had helped her to keep focused and to avoid the heady distractions of not just being in a new country, but also surrounded by pumped-up elite athletes, where drugs and alcohol were curtailed but sex was an ideal release for all that physical tension.

This time around, she was trapped and afraid, bound by a media hype of their own making – the golden couple, tipped to win. She had even read rumours in the press that Alex was planning to propose to her, and she hoped they weren't based on truth.

She had survived the last eight weeks by focusing intently on the skating and trying to ignore the sharp anxious feeling in her stomach that stabbed at her every time Alex looked at her displeased.

She knew she could get through this if she created her own

little bubble. Then, once the competition was over, regardless of whether they won or lost, she would find a way out of the web she was trapped in.

Katie stood outside and took a deep breath of the frozen air, feeling it chill her lungs and settle on her hair. It was still early but she was slightly jet-lagged so she had left Alex and gone for a walk around the athletes' village. She stuck her hands in her pockets, wishing she had brought her gloves with her, and strode out briskly into the dawn air. Despite the early hour, she passed athletes taking a morning jog, running off nervous jitters or trying to overcome their jet lag like her. Two leggy blonde girls walked past her, chattering away in Russian, their light-hearted laughter floating back towards her in the quiet of the campus. Katie stared back at them enviously, coveting their freedom and exuberance – just as she'd felt in her first Olympic Games. Her eyes stung in the cold air and she wished her dad were around. She walked faster, feeling her legs start to warm up from their early morning stiffness. She wiped away the tears that ran down her cheeks, barely registering them as they fell each time she blinked.

She must have been walking for an hour, not noticing where she went, following well-manicured paths around and around, when she heard someone call her name.

'Katie, wait up!'

She turned quickly, seeing Tristan Lomax waving at her.

Tristan trotted up to her with the eagerness of a puppy, his blond hair damp and clinging to his head, fresh from the shower. He hugged her.

'Great to see you! When did you arrive?' he asked, his hands still on her upper arms.

'Um yesterday,' she said, forcing a smile.

He looked into her face and frowned slightly. 'Everything okay? Jet lag? Nerves?' he asked, concerned. Katie hoped he couldn't tell that she had been crying, but she could feel the stiffness of the salt from her tears on her cheeks and her eyelashes.

She shook her head. 'Oh, it's nothing, really. How about you, Tristan? How are you feeling?'

He bounced up and down, his breath coming out in small puffs of fog. 'Psyched to be here. I have so much nervous energy!'

Katie couldn't help but smile at his joyfulness. 'And Angelica?'

Tristan laughed. 'She's the calm one. She's probably meditating in her room right now.'

Katie grinned. Tristan's skating partner was known for being obsessed with crystals, meditation, incense, anything to help her with nerves. Katie had always rather liked hanging out with Tristan and Angelica when they were on the competition circuit together, but Alex preferred not to, so she didn't any more either.

'Where's lover boy?' Tristan asked, with a wolfish grin.

Katie rolled her eyes. 'Still asleep. All right for some.'

They started to walk together, discussing the upcoming competition, Tristan making jokes about the other teams, causing Katie to sputter with laughter until her sides ached. She realised with a sad pang that she almost never laughed any more. Life with Alex hadn't been fun for a while.

'So, I hear Alex might have some big plans this competition …' Tristan trailed off, glancing at her.

Katie tried not to grimace.

'Oh, trouble in paradise eh?'

She didn't reply and didn't have the energy to lie or make excuses. It was easier to say nothing.

Tristan raised his eyebrows. 'Sorry. I shouldn't pry.'

'That's okay,' Katie said.

Tristan slung an arm around her shoulders and gave her a squeeze. She leaned in, feeling a moment of weakness when she was tempted to turn to Tristan and tell him, tell anyone, how bad things had been and how tired and afraid she was.

The moment was broken by Alex stepping onto the path before them.

Alex was silent all the way to their room. Katie knew him well enough not to expect sudden explosions. He had a long fuse that, once lit, took a while to come to a climax. It was like the tension in the air before a summer storm, hanging heavy and oppressive till that first crack of lightning split the sky.

He was like that all day, monosyllabic and taciturn, allowing the dark and malevolent thoughts to build up. Katie tried to act like nothing was wrong and made light conversation, hopeful that he would snap out of his dark mood. After all, she hadn't done anything wrong, she told herself. She had just been chatting to a fellow skater.

At the end of the day they walked back to their room, and Alex shut the door. Katie sat hesitantly on the bed, twisting her hands in the rumpled sheets. Their minds should have been on the performance tomorrow, but there was only a deathly hush.

He turned to face her and didn't say anything. She sat in silence and the clock ticked away the minutes.

'Alex ...' she started hesitantly.

He interrupted her before she could continue. 'What the hell, Katie?'

She flinched at the caustic edge in his voice and raised both hands to calm him.

He didn't give her a chance to talk. He folded his arms and started pacing the room.

'I mean, I chose you. Out of all the female skaters, I picked you to be my partner. I've given you everything, shared my life and my heart with you, and all you've ever done is resist me, question me, belittle me, and now make me look like a fool by playing around with Tristan?' He talked quickly with each turn around the room. Katie's eyes helplessly followed him as he rambled, pale and agitated.

He stopped and grabbed her arms, forcing her to look at him, levelling his eyes with hers.

'What more do you want?' he hissed through gritted teeth.

She winced as his spit grazed her cheek.

'Alex, please …' She whimpered as he squeezed her arms tightly, feeling his fingers curl around the bones. 'You've got this all wrong. Tristan and I were just talking.'

He gave her a shake and released her. She flopped onto the bed, rubbing the bruised flesh on her upper arms and watching him warily.

He shook his head and jabbed a finger at her. 'You're an ungrateful bitch, Katie.'

A hot flash of indignation stoked her anger. 'Don't you dare, Alex.' She stood up, even though her knees were shaking. 'I've only ever tried to please you and to live up to your impossible demands.'

He glared at her; eyebrows drawn low over his eyes. 'Impossible?'

'You're controlling, you never ask what I want, it's always your way or the highway,' she said, throwing her hands up in the air.

'That's only because I love you and want the best for you,' he snapped, running his hands agitatedly through his hair.

'That's not love, Alex!' Katie cried at him. 'It's …' She grasped for words as the tears started down her cheeks. 'It's bullying, the way you treat me. I'm sick of it.' She spat out the last words with a sob, her chest heaving at all the emotions she had been storing away and could no longer stop from pouring out.

'I want out Alex. After this, I'm done,' she said, looking at the floor, feeling it swaying beneath her as she breathed heavily, her mouth numb with panic.

Alex stared at her, his mouth open with confusion and shock. 'You don't mean that, Katie. You love me,' he said insistently, searching her face.

She took a deep breath through her nose and tried to stop her hands from shaking, pinning them to her sides. 'No, I don't, Alex. I don't love you. I don't want to skate with you, and I'm leaving you. As soon as this competition is over.'

In one stride, he crossed the room and shoved her down onto the bed, pinning her shoulders, locking her in place with his knees. She slapped at him with her hands as he bent over her, a wild look on his face. 'There's no way I'm letting you go,' he hissed, and leaned into her. Katie sobbed and pushed at him, feeling his strength as he pushed her down into the cover. 'Get off!' she wailed, violently thrusting her hips up and ramming her knee into his groin.

Alex bent double, gasping with pain. He lifted his hand and swung it blindly as hard as he could, catching her across the face. Her nose exploded in a hot wet mess. A stinging throb ran through her cheek and she gasped at the pain in her jaw as her head snapped backwards. She lifted her feet and pushed them against his stomach, managing to shove him off the bed. She ran to the bathroom.

She turned the lock with shaking hands, crying and holding her nose, watching the bright blood drop between her fingers. She ripped off some toilet paper and stemmed the bleeding, grabbing a flannel and dousing it with cold water to hold across the bright red mark now spreading on her cheek.

She heard Alex moan and then some scuffling as he left the room, slamming the door behind him. Katie sat on the toilet, gasping with shock and trembling violently. She felt saliva gush into her mouth and her throat constrict; she swallowed hard so she wouldn't vomit. She sat and counted the seconds passing by, trying not to think or feel.

When she crept out of the bathroom hours later, she found Alex crumpled on the bed looking utterly broken and contrite. She stood before him, making sure she was close to the room door, and waited.

'Katie, I'm so sorry,' he said, tears running down his face. 'I'm so nervous about this performance tomorrow, and I took it out on you. Please, please forgive me,' he pleaded.

He moved towards her to wrap his arms around her like he usually did, when she always gave in. Katie winced and took a step backwards, folding her arms. She didn't care if he was about to be crowned King of England. He was not getting away with this.

He paused, watching her hesitantly.

'You went too far this time Alex,' she said, as firmly as she could, hoping her voice didn't sound as shaky as her legs.

He nodded. 'Katie please, I'm sorry. It won't happen again,' he said mournfully. 'We both said and did things we didn't mean. Please don't throw away all our hard work because of a fight.'

He looked at her hopefully. 'You'll still skate with me tomorrow, won't you? You won't waste all these years of effort?'

She looked at the swirls on the carpet, thinking of all the early mornings, the late nights, the injuries and pain, and what she had put up with to get here. Just one day more.

Eventually, she looked up. 'I will skate with you tomorrow, Alex. And then after this competition is finished, we're finished too. Do you understand?' She pressed her lips together to stop them trembling.

He nodded and slid off the edge of the bed. She shuddered inwardly as he approached and stood before her. He leaned down and kissed the red mark on her cheek, and she could hardly draw breath as he did so.

'As you wish Katie,' he straightened up and looked at her sadly before leaving the room, shutting the door softly behind him.

Katie let out the breath she had been holding in, and slid to the floor, sobbing into the bed covers. After tomorrow it would all be over and she'd be free.

*

She had no idea where Alex went that night, where he slept or if he slept at all. She wasn't sure he would even be at the warm-up, but there he was, striding towards her, looking calm and confident and ready, though he was pale and there were dark smudges under his eyes.

Katie took a breath as he approached and tried to keep her composure. She had managed to apply some heavy make-up to disguise the awfulness of the day before. She desperately hoped that if they could hold it together for this programme, they could both depart the Games knowing they had done their best and break up with dignity afterwards.

Alex reached her and took a glance at her make-up, giving a slight nod of approval. He looked around at the other competitors, focused on their own anxieties, warm-ups and obsessive routines.

'Where did you go, Alex?' she asked in a low voice.

'It's not important,' he said. He stepped close to her and looked into her eyes. 'Please tell me you've reconsidered what you said last night, that it's not over between us,' he whispered urgently.

Katie had been up most of the night, running over and over the question she knew he would ask her this morning. As she thought of every outcome and answer, the ones where she ended up with Alex always made her heart sink. Although yesterday's argument felt like a bad dream, she knew his abusive and controlling behaviour would carry on and maybe even get worse. Katie bit her lip and considered lying to him so their performance would go smoothly, but she couldn't do it. She was a terrible liar.

She looked at him solemnly. 'I'm sorry, Alex. I meant what I said.'

A look of devastation ran through his face and she turned away, not wanting to see what he was thinking or feeling. They went to warm up together, Sergei staring at them, sensing there were greater issues than he could resolve at this late stage so he stayed silent.

Six minutes till the performance.

Alex said nothing. His skating was surprisingly smooth, hers was weaker than usual but she concentrated on every move, trying to block everything else out, focusing on warming up, preparing her body.

Just a minute remaining.

Their names were called. As they skated onto the ice, they could hear the scores from the previous performance being announced. Katie would usually have been totting up elements, working out if they could beat the pair before them, but right now her mind was a calm blank sea. The ice opened white and clean before her, benevolent and expectant.

She and Alex took up their starting position. Her heart thudded with nerves and all she could hear was the blood swooshing in her head, the sound of their breathing; the noise of the crowd dimmed and faded away.

Alex leaned down to her and whispered in her ear. 'Make the most of this, Katie. This is where it all ends for you.'

A shudder ran down her spine and she tried not to frown at his words, knowing the cameras were pointing directly at them. She was irritated that he was trying to break her concentration just before they began, but as the music started and the opening sequence began, she looked into his cold, angry gaze and felt a stab of fear at what his words might mean.

As their programme progressed, she felt herself relax into the routine and allowed her muscles to lead her through the motions. Katie felt a surge of triumph as they landed the triple axel side by side and heard the crowd roar their appreciation. A wave of sheer adrenaline flooded her and she prepared for the final aspects of the programme, counting, breathing, knowing the finish was near.

She prepared herself for the twist lift, feeling Alex's hands on her waist behind her, both of them working to propel her right above his head and into the rotations. But something was wrong. Katie caught her breath as she flew upwards far too quickly and over to the edge of the rink, unable to control her legs and her ankles flailing out to the sides.

There was no time to register the sensation. She slammed into the barrier and everything went dark.

It was the pain that woke her up. She was groggy and disoriented, but she could feel her leg screaming at her, flashing sirens of pain jolting through her nerves.

She gasped in pain and tears started down her cheeks as she looked at her leg, swathed in white.

'Oh, I know that hurts,' said a nurse sympathetically, bustling in through the door.

'How long have I been in here?' Katie asked.

'Just a day,' the nurse replied in a heavy Russian accent, checking the chart at the end of the bed. 'We gave you some strong painkillers and it knocked you right out. You had quite a concussion.'

'What happened to my leg?' Katie asked, blinking hard, trying to remember.

The nurse looked at her sadly. 'The doctor will see you later this afternoon to talk to you about that in more detail.'

Katie nodded and lay back. She stared at the white ceiling, wondering where the hell Alex was, and waited for the doctor.

She didn't know how much time passed. She drifted in and out of a light sleep, indistinct dreams of slamming into the ice foot first haunting her and jerking her awake periodically. She woke up sweating, with Alex's eyes burning into her mind, and she was still trying to shake herself from her nightmare when the doctor came in.

His manner was clipped and efficient, his English perfect. He held up her X-ray results in front of her unfocused eyes. She understood each individual word but to fathom the meaning of them all strung together and the impact it would have on her was impossible. She nodded along numbly and took in nothing, refusing to believe that never skating again was a possibility.

Day three and no sign of Alex. Katie lay mute and unoccupied, surrounded by cards she hadn't opened and flowers she didn't want to look at. She lay looking at the ceiling, vegetating, dreaming, and uninterested in eating.

She was on strong painkillers and her mind was foggy. Sometimes she thought she could feel Alex's eyes or hands on her, but he was never there in her small white room. Whenever her mind started to clear she could feel the pain from the doctor's words in her heart and the violent throbbing of her leg, and she would simply press the button at her side for a new dose to take her away to her dreams again.

She had taken another dose of pain relief when the door opened and two men marched in, wearing dark blue suits and carrying various papers with them. They seemed to loom over her, filling her vision with pinstripes and oiled hair.

'Katie? I'm Jon Slater of Harper and Randall. I'm here to talk to you about … your options,' one of them began, as they both dragged hard plastic chairs to sit beside the bed. He was lightly tanned with perfectly straight teeth and the neatest fingernails she had ever seen on a man, the perfect pale crescents tapping against the papers in his hand.

She frowned at him, feeling woozy. 'Options?'

The men looked at each other and the other one, tall and blond with eyes the colour of the ocean, cleared his throat. 'Katie, we're from a law firm. My name is Christian Reid, and we're here on behalf of the Michaelson family.'

She glared at him, and they exchanged looks.

'The Michaelson family would like to express their sincere sympathies for the injury you've sustained, which as you know by now, is potentially career-ending.'

'Sincere sympathies? What the hell is this?' Katie shouted at them angrily, spitting at them as her face numbed and her lips loosened from the painkillers.

Mr Slater continued. 'The Michaelson family would like to offer you a sum of money to help you ... adjust to life after skating.'

Katie stared at them blankly.

'For whatever your needs may be – a place to live, payment for additional private medical treatment and therapy, costs of starting a new career,' Mr Reid clarified.

'And what do they want in return?' Katie asked hoarsely, straining with the effort of concentrating on their words, knowing full well the Michaelsons wouldn't be offering this without something from her in exchange.

'A full non-disclosure agreement, effective immediately, that you will sign and adhere to in exchange for the lump sum of money.'

Katie closed her eyes and tried to pick her way through the words they were telling her through the cloud that had settled on her brain.

'Non-disclosure?' she asked, eventually.

The two men looked at each other. 'You won't say anything about the nature of your relationship with Mr Michaelson, nor about the, er incident,' Mr Reid replied.

Katie dragged air into her lungs, feeling as though she were breathing through soup, and wanted to scream that she wouldn't do it. Tears rolled down the side of her face into her hairline as she thought about being free from Alex, ending this nightmare and getting out of his grip on her life.

The clouds descending on her brain thickened, the fog curling around thoughts of her empty bank account and the cost of rehabilitative treatment that could, possibly, allow her to skate again.

'You want me to sign now?' she said, sleepy and heavy-lidded.

The men nodded and gave her a pen.

*

There was a throng of reporters waiting as she left the hospital days later, but Katie kept her sunglasses on and looked away as she was driven to the airport in a car with darkened windows. There was still Olympic Games marketing everywhere she looked, the thrill of the competition still palpable as the participants began to filter home after the closing ceremony.

Katie hadn't read or watched the news in days. It was too painful, not just to see her fall repeated over and over, but to see the medal winners standing on the podium where she had so desperately wanted to be herself, for which she had sacrificed, and stayed with Alex, all for nothing.

It wasn't until she was on the plane and nestled in First Class, thanks to the Michaelsons' money, that she grabbed one of the complimentary English-language newspapers and decided to read the headlines.

"Skating Pair Split Over Accident". The article continued: *"Alex Michaelson has today confirmed that he and Katie Saunders are no longer an item on or off the ice, due to the serious accident Katie sustained at the Winter Olympics in Russia.*

Katie is reported to be flying home today but the extent of the damage means she is unlikely to compete again.

Such is her devastation over the incident that she is refusing to speak to Alex, her long-term partner both on and off the ice, who blames himself for the accident.

'I take the blame for that. You're supposed to save your partner and protect them, and I guess I got carried away on the ice out there. I'm not surprised Katie won't talk to me. I hope in time she can forgive me because I'll never forgive myself.'"

Katie ripped up the newspaper, ignoring the stares of the people around her, and dry-swallowed some sleeping pills so she wouldn't wake again until she was landing back at Heathrow.

Chapter Seventeen

'So, there you have it,' Katie said, draining the last of the wine in her glass as she and Jamie sat on her small sofa, the cushions sagging inwards so each of them perched on the outer edges to avoid falling into each other. He had driven her home and she had told him everything – the first person she had revealed the truth to.

He shook his head in disbelief. 'All this time Alex has been playing the victim. What a shit,' Jamie said angrily, his eyes flashing indignantly.

Katie ran her finger around the rim of the glass and nodded. 'Yes. And everyone thinks he's wonderful. So now you see why I don't want to skate with him or even be in the same room as him.' She grimaced.

'But, I don't get it – you've never said anything all this time? To anyone?' Jamie asked incredulously. 'How can you stand it?'

Katie frowned. 'Believe me, I've wanted to speak out, many times. But I signed that agreement and they gave me the payment, which I really needed to get away from him. If I break the agreement ...' She paused. 'I don't know what they'll do but I don't have the money to challenge them.'

She looked at Jamie and sighed. 'You know his dad is hugely wealthy right? He can throw all those fancy lawyers at me. I feel like my hands are tied. I wish I'd never signed it, but I had no advice, was on my own in a foreign country, and goodness knows how many painkillers I was on at the time.'

'And now?' asked Jamie, raising his eyebrows.

'The lump sum they gave me didn't last too long,' Katie admitted, feeling embarrassed for her legal naivety and her poor money-management skills. 'It allowed me to recover, to set up some coaching students, to put down a deposit on this flat.'

She put her empty wine glass on the worn coffee table in front of them. 'And lo and behold I did it again – I got myself locked in a contract with the show because I needed money and it's come back to bite me on the bum.' She shook her head, frustrated at her incompetence.

'You really need to learn to read the small print,' said Jamie, half-jokingly.

She gave him a weak smile. 'Tell me about it.'

He paused for a moment. 'Were you in love with Alex?' He held up his hands apologetically. 'Sorry if that's too personal. It's just, you two did seem happy together, once.'

She thought about it for a moment. 'I don't know,' she replied eventually. 'I was pressured into a relationship with him and then I was stuck, I suppose. I felt the weight of public opinion pressing down on me, then I got myself in too deep and before I knew it, I felt … trapped.'

Jamie looked at her sympathetically.

She gave him a sad smile. 'It was hard being in a relationship with him. His love was … possessive, angry, controlling.'

'That's not love at all,' said Jamie, shaking his head vehemently. 'It's not supposed to be like that with someone you love. Sure, you have bad times and arguments, and people make mistakes, but what he did wasn't normal. It was downright abusive.'

Katie nodded, letting his words sink in. All this time she'd wondered if she had misinterpreted what happened – if it somehow had become warped in her mind and twisted by memory. Hearing Jamie use the word abusive made her feel clearer and stronger. It reassured her that she was the one in the right, that it hadn't all been in her head and that she wasn't being unreasonable.

Katie looked at him, grateful for his support. 'I was genuinely afraid of Alex. All the time. It wore me down till I didn't know how to break free from it and he knew that dangling my Olympic dream, my one passion and goal in life, would keep me blinded.' She sighed. 'Skating with him again is terrifying. It takes me back to where I once was. I'm afraid he will wear me down again,' she said, admitting to both herself and Jamie that Alex could still inspire fear in her heart with just one glance.

Jamie's jaw clenched. 'He won't. You're stronger than you know, Katie – stronger and braver than you give yourself credit for.'

She nodded, allowing an ember of self-belief to warm her heart. Jamie was right. It was nice to have someone in her corner again, encouraging her. She had needed a friend like that for so long.

'How did he manage to throw you just right so that he would cause a career-ending injury?' Jamie asked, furrowing his forehead.

Katie shrugged. 'I assume his plan was to drop me during the lift and hope the damage would be sufficient to punish me for wanting to leave him. He did a good job, but thank goodness I can skate again now,' she said, wryly.

'Do you have a copy of the contract you signed with the Michaelsons?' Jamie asked, suddenly, sitting forward.

She was surprised by his question. 'I guess so, somewhere.'

'Have you ever had anyone look at it?'

She shook her head. 'No, I can't afford a lawyer.'

Jamie grinned. 'You know Harriet is an amazing lawyer. I bet she would take a look for you.'

Katie bit her lip. 'Do you think it's worth her doing that?'

Jamie gently took her arm and looked in her eyes. 'What Alex did to you was unforgivable. And now he's still trying to manipulate you and bully you through the show.'

She nodded, with a grim smile, thinking of how even now he was trying to pull the strings on her life. A small spark of anger danced in her heart and the possibility of finally standing up to Alex made her tremble with both fear and excitement.

'Maybe it's time to fight back,' she said, as Jamie nodded eagerly.

Alex's usually calm demeanour was momentarily perturbed to find Jamie at the rinkside with Katie. He blinked in surprise then quickly changed his expression to neutral.

'Katie,' he said coolly, glancing at Jamie. 'You know I prefer practices to be unobserved. It helps my concentration.'

She stared at him and folded her arms. 'Jamie is so keen to see how you skate, Alex.'

Jamie grinned at him. 'Surely you don't mind?'

Alex gave a curt nod and headed onto the ice, his back rigid with annoyance. Katie made to follow him and Jamie grabbed her arm. 'I'll be here the whole time,' he said softly.

She could have cried with relief knowing that, for the first time since she started skating with Alex years ago, she finally had someone on her side. Feeling more confident, she glided onto the ice to start practising with Alex, knowing that he wouldn't try anything with Jamie watching.

Alex stared at her as she approached him to start their rehearsal, and she met his gaze defiantly. It was time to start standing up for herself.

'I don't believe you.'

Katie blinked in surprise. 'Excuse me?'

Harriet leaned across the table. 'Are you prepared for people to say that to you if you go public? Because they will. They'll say that you looked so happy together, that you're being vindictive. It'll be your word against his.' She leaned back in her chair, twisting a pen through her long fingers.

She pointed the pen in Jamie's direction. 'It happened with him when that cheating story came out. People didn't believe him – they believed what the media told them. Even his own wife took their word over his.'

Jamie flinched. 'All right, Harriet.'

Katie looked at him sympathetically. 'I guess people might take Alex's side,' she said hesitantly. 'They've been on his side for a long time.'

Harriet paused and folded her hands together. She had listened gravely while Katie had told her the story of her and Alex, about the so-called accident, and she had tapped her gleaming red nails on the non-disclosure agreement Katie had signed, frowning occasionally.

'Any other proof to add to your story?' Harriet asked. 'Anyone who can back you up? Just in case Alex's daddy decides to do something crazy like sue for defamation.'

Katie shook her head despairingly. 'I've got titanium holding my ankle together. I'd hope that was proof enough.'

'Didn't you tell anyone? Confide in anyone? A friend maybe?' Harriet asked.

'Nope,' Katie said. 'I didn't really have any friends – I was always so busy with skating.' She paused. 'The only person who knew what was happening was Sergei.'

'Your coach?' Harriet asked.

Katie nodded. 'But he was absolutely devoted to Alex. He would always take his side. He always turned a blind eye to what was happening with us though he must have known. In fact,' Katie said, tapping her chin thoughtfully, 'I'm pretty sure Alex probably stayed with him the night before our Olympic performance – there was nowhere else Alex could have gone without risking people knowing that something had happened between us.'

'Where is Sergei now? Does he still work with Alex?' Jamie asked.

'No, he retired after the Olympics. I never saw him again after that.'

'Hmm,' Harriet said, thoughtfully. 'It might be worth trying to track him down, see what he says.'

'So, does this mean you think my hands aren't completely tied by this agreement?' Katie said hopefully.

Harriet laughed and waved the contract around. 'Oh dear, of course not. This is worthless. Besides, if they do come after you, I'll be happy to take them on for you.' She glanced at Jamie, who looked delighted. 'For free,' she added.

Katie felt overwhelmed by her kindness. She was grasping for the right words to say so when Harriet put up her hand. 'Please, no gushing thank yous. The best reward will be when we get to see that little snake pay for what he did.'

Jamie thumped the table with his fist. 'Damn right!'

He looked at Katie, who had a stunned expression on her face. 'Now it's time to talk about what you want to do next.'

She turned to him and a grin spread across her face, lighting up her eyes. 'It's time people knew who Alex really is,' she said. 'I want to hit him where it hurts – his public image.'

'What are you thinking?' Jamie asked.

Katie paused and thought for a moment. 'Is your agent any good at arranging TV interviews?' she asked.

Jamie grinned and dialled Matt's number.

Chapter Eighteen

'Well done!' Katie hugged Jamie as they came off the ice, breathing hard from their fourth-week performance. The audience's applause echoed warmly around the rink as she squeezed him close. 'You did so well.'

Jamie felt brilliant that he had managed to pull off another performance with aplomb, despite their limited rehearsal time that week. Katie gazed at him proudly and he grinned back at her.

'That was good, right?'

She nodded, beaming, though her smile quickly crumbled away as Alex approached them while the advert break began.

'Good job, Jamie,' he said, a sarcastic edge to his voice. 'Katie, you'd better go and get ready for *our* performance.'

She nodded tersely at the command and bit her lip. Jamie tensed up and she put a gentle hand on his arm. He would give anything to throw a punch at Alex, but he knew Katie had better plans for him.

Alex stared at Jamie and he glared back, unblinking, wishing he could tell Alex what he thought of him, that he knew what he had done.

'See you in a few minutes, Katie.' Alex smirked, and strode away confidently, as Katie sighed with relief.

'I could so easily throttle him,' Jamie said, his hands balled into tight fists.

Katie turned to him. 'Leave it J,' she said, running her hands down his arms and squeezing his hands before quickly letting go, looking embarrassed at being so tactile. 'We'll show him soon enough.'

Jamie nodded, and wished she hadn't let go of his hands quite so quickly. 'I'm off to the waiting area. You'll be okay?' he asked her, looking concerned.

'I'll be fine,' she said, giving him a reassuring smile and heading off backstage.

Jamie watched her leave and reluctantly went to wait with the other participants in their spectator room.

'Hey Jamie, sit here,' Theo said, beckoning him over to the green sofa where he was sitting with Lara, Vicky and Eric. Vicky had her head in her hands, bemoaning her performance that evening while Eric tried to comfort her.

'It wasn't that bad,' he said, patting her shoulder with his large hands and looking upset. Vicky had fallen during the routine and flailed around awkwardly on the ice afterwards, her confidence shaken. 'At least you weren't as bad as Rory,' Eric said, speaking quietly and glancing at Rory in the corner where he chatted with Andy.

'We can't wait to see what Katie and Alex do,' Lara burbled excitedly as Jamie sat beside her. She gently brushed a hand against his thigh as he sat next to her and he shifted uncomfortably in his seat, remembering the awkwardness of their hotel encounter not long ago. She gave him a sideways glance, but he avoided her gaze and downed a can of Coke, letting the bubbles burn his throat. He didn't want to watch the show, but he knew he had to act normally. He tried not to grind his teeth in annoyance as Faith announced the performance.

'You voted for Alex and Katie to skate together this week. Here they are, together for the first time in years – Katie Saunders and Alex Michaelson!' she announced triumphantly, as the camera zoomed in on the pair in the centre of the ice and the crowd hushed expectantly.

They stood under a halo of spotlights in the centre of the ice, both dressed in black, the sequins on their costumes catching the lights and sending out sparkles with every move. Alex looked completely smitten with Katie, every move and every lift executed with a look of absolute adoration, and the audience was enthralled. Jamie felt sick, a hot, pounding anger coursing right through him, cutting into his stomach. He clenched his fists around his Coke.

Katie was like a blank white slate, her face completely impartial, but her body still responded to Alex's touch as they skated together. It looked like the dance of two reunited lovers long torn apart. Jamie could hardly breathe watching them together. He wanted to throw his drink at the screens and shout that she was his partner and that Alex had no right to skate with her any more.

The audience screamed their appreciation and Faith was moved to tears, as were some of the other participants. Deborah dabbed at her eyes at the judges' table, trying not to smudge her eyeliner. Jamie tried to nod appreciatively as he clapped, knowing cameras and eyes were on him, but inside he was a molten volcano of anger and envy.

Katie and Alex stood on the ice for a moment while the audience roared. Alex had his arm around her waist and she wanted to push him away but instead, she smiled brittlely for the cameras, counting the seconds in her head, waiting for it to end so she could get away from Alex. Her head was swimming with the memory of that day at the Olympics and she could feel her throat closing up. Only Alex could make her feel like that on the ice, she realised. Skating with Jamie was fun, and she had no fear that he would drop her on purpose like Alex had done. With Jamie, she had enjoyed skating again, but this performance with Alex took her right back to how she felt before – the feeling of being in his hands and the sense that he had the power to do whatever he wanted, even though Katie knew he wouldn't be foolish enough to drop her live on TV, again.

Alex dropped his head to whisper and she flinched at the warmth of his lips near her ear. 'They love us,' he murmured. She wanted to turn around and claw at his face, but she said nothing and didn't even acknowledge what he said. She would have her say soon enough.

They turned to skate off the rink and Katie moved ahead of Alex, his arm dropping from around her waist. As they came off at rinkside, people hurried up to congratulate them, but Katie swiftly pushed through to get changed. She could feel their bemused stares burning into her back as she scurried off, but she was desperate to get away from Alex. All she could think about was being near Jamie and feeling safe again.

After the show, Katie waited anxiously at the rinkside. People were still congratulating her on her performance with Alex as they passed by, and she wished they wouldn't. She wanted Jamie's efforts to be the focus – he had tried so hard that week and made so much progress. It wasn't fair it was being overshadowed.

Anna walked by, her sleek hair shining in the studio lights. 'Waiting for Alex, are we?' she said, raising an eyebrow.

Katie shook her head. 'Nope. Jamie.'

Anna looked surprised and carried on. Katie couldn't believe her and Rory were still in the competition. It had been another surprising week, with Vicky voted out even though Rory was still scoring the lowest. The audience truly loved the underdog.

Jamie emerged from backstage, striding off purposefully without seeing Katie, so she had to run after him quickly and grab his elbow. 'Jamie!'

He turned quickly, looking pleased to see her. 'Oh hey, I thought you might have gone already.'

'Nope. Erm, are you busy?' she asked hopefully.

'No, in fact, I'm beat. I was heading off home. Why?'

She shifted awkwardly from one foot to another. 'I didn't really feel like going home yet. I've got a lot of nervous energy building up.'

He smiled at her. 'Wanna hang out?'

She was relieved he'd asked her and had been hoping that he would. 'Yes! Is that okay?'

He nodded. 'It's no problem.' He hesitated. 'But I was going to go straight home tonight and not back to the hotel. I have a thing with Kick Start tomorrow morning,' he explained.

'Oh right,' she said, unsure what to do, hoping there was a way they could still spend some time together.

He rubbed the back of his neck. 'I'd be happy for you to come to mine and drop you off at yours afterwards,' he offered hopefully.

She smiled with relief at his suggestion. 'Perfect. I really hate that crummy hotel I'm in anyway. Would it be okay to swing by and get my bag? I'm actually already packed,' she said, playing with a strand of hair, still slightly crispy from hairspray though she had brushed most of it out.

He nodded. 'Sure, of course.'

Katie followed him out to his car and a little shiver of happiness ran through her as she slid into the passenger seat beside him.

'I'm starving,' Jamie said as they walked into his cavernous kitchen. 'Do you want to eat?' he asked her.

'Sure, I could eat,' she said, sitting on one of the high stools next to the counter, grateful that he had decided not to stay at the hotel that night, grateful the drive had been smooth and quick as they glided along country lanes in the darkness. It was already 11 p.m. but she didn't want to go and be on her own just yet.

He waved a takeaway leaflet at her. 'Pizza okay?'

She nodded.

'Are you a meat feast kind of lady or a veggie classic?' he asked, picking up the phone.

'Actually, I always go for ham and pineapple,' she said. 'I like to court controversy.'

Jamie laughed and ordered the pizzas. 'Wine?' he asked as he hung up the phone.

'Thanks,' she said, and he turned to get some glasses and a bottle from a cupboard. Katie stared admiringly around the kitchen, amazed at how clean it was. 'Do you ever actually cook in here?' she asked curiously.

Jamie shook his head as he poured the wine. 'Not really. Cass used to do a lot of cooking and entertaining, but it's not really my thing.'

Katie sipped her wine. She would just have the one, she thought. She knew what happened when she drank too much and it was not pretty the next day.

'So how did you feel tonight?' he said. His top button was undone and as he leaned forward over the kitchen counter her gaze flickered downwards where she could see the defined muscles underneath. She flushed and quickly looked up, hoping he didn't notice.

'I hated skating with Alex but at least I knew he wasn't going to throw me again,' she said, sipping her wine and daring to look back at Jamie, who had straightened up so she couldn't be distracted by the gap in his shirt.

'It was a beautiful performance,' he said. 'You're so talented, Katie.'

She smiled. 'Thanks. You're coming along pretty well yourself you know,' she said. 'It was really good this week.'

He grimaced and shrugged his shoulders. 'I'm getting there. It's great to make it to week five. I didn't think I'd make it that far,' he admitted.

'Me neither,' she agreed, before clapping her hand over her mouth in horror at how rude it sounded.

Jamie threw back his head and laughed loudly. 'I knew it! From the moment you saw me you thought I was a big clumsy rugby guy who would fall on his face every time, right?'

Katie covered her burning cheeks with her hands. 'Oh no that came out wrong, Jamie! I thought that some of the others were stronger skaters, and ... er ...' she stammered.

He grinned at her. 'Don't worry, I think most people thought the same.'

'Well, you're proving us all wrong now,' she said, smiling at him.

He shrugged. 'I'm no Theo Jarvis, you know,' and she gave a derisive laugh.

'He can skate but he's so boring!' she said, giggling and rolling her eyes. Jamie looked pleased.

'I'm so curious,' she asked him, leaning on her elbows on the counter and looking up at him. 'Why did you really sign up for this show?'

'Oh, just a long love of figure skating,' he said impishly.

'Seriously – how come?' she pressed.

'Well,' he said, 'a couple of reasons, I guess. They offered really good money, and this house costs a lot to keep, so I thought it couldn't hurt. But the real reason ...' He trailed off.

She nodded at him to continue.

'If I'm honest, I was in a bit of a slump before the show, you know, feeling unhealthy, kind of lonely.' He shrugged. 'I thought doing something new might help. I needed to get out of a rut. The money was tempting, but in my heart, I knew I had to do *something*, anything, other than sit around the house all day eating junk, thinking about Cass, and feeling sorry for myself.'

She nodded understandingly.

'I didn't get many offers in the eighteen months after the World Cup disaster,' he continued, looking down at his hands. 'Luckily I had saved enough to live off, but I was starting to think about what to do for a living if I couldn't do rugby. I didn't go to university and I've never really wanted to do anything other than play ...' He trailed off. 'I guess the offer for this show came just at the right time, both financially and emotionally. Perhaps it'll help me figure out what to do next.'

'You?' he asked, taking a mouthful of wine.

'I suppose money was the main thing for me. But if I'm being honest as well, there's this image of me in the public and I wanted to try to break that and be liked again. It's kind of pathetic, but I wanted to be in the public's good books again – like I used to be.'

'Before Alex twisted everything,' added Jamie.

'Exactly. I was made into this ice queen caricature by the media – but I was only ever trying to handle what happened between Alex and me and the fallout from the accident.' She sighed grimly.

'I must admit, I thought you were pretty stand-offish,' Jamie said, hesitantly. 'You know, from what I had read and heard, and you did seem a bit uptight.'

Katie nodded. 'Well I hope you don't think that now.' She searched his expression, but at that moment the buzzer for the gate rang and he went to get the pizzas.

It was fun, Katie realised, to sit with someone and laugh and joke and talk about things other than ice skating, other than Alex, other than the accident. To share pizza and talk about family, school, the best holidays, the biggest regrets. Katie's mind flicked back to the time she had shared pizza with Alex and he had cruelly made her believe she was fat. She knew now that it was just Alex's manipulative and controlling behaviour that had made her feel that way, although sometimes the old fears surfaced and she had to tell herself firmly not to pay attention to them. She glanced at Jamie and thought that he would never do such a nasty thing, nor would he take advantage of her if she drank too much either. In fact, the more she compared him with Alex, the more she wished she could have been with someone like Jamie a long time ago – someone she actually trusted. She realised that she couldn't believe the press stories about him being a cheat any more. The love rat stereotype just didn't fit the sweet, kind Jamie she was getting to know. She knew from experience how the press could get it so wrong and could have kicked herself for believing the gossip about him in the first place.

Jamie started to yawn loudly and checked the time. 'Wow, it's gone 2 a.m.'

She blinked sleepily. 'Oh, it's so late, I better get home. I can get a cab as you've had wine and are probably really tired too.' She reluctantly started to get up from the sofa.

'Stay,' Jamie offered quickly. 'I mean, I have loads of space. You should stay,' he repeated.

'Sure, thanks Jamie, that would be wonderful,' she said, delighted that he'd asked. She didn't want to go home just yet.

He got up and she followed him up the stairs where he opened the door to the guest room and indicated the en-suite. 'There are towels and things in there,' he said.

'This is lovely,' she murmured, turning to face him, their bodies so close in the doorway that she could feel his body heat. She looked up at him and breathed in the scent of his cologne and felt a shiver of longing.

'Sleep well, Katie,' Jamie said. For a moment he leaned closer and she thought he might be about to kiss her, but he turned instead to head down the hall to his own room.

Katie watched him go and wondered what he would do if she walked down the hall after him. She shook her head, dismissing the thought. She dived onto the king-sized bed and enveloped herself in the huge duvet. She sighed at its plump softness and the smell of fabric softener before falling into a deep sleep, aided by sheer exhaustion from the week's trials and the wine fogging her head.

The following morning, Jamie busied himself with preparing breakfast. The pale morning light was illuminating the garden and a smattering of frost topped the lawn.

He was delighted that Katie had stayed overnight. He had enjoyed the time spent with her, and had been surprised at how the evening had flown by so quickly. It had been a long time since he really connected with someone, and he never imagined it would be Katie given their rocky start.

She padded into the kitchen.

'Morning,' she said, slightly sheepishly, running her fingers through her hair.

Jamie looked up from making the coffee. 'Morning!' he said, happy to see Katie in his house, in her pyjamas. Katie looked pale and radiant without any make-up on, a stark difference to the perma-tan that Cassandra always sported. She would be beautiful to wake up to in the mornings, he thought longingly; then busied himself with the kettle, trying to push that thought out of his mind.

'Did you sleep well?' he asked her as he stirred the tea, remembering that she didn't drink coffee.

'So well,' she said, smiling blissfully. 'Thanks for letting me stay.'

'It's no problem,' he said cheerfully, passing her the tea. She took it gratefully.

She reached for the stack of morning papers on the counter and Jamie sucked in a breath through his teeth. 'What?' she said, looking up at him.

'You might not want to read those – there's lots of gossip about you and Alex,' he warned, pouring out his coffee.

Katie took a breath and opened up the first one despite his warning. Jamie watched her carefully, but she didn't react as she read the rumours about her and Alex, who was keenly stoking the flames of speculation with his comments. She closed the paper carefully and sipped her tea in silence.

'You okay?' Jamie asked, as he popped bread into the toaster.

She looked up at him and he saw a change in her expression – determination rather than resignation.

'Let him say what he wants. They are all going to get a shock tomorrow,' she said, firmly. Jamie grinned at her and she smiled back. He couldn't wait for her to bring Alex down.

Chapter Nineteen

'Donald,' Hannah said quickly and quietly, closing the office door behind her with a gentle click. He looked up expectantly as she walked to his desk, feeling jittery about what she'd heard from the media team. It was only just gone eight that Monday morning and already her mobile had rung several times as she dashed to the office, knowing Donald would already be there.

'I've heard Katie is going on morning TV in thirty minutes. To talk about Alex ...' Hannah trailed off, her eyes dancing.

Donald thumped triumphantly on the desk. 'I knew it! I did it! I am a genius. We've reunited Alex and Katie.'

Hannah nodded, still grinning manically.

'Is Alex going to be with her?' he asked.

Hannah shook her head. 'I don't think so. I just got the call now. I can't wait to see what she has to say!'

'You can do this,' Jamie said, giving Katie a firm reassuring nod.

She felt intensely grateful that he had agreed to come with her to the studio for the TV interview that Monday morning. It wasn't so much that she needed him there as she knew she could do this on her own, but she wanted his calming presence and support.

'Thanks, Jamie,' she said, sipping her water, a slight tremor in her hands betraying her nerves. She wasn't particularly good at interviews, let alone doing one on live morning TV like this. Her stomach was churning and she hoped fervently that she wouldn't be sick.

A text pinged into her phone and she grabbed it from her bag.

Good luck. Show that bastard what for.

Katie grinned and turned her phone around to show Jamie.

He leaned in and laughed as he read the message. 'Harriet is the best,' he said, smiling.

A runner popped his head around the door. 'Katie? Follow me please, we're ready for you.'

She got up and took a deep breath, glancing back at Jamie as she walked out of the door. He gave her a thumbs-up.

She followed the runner to the set and sat under the heat of the studio lights, hoping she wasn't sweating through her dress. She tried to relax her shoulders and breathe deeply, but her heart was racing so fast that she could feel pins and needles tingling at the edges of her lips. She was sure that her pulse could probably be seen by millions of viewers as it pounded away above the high neckline of her dark green dress.

The presenter Louisa joined her during the adverts, ready to start her interview as soon as the break finished. Louisa sashayed towards her and shook her hand, looking bright and glowing in a tight scarlet shift dress. 'So nice to have you with us, Katie. We'll be back on in just a moment, okay?'

Katie nodded and tried to smile with her frozen lips. She fidgeted gently on the vibrantly coloured sofa and gazed around at the brightly lit set. Louisa sat and sipped some water, checking her phone, and was counted back in when the adverts were over. She turned to the camera with a smile.

'Good morning, we're delighted to welcome Katie Saunders with us today. You've probably seen her skating on the hit show *Sport Star to Skate Star*, where she's partnering with former rugby star Jamie Welsh.'

Louisa turned to Katie. 'We're delighted to have you on the show this morning to talk about your skating comeback, your time on the show, and of course all those rumours flying about you and Alex.'

Katie nodded. 'It's good to be here,' she said, feeling her legs shaking.

Louisa leaned in with a smile. 'I saw your skating performance with Alex on Saturday night and nearly everyone was in tears. It was beautiful! How did it feel to skate with Alex again?'

Katie hesitated and knew that she could still back down, she could still cave in and not tell the truth. She thought of Alex's anger and his manipulation and knew she couldn't let him get away with it any longer. Katie unfolded her legs and leaned towards the camera, her eyes wide. This was no time for nerves or hesitation.

'Let me put something straight. I know there are a lot of rumours about Alex and I being reunited after that performance.' Katie put her fingers in air quotes around the word reunited. 'But if I could have avoided skating with him, I would have.'

Louisa looked surprised and a little disappointed at the negativity of the response. Before the presenter had a chance to respond, Katie carried on. She didn't want to be interrupted. The courage to speak out was with her now, and she knew she needed to make the most of this moment.

'Alex was a nightmare to be in a relationship with. Behind all his loving social media posts and gushing interviews, he was abusive, manipulative and controlling. I spent years trying to please him, but his behaviour increasingly turned from emotionally manipulative to physically violent.'

Katie swallowed, her throat dry and tight. The memories were still so vivid that talking about them made her shudder still, even years later. She took a deep breath, clasped her hands together, and continued. 'I carried on with the pretence because my skating career was all I had. I had sacrificed everything for it, and I kept thinking that if I just did what Alex wanted then we could get to the Olympics and maybe we, I, could be winners again. But ...' She trailed off and blinked hard. 'But that night before we were due to skate, he was so abusive towards me that I knew I had to end things with him. I just couldn't take it any more. I couldn't carry on with the fear that I had all the time, no matter where I was and what I was doing. I told him that we were over and I only agreed to skate with him the next day because I didn't want those years of training and putting up with his behaviour to go to waste.'

Katie glanced at Louisa, who looked rapt, her eyes wide and nodding at her to continue. 'But Alex didn't let me finish the programme that day. His desire to hurt me overcame his desire to win, and he threw me on the ice to punish me.'

Louisa leaned back in her seat and cleared her throat. Katie gave an almost imperceptible nod for her to continue the interview.

'Well, Katie, this is a, er, shocking revelation,' Louisa said, stuttering a little over her words, clearly trying to think of her next question. She paused for a moment. 'Are you saying that Alex deliberately threw you at the Olympics?'

Katie nodded firmly. 'I am, and he did.' She willed her voice to stay level, reminding herself to speak clearly and firmly and not too fast.

'It was no accident. When we were waiting on the ice for our music to start, he told me that it was the end for me. I am absolutely certain that he meant he would find a way to injure me. I have no doubt. And if you look at the lift and the fall carefully, any seasoned skater can see that it was entirely preventable.'

Katie lifted her chin defiantly to the camera. 'Look at the footage if you don't believe me. Get it analysed by lip readers to see what he says. Zoom in close and you'll see the mark across my face where he hit me the night before – it's covered with make-up and not obvious but if you look for it you can see it. Get skating professionals to look at the throw and see if they think it was something that could have been done intentionally, if someone really wanted to try to hurt their partner.'

Louisa folded her hands over her knees and raised her eyebrows. 'Why didn't you say anything before, Katie? You've kept silent these past few years while Alex has openly talked about it as an accident. Why has it taken you this long to put things right?'

Katie was prepared for this question and held up the non-disclosure contract she had brought with her and had next to her on the sofa. She unfolded it with trembling hands. 'When I was in the hospital, on heavy medication and alone in a foreign country, Alex and his family sent lawyers in to offer me a lump sum in exchange for a non-disclosure agreement, binding me not to talk about our relationship or the nature of the incident. I was sedated and desperate and alone, and I signed it.'

Katie grabbed the edges of the agreement and ripped it right down the middle, something she wished with all her heart she had done years ago in that hospital room. 'Having consulted with a lawyer for the first time, I have been advised that this contract is void because I was not in a fit state to sign it at the time. So now I am choosing to speak out and tell the truth about me and Alex.'

She held out the two pieces of the contract in triumph and looked straight down the camera, imagining and hoping that Alex was watching and she was speaking to him directly. Her eyes flashed bright and hard like steel as she said: 'I won't be silenced any longer.'

'Oh no, oh no,' Hannah muttered, hands up to her face, looking fearfully at Donald's office for his reaction. Her heart pounded and her almond-milk latte swirled nauseatingly in her stomach. It didn't take Donald a minute to throw open the door and call her in. She staggered to his office, where he stood with his arms crossed.

'Well, that was … unexpected,' he said, slowly.

She nodded, waiting for instruction, chewing on her bottom lip and smudging her lip gloss.

Donald linked his hands behind his back and did a few slow turns in the centre of the office, thinking. 'Okay. We need to do some damage control here.'

Hannah nodded, picking anxiously at her nail varnish.

'We will issue a statement in support of Katie to say we are horrified at the allegations and Alex will be suspended from the show until further investigation.'

'Suspended?' Hannah gasped. 'Can we do that? After all, it's her word against his.'

Donald gave a derisive snort. 'Of course we can do that. We have to be seen to be doing something.' He carried on. 'We'll push the narrative that the show empowered Katie to find her voice and that it brought Jamie and her together and he has been her rock throughout this whole ordeal.'

'Okay,' Hannah murmured, taken aback at how fast Donald could change his tactics.

'From now on the angle is that she's back in the spotlight, her close friendship with Jamie helped her and they are dark horses to win the show,' Donald finished triumphantly. 'How does that spin it?'

'Perfect,' said Hannah.

'Leave it to me to suspend Alex. I suspect he won't be pleased,' Donald said with a curt laugh, and Hannah nodded, relieved she wouldn't have to do it. If what Katie said was true then Alex was a nasty piece of work.

Hannah headed to brief the production team and media department, her mind running over the details of what Katie said in the interview. She felt a pang of guilt for not believing her, remembering the way she looked when she begged not to be made to skate with Alex, and when they prevented her from quitting the show when she found out he was a judge. Hannah hurried down the corridor and hoped that Alex would get what he deserved. And that the ratings wouldn't suffer either.

'I can't believe you're going to let her get away with this!' Alex shouted, his face turning an ugly shade of puce.

Henry Michaelson calmly looked up from the paperwork

on his gleaming walnut desk and folded his hands, watching as Alex paced the study, running his hands through his hair.

'My career is ruined, and so is my reputation. All the sponsorships and commentating roles I lined up over the past few years have now been withdrawn, and I'm too old to go back to Olympic training! What the hell do you expect me to do?'

'Alex,' Henry's voice was calm and level, the tone he used with upset and unreasonable clients. 'We've supported you all these years because of your talent. But I cleaned up your mess last time because you were ill-disciplined and you lost control of yourself.' He looked at his son with cool disdain.

'If you had just left her alone maybe she wouldn't have needed to go public, but you kept on goading her. I'm not stepping in again to deal with this,' he said, resolutely.

Alex placed his hands on his father's desk and pleaded. 'But we can sue for breach of contract, right? And maybe defamation too? We have to do something to challenge this!'

Henry shook his head. 'I'm not going up against Harriet Laine. Face it, Alex, the public and the law aren't on your side here. You'll have to deal with it.' He gazed sternly at his son, disappointed in his inability to control his emotions.

Alex stormed out in despair, slamming the door behind him, and stood on the patio clenching his fists, hot angry tears running down his cheeks.

Chapter Twenty

Katie's phone buzzed incessantly until she finally retrieved it and switched it off, sighing. She was trying not to look at social media, her email, the news, anything where she could see the overwhelming inundation of both supportive and abusive messages. #TeamKatie and #TeamAlex were trending on Twitter, with some people on her side and some people accusing her of lying, of being a drama queen, of making everything up to salvage her career. She tried not to think about those comments.

After the interview, when she had emerged from the studio lights shaky and damp with nervous sweat, Jamie had scooped her up in a bear hug and driven her to his house, knowing the resulting publicity would lead to her being hounded by journalists and photographers for a few days. She hadn't protested, grateful for the privacy and security his gated house offered. Photographers were camped outside the gates, and Maddie had kindly braved the gauntlet of paparazzi to collect some of her things from her flat and bring them to Jamie's house.

Her interview had made headline news. A stack of newspapers lay in the living room and if Katie glanced over at them, she could see her face splashed across the pages, the headlines screaming dramatically about her allegations against Alex.

Given that not everyone seemed to believe her, she was taken aback when Donald phoned and told her that Alex was suspended. He had urged her and Jamie to carry on in the show, so they planned to restrict their practise sessions to the studio rink to avoid too many prying eyes.

The morning after the interview, Katie was curled up on Jamie's sofa, feeling restless and trying to process what was happening while he brought her endless cups of tea. She smiled at him as he sat down next to her, fresh from a workout in his home gym, his hair damp from the shower.

'What's new today?' Katie asked him as he scrolled through his phone.

'Well, my agent has been contacted for comment about whether or not you and I are now dating, especially since you've moved in with me,' he said, grinning and raising an eyebrow.

'Wow, that didn't take long for rumours to start,' she said, unimpressed.

'I know, can you imagine? Me and you?' He laughed, and Katie took a breath, feeling stung that he was so dismissive. She laughed along weakly.

'For the moment, Matt is holding the press at bay. He knows you don't want to do any more interviews just yet.'

Katie nodded, thankful for Jamie's agent and his advice. He had been instrumental in arranging the TV interview and had eagerly agreed to help manage the resulting press interest. The show's producers had offered support, but Katie wasn't inclined to accept much help from Donald after the way he had been so dismissive of her pleas not to skate with Alex. She didn't trust him one bit, and preferred to deal with Matt. He was busy issuing comments and fielding requests for more interviews, and Katie trusted his opinion on how to handle matters.

Jamie switched on the TV and flicked through the channels, studiously trying to avoid the news, when Katie sat bolt upright.

'Wait!' she said urgently. 'Scroll back!'

Jamie turned back a channel and Katie's mouth dropped open to see Sergei being interviewed. She grabbed the remote from Jamie and turned up the volume.

'Yes. That's what I saw.' He was nodding, speaking via a video connection from his home in Romania.

Katie sighed and shook her head resignedly. She knew Sergei would come out in support of Alex.

'Katie is telling the absolute truth,' Sergei finished, and she looked up in shock. He was supporting her? She hadn't seen Sergei since the day of their performance and was certain that he would always come out on Alex's side.

'I knew something was very wrong with Alex and Katie. I could never be sure but their relationship was never ... healthy. I have long had suspicions that this was no accident, when he dropped her on the ice,' Sergei said, calmly.

Katie looked open-mouthed at Jamie, who was punching the air in triumph. Team Katie was winning.

The chatter dimmed as Katie entered the studio and she could see Maria glaring at her from across the room. Maria had spoken out in support of Alex and had accused Katie of being a liar and a drama queen. Katie sighed inwardly, disappointed that so many of the people who didn't believe her were women. So much for sisterhood, she thought, and walked to the rink, trying to ignore people's stares.

Katie sat down on the bench at rinkside and started to tie up her skates, concentrating on the laces, trying not to look up or hear the murmurs around her, knowing her face was still warm from the scrutiny. A pair of feet came into view before her and she looked up to see Anna. Katie was not in the mood for any confrontation and opened her mouth to say so, but Anna spoke before she had a chance to say anything.

'Katie, about Alex,' Anna said, sitting down beside her on the bench. 'I had no idea. Like absolutely no clue.'

Katie stared at her and stayed silent, wary of Anna's intentions given how smitten she had been with Alex.

Anna looked at her earnestly. 'I always thought you were being a snotty cow, but I totally get it now. I'm really sorry about what you had to go through.' Anna reached across and squeezed Katie's hand, giving her a genuine smile.

'Thank you. That means a lot,' Katie replied softly.

'My sister was in an abusive relationship,' Anna said, looking down at the ground and picking her words carefully. 'She didn't say anything for years. We had no idea until she turned up at my parents' house with a bag of possessions and a dislocated shoulder.'

Katie grimaced. 'That's terrible,' she murmured.

Anna nodded. 'You were brave to speak out publicly, Katie. I hope it helps women like my sister to know other people are going through the same thing.'

Katie didn't know what to say. She had never thought about how her words would impact other women experiencing emotional and physical abuse. Before she could reply, Anna stood up to go to hair and make-up.

'Good luck tonight,' Anna said, and walked away.

'You too,' Katie called after her. She breathed a little easier, relieved and encouraged by the small show of support, Anna's words tumbling around in her mind. She thought of other women like her, maybe too afraid to leave their partners, who might be watching her skate this evening. She was determined to hold her head high, no matter what people believed or didn't believe, and show those women, unknown in name and number, that freedom and healing were possible.

Once Anna had been over, Katie was approached by others, some directly addressing what had happened, others just giving her a reassuring pat on the back or a smile, including the crew. A few people avoided her gaze and walked away when she was nearby though, and she knew not everyone was on her side.

Jamie approached her, ready to warm up for their performance. He was dressed and ready for the show in an olive-green shirt that showed off his eyes and clung tightly to his newly-defined muscles. She looked at him admiringly, feeling a flush of pride at him being her skating partner and friend. That spark of lust she had felt for him the other night was stoked afresh as she found herself unable to look away from him. Katie couldn't help but feel slightly flustered at how attracted she was to him.

He caught her looking and grinned at her with a raised eyebrow. 'Like what you see?' he said, and she blushed at being so apparent.

'Looking good J,' she said, wishing the heat in her face would subside.

He smiled back and didn't try to hide his own lingering appreciative glance as he looked at her. 'You look pretty stunning yourself,' he murmured.

They stared at each other for a moment and Katie thought she saw a flicker of heat in his gaze, a look that suggested something more than friendship was on his mind, but then he looked away at the other competitors doing their warm-ups and she wondered if she was mistaken.

'If we can get through this week,' he said, 'we'll be in the final.'

She held up her fingers, crossed together, and suddenly it didn't matter any more what the newspapers or Twitter or gossip magazines said, because she had Jamie in her corner.

Katie and Jamie pushed open the glass doors to the car park and walked into the cold night air, refreshing in comparison to the heat and noise of the studio that still buzzed excitedly behind them.

'I still can't believe I'm in the final,' Jamie said, shaking his head in disbelief.

Katie looked at him and grinned. 'You deserve your place, Jamie,' she said, delighted for him. She couldn't also help but feel the result was somehow a sign that the audience was on their side.

Jamie nodded. 'Shame for Lara though. She looked pretty upset.'

'I did feel really sorry for her when she started crying on camera. It's a good thing the cameras weren't on to capture what happened afterwards – that was pretty shocking!' Katie exclaimed, still surprised at Lara's uncontrolled reaction.

Lara had thrown a screaming fit at being voted off after the show had finished. The other participants had looked on, embarrassed, as she wailed about the unfairness of the public vote, questioning how Rory could still be in the show and she voted off.

While everyone was distracted by Lara, Katie and Jamie had decided to make a quick getaway back to Jamie's house, where Katie was still staying. They had forgone the hotel this week, preferring the long drive to the studio while the headlines about Alex and Katie still appeared daily.

'Oh wait,' Jamie paused mid-step. 'I forgot my jacket. I better run back and get it.'

'No problem. I'll meet you by the car,' Katie watched him hurry away with a smile. They were both so astounded at the results and taken aback at Lara's reaction that she was surprised they had remembered anything at all that evening.

She carried on walking, taking deep, slow breaths of the crisp air, grateful to be outside in the silent freshness. When she got to Jamie's car, she realised he had taken the keys with him, so she leaned against the door and pulled out her phone to see what people were saying on Twitter about the results. She was scrolling down her feed when she heard the crunch of footsteps behind her, and whipped around as Alex emerged from the shadows near a concrete pillar. A tremor of fear crawled down her spine and her eyes swivelled quickly to see if anyone was nearby, but the car park loomed empty.

She made to move away from the car, but Alex approached her swiftly and stood in front of her, glaring, his arms folded. She placed her hands behind her, wishing the car was open, and stared at him, wincing at the rage that glowed in his eyes.

'Alex, what are you doing here?' she said, hoping her voice didn't tremble.

Alex gave a short laugh. 'Waiting for you so you can explain yourself.'

'Explain myself?' Katie said incredulously.

'That little stunt you pulled on TV ruined my career,' Alex said furiously. He took a step closer to her.

Katie wanted to shrink back at his closeness, but a wave of hot anger rose in her stomach as she looked into Alex's eyes. She could see that he still expected her to give in to him, that he wouldn't admit that he was the one in the wrong. She stood up as tall as she could and held her head up high, holding her arms stiffly so they wouldn't shake.

'You deserve everything you get, Alex. I only wish I had told people sooner what an abusive lying bastard you really are.'

He looked furious and made to grab her arm, but she shook him off.

'Don't you *dare* touch me!' she shouted at him. She stepped towards him and shoved his shoulders. He was solid and unmoveable, but he looked taken aback at her retaliation. 'I'm not afraid of you any more, Alex. You can't bully me. If you try anything, I'll scream so loudly that everyone will hear and I'll make sure you're arrested. Do you want to go to prison?' she said.

He stood looking at her, a tumult of emotions flickering in his face, his mouth contorting as if to speak, but no words came out.

'Leave me alone. Never contact me or speak to me again,' she said forcefully.

Alex gaped at her. 'And what, now you're shacking up with Jamie? Let's hope he doesn't cheat on you like he did his wife,' he sneered.

Jamie's hand landed on his shoulder and pulled him around, practically yanking Alex off balance.

'What the hell are you doing?' he said through clenched teeth, looking at Katie to make sure she was okay.

She stepped forward and put a hand on Jamie's arm. 'Leave

it, Jamie. Alex was just going,' she said, giving Alex a firm look.

'Don't do anything,' she murmured to Jamie, knowing that if he did, Alex could use it against him. Jamie took a breath and released Alex's shoulder, glaring at him.

Alex shook himself and gave a derisive snort. 'You two deserve each other,' he snapped, and marched off into the darkness with his fists clenched. Katie let out a long shaky breath, the adrenaline, anger and fear still pounding through her veins.

'Are you okay?' Jamie asked her urgently. 'Did he hurt you?'

Katie shook her head. 'No. I have a feeling I won't be hearing from him again,' she said, and turned to Jamie with a faint smile. 'Let's go home.'

'I can't believe you're still in the show,' Greg said, shaking his head in disbelief.

'I know,' said Jamie. 'It's insane. I never thought I'd make it past the first week let alone get to the final.'

Greg had invited him and Katie round for a drink and Jamie knew he was keen to find out more about the gossip around the show. Katie's allegations about Alex were still headline news, and the paparazzi were still camped outside Jamie's house, the camera bulbs flashing eagerly anytime he and Katie emerged from the gates. Alex had gone to ground after his suspension, staying silent as he plotted his next move, Jamie imagined.

Katie seemed pleased when Jamie invited her to his friend's house. It was a welcome distraction for both of them from the show and all the media over the past week. Jamie made sure to ask Greg and Clara not to mention Alex, and he was heartened to see Katie talking animatedly to Clara, a glass of wine in hand, looking relaxed and happy.

Jamie watched her from across the room and she caught his eye and grinned at him.

'It's been a crazy few days,' he said, turning back to Greg.

Greg nodded. 'I'll bet. Is she still staying with you?'

'She is but only for another night or two while things calm down. I think she said she would go home tomorrow.'

Greg sipped from his cider and looked at Jamie intently. 'So …?' he asked.

'So what?'

'Are you two …?' Greg nodded in Katie's direction and raised his eyebrows.

'No mate.' Jamie grinned. 'You should know better than to believe everything you read in the papers.' Despite Matt denying that there was a relationship between them, the rumour mill was still grinding out stories that he and Katie were together.

'Shame. You two seem pretty good together,' Greg said in a low voice so Katie couldn't hear.

Jamie shrugged. 'I don't think she's interested. I'm not her type.'

'Tall, dark and psychopathic? Sounds like that's a good thing.' Greg laughed and offered him another cider.

'Would you be interested though, if she was?' Greg asked casually, as he grabbed the bottles from the fridge.

'I don't know. Maybe. Probably,' Jamie admitted, looking over at Katie, who was dressed down in skinny jeans and a white jumper, her hair falling down her back in dark waves. Jamie thought she was at her prettiest when she wasn't made-up for their performances, when her hair was loose and her natural radiance shone without make-up. He couldn't deny the increasing spark of attraction he felt for her, not just a physical lust but something deeper, that had grown as they had gotten to know each other and as she stayed longer at his house.

Clara straightened up and headed for the kitchen to pour some more drinks. She smiled at Jamie.

'You know, Jamie, I saw Cass the other day. She was asking

about you,' she said, popping the cork out of the red wine and refilling her and Katie's glasses.

Jamie was surprised. He hadn't actually thought about Cassandra much over the past few weeks as he'd been so busy with the show.

'She was talking about how great you looked on the ice. She seemed really impressed.'

Jamie felt a warm glow of delight that his ex was complimenting him and then felt irritated at himself for still caring what she thought.

'Good to hear,' he said evenly. 'How is Cass doing?'

'She's great. Busy planning her wedding,' Clara said carefully, not wanting to open up old wounds.

'Right,' said Jamie, remembering when Cassandra had planned their own wedding – two years of carefully thought-out colour schemes and flower arrangements for a fancy hotel in Sussex on a bright summer evening. She had been so hung up on all the major and minor details, but all Jamie had cared about was marrying her.

Clara took the wine back to Katie.

'Cass has moved on mate,' Greg said. 'Maybe it's time you did the same.'

'Maybe,' Jamie said thoughtfully.

'You should see if Katie's interested,' Greg said. 'You could use a little fun.' He winked.

'I'm not looking for just a little fun,' Jamie said thoughtfully, looking over at Katie and thinking about the possibilities, the pleasures, the potential. Was there a chance signing up to this show could have a bigger impact on his future than he had planned?

Chapter Twenty-One

'I'm really pleased with the performance, and the scores, and I hope people at home vote for us!' Jamie said, smiling at the camera. He was aching all over and dripping with sweat but he felt calm and happy about his performance, with their final routine. He realised with a pang that this was the last time they would skate together and he glanced at Katie, but she was looking straight ahead, focusing on Faith as she brandished her microphone in Katie's face.

'Katie, this has been a huge competition for you in the sense that there's been a lot of personal drama. How do you feel now it's coming to an end?'

'It's been a difficult and challenging experience.' Katie turned to Jamie and smiled up at him. 'But I've made a really good friend. And I'm really going to miss spending so much time with him. He's a great guy.' She rubbed his arm as Jamie grinned back at her, a warm glow of satisfaction spreading in his chest at her calling him a "great guy".

Katie continued talking into the camera. 'We both felt that skating to "Wind Beneath My Wings" for our final performance was the perfect song choice for us, because it's really a song about friendship and support, and Jamie's been a great support to me in the past few months. We've become good friends.'

She squeezed the arm that she'd not stopped rubbing and Jamie felt hotter than ever under the bright studio lights. He noticed, with a slight sinking feeling in his stomach, that she used the word friend a number of times, and wondered if she was trying to tell him something.

They finished their interviews and went backstage to wait for the results part of the show.

'You look really beautiful,' he said softly as they walked to the waiting area. Katie was wearing a floaty white dress, the top half a shimmering corset that sparkled like diamonds reflecting a thousand lights. Her hair was braided down her back with strands around her face, and her blue eyes were luminous under the light of the studio lamps.

'Thanks, Jamie.' She smiled at him.

They paused in the corridor leading to the participants' viewing area, where a constant stream of people hurried past them. Katie and Jamie stared as Kiara Jacobs, a popular singer, passed by with her entourage, getting ready for her performance while the results were tallied. She waved at them and gave them a thumbs-up. 'Good luck you guys!' she said with a grin. 'You're my favourites.'

Katie smiled. 'Wow, we've got a famous fan.'

'I can't believe this is the final – the last time we'll skate together,' Jamie said, leaning against the bland cream wall.

Katie folded her arms. 'I know. I'm a little sad about it coming to an end, despite all the craziness.' She gave a wry smile.

'Me too.'

They paused for a moment, and Katie's eyes met his. She had been increasingly tactile with him for the past few days, and he often found her looking at him with what he thought might be desire, but he couldn't be sure. More than once in their practice sessions he had to grit his teeth and tell himself to maintain self-control as he found himself more and more tempted by their on-ice embraces. It had been a struggle to stay professional and focused, but he wasn't sure she felt the same. He wondered if he should say something now, before the show ended, but the moment was interrupted by Theo popping his head out of the waiting area.

'Hey guys, you coming in?' he asked.

'Sure,' Katie said, and they both reluctantly went into the room, leaving sentiments and words unsaid hanging in the corridor outside.

*

The studio was silent and dark with the final three couples in the middle of the rink, illuminated in the hot studio lights, each person tense and nervously awaiting the final result. The air was thick with anticipation as the audience waited.

Jamie stood behind Katie with his arms wrapped around her. She could feel Jamie's warmth through his shirt, could sense the throb of his heartbeat close to her back, and she wanted to bury her face into his chest and breathe him in. She could feel his breath on the back of her neck and it made her skin tingle, sending sparks of yearning running up and down her spine. His closeness was so distracting that it took her a second to register the results being announced.

'Congratulations ... Rory and Anna!' Faith called out, trying to keep her face from showing her shock at the surprise result.

The tension dissipated like a popped balloon and Jamie and Katie looked at each other, smiles wide, their eyes full of laughter. Rory looked stunned as Jamie shook his hand.

'Oh wow,' Anna murmured in Katie's ear as she gave her a congratulatory hug.

'Good for you,' Katie whispered back. 'Enjoy it.'

A shower of silver and blue confetti shimmered down over the winners and Katie turned to Jamie to leave them to enjoy their victory. They skated off together in tandem with Theo and Maria, who had managed only stiff congratulations with peeved expressions, shocked to have been the favourites and to have lost to the underdogs.

'I'm sorry you didn't win, Jamie.' Katie turned to him as they left the rink. Maria and Theo clomped off behind them, irritated at victory being snatched from them. Katie and Jamie watched them leave.

Jamie chuckled and shook his head. 'It really doesn't matter. I'm happy for Rory,' he said, gently removing a sliver of the confetti that had landed in Katie's hair. She thought for a moment that his hand lingered there but perhaps she was just imagining it.

'Thanks for being such a great skating instructor,' he said, wrapping his arms around her. Without thinking, she pressed herself right into him, enfolded in his chest, and hoped he wouldn't let go too quickly. Her hands felt the solidity of his muscles in his back as he held her close, and her imagination was firing what it would be like to be held by him like this in the bedroom. Eventually, he released her and they both stared awkwardly at the ground for a moment.

'Are you coming to the wrap party?' Jamie asked hopefully.

Katie nodded. 'I'll be there,' she said. 'I need to go and get changed.'

'See you in a bit then.' Jamie grinned and walked off. Katie watched him go, thinking of how good it felt in his arms and hoping the after-party might be her chance to take things a little further.

Hannah straightened her dress and looked around in delight at the wrap party, which was in full swing. The tension of the past few weeks had been released and people were letting go, downing alcohol from the free bar. She took a large gulp of wine and started to relax for the first time in weeks. The show had been hard work, with more twists and turns than she had planned, but it had been worth it.

Donald marched over to Hannah, and she quivered slightly as he approached, wondering about his reaction to the results.

'Hi Donald,' Hannah said, slightly nervously. 'Can you believe Rory won? Maybe we gave too much power to the public,' she said, shaking her head.

'I don't care who won the actual competition. We're the ones who struck ratings gold,' Donald said, looking triumphant and sweaty in a grey suit and shiny burgundy tie that matched the wine in his hands. He turned his head to look at Katie, who was drifting through the crowd of people.

'Based on these ratings we can definitely go ahead with a second series next year. And I bet Katie would be ideal as one of the judges,' Donald said.

Hannah nodded, but she doubted Katie would want to be involved with them after they had forced her to skate with Alex.

'Make her an offer she can't refuse and get her locked into a contract,' Donald said.

Hannah nodded. 'I'll talk to her ASAP.' It looked like her work wasn't quite over yet. She put down her wine and went to find Katie.

Katie couldn't see Jamie anywhere in the midst of the party. Trying to ignore her disappointment, she headed to the bar to take a tall glass of prosecco. A hand grabbed her arm.

'Hi Katie,' a voice chirped in her ear and Katie turned to see Lara, who was wearing a white dress that clung tightly to all her curves. She looked tanned and glowing; her blonde hair left loose. Katie felt drab and pale in comparison.

'Hey Lara, good to see you,' she said politely. The two of them hadn't spoken much during their time on the show and Katie was surprised that she seemed so keen to talk to her now.

'So, have you seen Jamie this evening?' Lara asked, her eyes scanning the room over Katie's head.

'Not yet,' Katie replied warily.

'I'm hoping he and I can pick up where we left off a few weeks ago,' Lara said, grinning widely, her teeth bright white against her red lipstick.

'Oh um, I didn't realise that you two, erm ...' Katie stammered, the blood rising in her cheeks and her heart thudding with jealousy.

'Well, we had a moment a few weeks back and I know Jamie didn't want to pursue it because we were competing, but now the show has ended so I figure we can ... reconnect.' Lara smiled. 'Unless you can think of a reason why he wouldn't want to?' she asked pointedly.

'Like what?'

'You know, like you two being involved?' Lara raised her eyebrows.

'No, we're just friends,' Katie said, feeling wretched and wanting to yell at Lara to stay away but knowing she had no right to.

'Fabulous! Well, I must dash and go find him.' Lara winked at Katie and headed off into the crowd.

Katie put her prosecco glass down and tried to fight off visions of Lara and Jamie together. She knew it shouldn't matter to her, but it bothered her immensely. She made up her mind to find Jamie before Lara. She moved quickly through the crowd of people, but kept getting sidetracked. Carmen bounded up to her and hugged her tight, bombarding her excitedly with questions about Alex, then Andy joined them and Katie tried to excuse herself but it seemed impossible. Her agitation rising, she looked over Andy's shoulder to see Jamie and Lara in a darkened corner, their heads close. Lara's hand was on Jamie's chest. Katie's throat tightened and she didn't hear Carmen's question.

'Katie, hello?' Carmen said, waving a hand in front of her face.

'Pardon? Sorry, I er didn't hear,' Katie stammered, trying to tear her eyes away from the corner where Jamie was, yet unable to look away.

'Please excuse me, I have to ...' she muttered and trailed off as she walked away from Andy and Carmen.

'What's her problem?' Carmen said to Andy as they watched her leave and head to the exit.

Andy shrugged. 'She's always been a bit odd. I thought maybe now the whole Alex thing was sorted she might be a bit cheerier, but maybe she's just weird from all the years of competing,' he said.

Katie hurried through the warm crowd and pushed her way through the doors to the night outside. The pavement was slick from recent rain and reflected the street lights. Moisture hung in the air and Katie shivered, pulling out her phone.

'Katie, wait!' Hannah dashed after her, tottering on black patent stilettos. 'Are you leaving already?'

'Um, yes I think so,' she murmured. 'I was about to call a cab to go home.'

Home for Katie was back in her own flat again. She had loved staying with Jamie, but she knew she couldn't impose on him too long and had gone back to her apartment a few days before the final. She wished that she was going home with him tonight but that didn't look likely. She frowned as she tried not to think of him taking Lara back with him instead of her.

Hannah shot her a look at seeing her strange expression. 'Can I talk to you while you wait for your taxi? I have an offer you can't refuse.'

Chapter Twenty-Two

'So, when are you going to tell her then?' Phil asked Jamie. The family had joined Jamie for a big barbecue at his house to celebrate the end of the show, and to make the most of some unseasonably warm spring weather.

Jamie pressed a burger onto the hot grill, the juices sizzling pleasurably. 'Tell who what?'

Phil smiled. 'Tell Katie how you feel.'

Jamie looked up; his face reddened from the heat of the barbecue. 'You've got the wrong end of the stick, Dad.'

'Have I?' Phil raised an eyebrow. 'I think you two would be good together, Jamie.'

'I don't think she's interested,' Jamie replied, focusing on the meat. He had texted her loads of times to try to find her at the after-party, but she had disappeared and hadn't replied until the next day. He had been stung by her dismissiveness – he had been looking forward to seeing her at the party, sharing a drink with her, hoping their inhibitions would loosen enough for him to be able to tell her what he was thinking about her.

In the end, it was Lara who had sought him out again, making clear her intentions, but she wasn't the one Jamie wanted. It was Katie he had looked for after telling Lara nothing could happen between them, it was Katie he had spent the night texting and thinking of, checking his phone every ten minutes and leaving the party disappointed. He had really thought that perhaps there was a chance, but her behaviour was a clear sign that he was barking up the wrong tree.

'Don't ask don't get,' his dad said, sipping from a bottle of beer before walking off, leaving Jamie to think about what he had said.

He pulled his phone out of his pocket and started typing a message to Katie. He deleted it and started writing another one, then sighed and rewrote it, shaking his head. Finally, he jabbed the send button.

Katie picked up her phone as it pinged and smiled to see a text from Jamie. He had messaged her loads of times after she left the party and she was kicking herself for leaving so soon. Even though she'd seen Jamie and Lara looking so cosy together, the barrage of messages from him suggested that it was her he had wanted to see that night. Unfortunately, her phone had died on the way home and she hadn't seen them till the next day. She wondered what he must think of her. She read his latest message.

Meet soon for a drink?

Sure. When/where? she typed quickly.

His reply came back instantly.

Mine? Tomorrow night?

She sent a thumbs-up emoji and had already started thinking about what to wear, when her phone rang, interrupting her thoughts. It was an international number she didn't recognise, and she hesitantly answered the call.

Katie drove up to Jamie's house in her new car. He bounded out when he saw her pulling into the drive.

'Woooow, I'm impressed, Katie!' he said, looking over her car as she got out.

'Don't get too excited. It's just a rental,' she said, smiling at his excitement. 'I was sick of taking the bus.' She followed him inside, hurrying as fat droplets of rain started to pour down from a leaden sky.

He seemed slightly on edge and distracted as she sat down on one of his enormous sofas, sinking into the soft leather. He rushed off to make her a cup of tea and returned quickly, popping the steaming mug on a table before her, sloshing the contents over the side and onto the wood, although he didn't seem to notice.

'I heard from Alex's lawyers today,' she said as he sat down next to her.

'And?' He leaned forward expectantly.

'They're not going to do anything,' she said, grinning triumphantly.

'Yes!' he said, holding his hand out for a high five which she returned gleefully. 'That's such good news.'

'I owe you and Harriet a big one,' she said.

'Nope. We were happy to help,' Jamie said smiling. 'Just do me a favour and don't sign any more contracts without reading the small print, okay?'

She laughed and sipped her tea, feeling small droplets from the spill drip onto her jeans from the bottom of the mug. She rubbed her fingers over the small damp patch.

'I wanted to talk to you about something,' Jamie said awkwardly, rubbing the back of his neck.

'I wanted to speak to you too,' Katie said, smoothing a thumb around the rim of the mug.

Jamie held his hand out to her. 'Ladies first, of course.'

Katie took a breath. 'So, I got an amazing offer after the show ended,' she began.

Jamie nodded. 'And?'

'Well, actually I got two offers,' Katie said. 'Firstly, they've asked me to judge the next series.'

Jamie laughed. 'That makes sense. What did you say?'

'No way! Those producers made me skate with Alex when I begged them not to. I don't want to work with people like that,' Katie said, wrinkling her nose. It had been incredibly satisfying to tell Hannah where she could stuff her offer and to see the shock on her face. Katie only wished that Donald had been there too.

Jamie grinned. 'Sounds like the right decision. What was the other offer?'

Katie paused. 'I got a call from Ivan yesterday,' she said.

'Your old coach?'

Katie nodded. 'He's living in Canada and saw all the news about the show. He got in touch to ask if I'd like to explore skating properly again.' Her eyes widened with excitement. 'It's two years till the next Olympics and Ivan is technically retired but he wants to go for gold again.'

Jamie nodded slowly. 'Do you think you can get back up to that level and qualify in two years?'

Katie nodded. 'All those mornings before you showed up for practice, I was honing my doubles and then working on my triples. I can still do it.'

'And your ankle?' Jamie asked cautiously.

'I went to the doctor last week and everything is holding together as it should. There'll always be a risk of course, but I think it's one I'm willing to take.'

'Katie, if you think it's the right thing to do, then you've got to do it,' Jamie said, firmly. 'You could get back on that podium again.'

'That's always been the dream. It's never been about money or fame for me. It was always about being on the ice and being the absolute best I could be.'

Jamie grinned and reached across to give her a hug. 'This is such great news. I'm so happy for you that you'll get another shot.'

Katie leaned her head on his shoulder and wished the hug wouldn't end, but he released her and leaned back. 'There's just one drawback really,' she murmured.

'Whatever it is I'm sure you'll find a way around it,' Jamie said confidently.

'I'll be moving to Canada for the training for the next two years.'

'Oh right,' Jamie said. His tone was less enthusiastic, and although his expression was neutral Katie thought she saw a flicker of emotion.

When she'd got the call from Ivan, the only thing that had held her back from saying yes immediately was the thought of

Jamie and the feelings that she knew she was fast developing for him. But she had no indication that what he felt for her was anything other than friendship, and she had made the mistake before of putting one man's feelings before her own desires and it hadn't led to anything good. As much as she liked Jamie, this was her one last shot at the Olympics and her head told her to take it, even if her heart was screaming at her in protest. She knew this opportunity wouldn't come again. She would be twenty-five by the next Olympics, and in figure skating terms that was old. It was her last chance.

She knew that what she was about to say would most likely kill off any option for them other than being friends, as she couldn't expect Jamie to wait around for her for the next two years, especially not now he was seen as hot property. The show had totally reversed his reputation, the public loved him, and his charm, good looks and tall, muscular body had won him countless female admirers. There was no way she could expect someone like Jamie to hang around for her when he could have his pick of any number of women.

'It'll be really full-on. I won't have much time to come back or you know, do much else other than skating,' she said, wishing she could have both Jamie and her Olympic dream, and feeling utterly torn between the two.

Jamie nodded. 'You have to follow your heart, Katie,' he said encouragingly, but she thought perhaps his smile was a little weaker than before.

'Thanks, Jamie. I'm lucky to have a friend like you,' she said. 'What was it you wanted to talk to me about?'

'You know what, I can't remember,' Jamie said, shaking his head.

She smiled at him. 'So, what are your plans? I bet the offers have come flooding in, haven't they?' she asked. 'You're certainly very popular right now.' She grinned and showed him a news story on her phone which had labelled Jamie "Sports Heart-throb of the Year".

He laughed. 'Heart-throb? I don't know about that.' He shook his head, amused, and Katie loved how modest he was, even though it was clear to her and everyone else how accurate the label was; Katie was a little embarrassed by how much she had stared longingly at the photo of him on the news story.

'But yes, you're right, Matt has been inundated with offers for me,' he said.

'What are you thinking of doing?' she asked.

'Well, the stuff that interests me most are the offers relating to rugby, of course. I've been asked to work on the Six Nations coverage, which is amazing. Plus, I've been asked to do ambassadorial work for the Rugby Football Union.'

'That's wonderful!' Katie said warmly. 'I'm so proud of you.'

'Oh, and I've had some great offers to do underwear modelling.' He winked at Katie and her cheeks burned because she knew she would love to see Jamie in his pants.

She giggled. 'Well, I look forward to seeing that.'

He lifted his mug to hers. 'Here's to chasing our dreams of medals and underwear modelling.'

'Going for gold.' Katie clinked her mug against his.

Sitting on the sofa with Jamie, toasting their new opportunities, Katie felt a mixture of emotions churning in her heart. She was excited about training with Ivan again, but her head was spinning with how much she wanted Jamie. He leaned back on the sofa and she tried not to look as his T-shirt rode up slightly, revealing the defined abs that nestled above the waistband of his jeans.

Katie wished she could simply tell him how she felt, but instead she knew that it was time for her to go, time to pack and get ready for her flight the next day.

'I'd better go, J,' she said, sadly. 'I have to pack. I managed to get a last-minute flight for tomorrow afternoon.'

He glanced at her and swiped a hand through his hair, looking at her with a smile that didn't quite reach his eyes. 'Sure,' he said, getting up and walking her to the door.

The rain pelted down outside, thundering against the windows and onto the gravel with a dull roar. Katie shivered and turned to Jamie, hating that she was going to have to say goodbye.

'Bye Jamie, and thank you. For everything,' she said, her breath almost catching in her throat. He leaned in and wrapped his arms around her, holding her close. She closed her eyes and savoured his touch before pulling away.

He swallowed hard and looked genuinely upset that she was leaving. 'Good luck,' he murmured, and kissed her on the cheek.

She turned and left the house quickly so he wouldn't see the tears that threatened to spill down her cheeks. She hurried to the car under her umbrella, scrabbling in her pockets for the car keys. It took her a moment to find them and she thought she heard something over the pounding of the rain. She realised that Jamie was calling out, hurrying down the path towards her. She looked up in surprise as he dashed to her. The rain was running down his face, his T-shirt clinging tightly to him, already soaked through.

'Wait!' he said urgently.

'What's the matter?!' she asked, alarmed at the intensity in his gaze.

'Katie, I ...' He ran his hands through his hair with an agonised expression. 'I can't let you go without telling you the truth ...'

He trailed off and she stared at him, wide-eyed. He took her hand, his skin surprisingly warm against hers despite the coolness of the rain.

'The truth is that I've fallen for you,' he said eventually, looking at her earnestly. 'Completely, head over heels. I'm in love with you.'

Her mouth opened in shock, and she let her umbrella drop to the ground.

He looked at her searchingly. 'Don't you have anything to say?' he asked, looking slightly hurt.

'Oh, Jamie,' she began, and she was suddenly grateful for the rain on her face hiding the tears that coursed down her cheeks. She stepped towards him and stood on tiptoe to press her mouth to his. He wrapped his arms around her and lifted her clean off the gravel, kissing her deeply, leaving her gasping for breath.

'I know you have to go,' he said. 'But please don't go just yet. Stay here with me, tonight,' he pleaded, before kissing her again. He rested his forehead against hers and murmured in a voice husky with emotion. 'I'll wait for you, Katie. I'd wait longer than two years if I had to.'

She wrapped her legs around him and stroked the side of his face, feeling the slight rasp of stubble under her fingertips. He swung around and carried her into the house and upstairs, laying her on his bed, where their rain-soaked clothes marked the luxurious cotton sheets and thoughts of packing and flights disappeared from her head as she melted into his embrace.

Chapter Twenty-Three

Two years later

The energy in the athletes' village was high, and Katie felt that same buzz of competitive tension in the air she remembered from her previous Olympic competitions. The difference from the last Games was that this time she was free from fear and anxiety about appeasing Alex. She thought about the amount of time and energy she had dedicated to keeping him stable and happy rather than focusing on their skating, and she still burned with anger at him for ruining that last competition for them both.

At least now she had one more shot; this time tempered with something else – the weight of expectation for the great comeback story that she was supposed to produce for the public at home. She hoped that she could deliver for them.

It was the day before her performance and Katie was free to go to the rink and practise, her mandatory drug tests over. She laced up her boots and chatted with Ivan before she got on the ice. She knew her short and long programmes inside out, but the famous triple axel would be difficult to deliver. The past two years had been intense work but it had been so good to team up with Ivan again. They knew each other well and he understood how to work with her and get the best from her – he always had ever since she was young. It was even more precious to her that he had known and respected her dad too. She knew they both felt his absence from their training this time around and she often looked at his photo at night, determined to make him proud if he was somehow able to see her.

Jamie was never far from her thoughts either. She was always focused on her training during the day, but at night she thought endlessly of him, missing his smile and his touch.

They had only seen each other a handful of times since she left, fitting fleeting visits around international competitions, but those snatched hours, a day or two here and there, those had sustained her. It wasn't enough, she could never get enough of Jamie, but it would have to do, for now.

As she skated onto the ice to practice, she waved across at Lexi, one of the younger Team GB skaters. 'Good luck!' Lexi called out cheerily. Katie liked Lexi. She was a talented young skater, not tipped for a medal this competition, but she had great potential. Katie felt a little sorry for her, as her parents couldn't make it to the competition. Lexi's dad was ill, and Katie knew what it was like to feel alone and a bit lost at the Games, so she had made sure to befriend the girl. Lexi hung over the barriers, watching Katie eagerly, and Katie grinned at her as she began her practice.

She felt calm and confident, certain that this was the winning routine. Her timing was perfect and her jumps smooth. She allowed the music to guide her, feeling the rhythm in her heart and mind, not allowing herself to think of anything but the ice and her mastery of it. She was ready for this and she wouldn't allow anything to distract her now.

'Have you texted Katie yet?' Harriet asked, waving her chopsticks at Jamie and finishing her mouthful of food with gusto.

'Nope, I didn't want to distract her.' Jamie shook his head, staring around at the bustling restaurant, a medley of foreign languages rising from the full tables that were heaving with Olympic visitors and tourists.

'Don't be silly, just pop her a text and tell her you're here,' Harriet said, rolling her eyes. 'You know she'll be happy to see you ...' She winked at him.

Jamie shifted about on the narrow stool. The truth was he was desperate to get in touch and let Katie know he was here, having assured her that he would be there to see her skate and cheer her on. He couldn't wait to see Katie compete, and more than that he couldn't wait to hold her in his arms again. Two years had passed at a glacial pace and he had missed her every day. They kept in touch almost constantly but FaceTime calls and WhatsApp messages weren't the same as having her by his side. Although he had been busy himself and was never short of work, there was a void in his life that only Katie could fill.

Harriet waved at him as he stared at the chefs in the kitchen, their swift mastery of their knives almost hypnotic. '*Hello? Anyone there?*'

He snapped out of his reverie and pulled his phone out of his pocket. 'Maybe you're right,' he said to Harriet, tapping out the text. 'I'll just let her know I've arrived.'

He put his phone back down on the table and tried not to check it every five minutes. He didn't expect a reply, knowing that Katie would be busy preparing and wouldn't want to be distracted by her phone.

It wasn't long till he would see her anyway, out there on the ice. He felt a gleam of pride as he thought of her bravery, her talent, and her dedication, and he knew she stood a real shot at getting a medal this time. He couldn't wait to cheer her on.

Katie left the ice, out of breath but pleased with the way the practice had gone. She knew she could complete the programme cleanly, she just had to do it out there in front of the eyes of the world.

Ivan nodded at her as she came off the ice. 'Good job,' he said, with a smile. His praise was as restrained as ever, but she knew from the sparkle in his eyes that he was feeling as positive as her. 'Now make sure you get some rest before tomorrow.'

She nodded. 'Will do.' As she leaned down to unlace her skates, a shrill scream made her whip round towards the rink. It was a heart-wrenching shriek of pain that could only come from a competitor experiencing a serious injury; a sound Katie knew all too well.

She saw Lexi sprawled on the ice and she raced towards her. Her coach was gesturing urgently for help as Lexi lay prone, sobbing and whimpering in pain. Katie knelt by her side and grabbed her hand, squeezing it tightly.

'What happened?' she asked, attempting to sound calm.

'My landing was off!' Lexi cried. 'I think I've broken something!'

Katie tried to talk to her soothingly. 'It'll be okay, don't worry,' she said, stroking a strand of hair away from the girl's forehead. 'Try not to panic. Help is on the way.'

Lexi nodded miserably, tears rolling from her eyes down onto the ice. Katie waited with her until help arrived and stood back as Lexi was loaded onto a stretcher to take her to a waiting ambulance. Her coach got in with her, but Lexi waved urgently to Katie, her eyes wide and her face stricken with fear and pain. 'Katie, please! Come with me!' she cried out desperately.

Katie didn't hesitate to leap into the ambulance with her and took her hand once again.

'I'm here,' she said, and Lexi nodded, wrapping her fingers tightly around Katie's.

Katie remembered the utter fear and despondency she felt when she was injured, the terror of her career being over, the loneliness of being in a hospital in a foreign country. There was no way she would leave Lexi if she wanted her there.

She stayed with Lexi in the hospital, through checks and tests and X-rays, as the clock ticked away the afternoon, then the evening. The hours bit into the night and still she stayed, leaving for the village only when Lexi was comfortably asleep, her dislocated kneecap putting her out of the running for these Games. As Katie left the hospital, dawn was creeping over the horizon. It was performance day and she had barely slept at all.

Katie took a deep breath as her name was called. Despite being up most of the night, her mind was clear and she felt tired, but calm. She knew she wasn't in the absolute best shape to compete that day, but she couldn't regret staying with Lexi, not when it was the right thing to do.

She wasn't nervous. It was nothing like her last Olympics where Alex had robbed her of her joy of skating and her self-esteem. Regardless of how tired she was, everything about today just felt right, from the crisp golden dawn that had warmed the freezing air as she returned to the village that morning, to the way her boots felt as she laced them up, hugging her feet, melding with her skin and bones, becoming part of her.

Her costume was one of the best she had ever worn. It was a shimmering orange, red and gold bodice, glowing like fire under the lights, with a skirt of blazing scarlet that danced with her as she moved. It was, as the designer had explained, meant to represent the phoenix, "one who rises from the ashes, triumphant". It was perfect.

Katie made a final check on her laces and stepped onto the ice. She glanced around at the packed arena as she skated to the middle of the rink. The audience was packed, a distant blur of flags and strangers' faces. But amidst the crowd, she knew Jamie was there somewhere, and she wished she could see his smile encouraging her.

Her name echoed around the rink and the crowd fell silent, expectant. It was only a short moment before her music started, but the seconds seemed to stretch unbearably. Katie told her mind to let go of any thoughts other than the programme she needed to complete. She let go of Jamie, and Lexi and Alex, and Ivan, and her dad, and allowed the opening bars of the music to fill her head. She closed her eyes and breathed deeply, imagining the oxygen infusing her muscles for the challenging but achievable programme she and Ivan had created.

She felt free as she flew around the ice, just like when she was little and her dad had stood watching her for hours, patiently tucking his hands into his old coat, while she soared and spun like a superhero. Her body was fatigued, but her heart was joyful, and the smile on her face wasn't forced for the benefit of the judges and cameras. This was her moment. This was where she was meant to be.

Katie readied herself for the challenge of the triple axel and powered upwards into the rotations. She landed heavily on her ankle and felt a slight shimmy of the blade edge, and the tremor through her hip meant her free leg didn't extend fully backwards. She managed to stay upright, and she could hear by the resulting cheers that the crowd considered it a clean landing, but she knew that the judges would have seen the tiny error.

She pushed the mistake from her mind and whipped into the final spin, stopping dead on time with the music, a clean halt, to a cacophony of applause. Whether she made it to the podium or not, she had done what she came to do. She raised her arms and bowed to the crowd.

She wasn't sure if she had done enough, and the competition was fierce. The slightest error could make the difference between her dreams being dashed or fulfilled. But she knew in her heart that she had done all she could. She was free from regret, free from past mistakes, and she wanted to relish this moment that she had worked so hard for and never thought she would experience again.

She bowed once more and a crescendo of applause roared through the arena as the audience stood, and she was embraced by their cheers. Spectators behind every flag applauded her, acknowledging her attempt, telling her she didn't need to do any more. Her revelation about Alex's abuse had made headlines around the world and she knew the applause was both for her performance and because of her journey to be there to complete it.

Katie turned and skated off the ice, heading towards Ivan, and for a fleeting moment she thought she could see her dad standing there beside him, nodding his approval, his eyes bright. She blinked away tears and the apparition vanished, but she knew in her heart that, somehow, her dad was there with her for her final Olympic performance.

Jamie watched Katie skate off the ice, his heart pounding with pride at her performance, clapping so hard his hands began to ache. To him, it had looked flawless. He was sure that she had to medal. She was clearly one of the best out there, with very few left to compete. He watched as she received the scores, sitting by Ivan, waving to the camera and teary-eyed with emotion. Her face was bright with hope as the scores came in and both she and Ivan leapt to their feet to see that she was leading the table in gold medal position. Jamie fist pumped the air and cheered, Harriet laughing beside him at his delight.

'Now all Katie has to do is wait and see what scores the Russian and Korean skaters get,' Harriet said, placing a hand on his arm.

Jamie nodded. 'I hope she's done enough,' he said, drinking in Katie's joyful expression on the screen, and crossing his fingers.

Chapter Twenty-Four

Katie bent low and felt the ribbon slide over her hair and the weight of the medal hang around her neck. She stood upright again and raised her arms, soaking in the cheers. Katie clutched the silver medal tightly and kissed it, holding it aloft, hardly able to breathe, wondering if she was in fact just dreaming.

The skater next to her mounted the podium for her gold and Katie clapped her wholeheartedly. The young Russian had won by the narrowest of margins, a mere sliver of a point ahead of Katie, but her triple axel landing was cleaner, her programme was strong, and she had choreographed all her jumps into the final moments of the programme for bonus points. She had won fair and square, Katie thought, as she smiled at her competitor.

Katie was exhausted but euphoric as she completed her interviews, posed for photos, fielded congratulations. The evening was overwhelming in its perfection, aside from the absence of Jamie, whom she hadn't had a chance to see yet.

It wasn't until she left the medal ceremony that night, walking out of the stadium under a clear, starry sky, that she saw him, silhouetted against the lights of the entrance, where his text said he would be waiting for her. Although there were crowds streaming from the stadium she recognised him instantly, seeing his broad shoulders and his blond hair, taller than most around him, a beaming smile on his face as he turned to see her approaching.

She hurried eagerly towards him, her breath puffing out in cold white streams, her medal safe and warm against her skin underneath her coat. She dashed through the crowd and straight into his arms, where he caught her in a hug and lifted her off the ground, his hands around her waist and his mouth finding hers with a kiss that left her breathless.

'Well done!' he said delightedly as he pulled back with a

grin. 'I'm so proud of you, Katie.' He stared at her intently and she smiled so hard her cheeks ached, finally convinced she wasn't in a dream, as no imaginary kiss could be so fiercely passionate.

'I'm so glad you're here,' she murmured, wrapping her arms around his neck and pressing her cheek to his, delighting in the warmth of his skin against hers.

'I told you I would wait for you,' he said.

'Well, the wait is over,' she said, running her fingers through his hair.

He gently put her down so her feet were on the floor again, and ran his fingertips down the front of her coat, brushing the shape of the medal that hung underneath and making her knees shake with desire at his touch. 'Are you happy with the result?' he asked her.

She nodded. 'The best woman won, and besides, silver always suited my complexion better anyway,' she said with a laugh and no trace of bitterness.

'That's good to hear,' he said, reaching into his pocket and taking out a small box. 'Because ...' He opened it to reveal a white-gold ring nestled in dark velvet, the diamonds studded around the band catching the stadium lights, glittering like the stars that were above them. Though the crowds still thronged around them, at that moment Katie could see only Jamie kneeling before her, as if they were completely alone.

'You were worth the wait,' he said, looking up at her. 'And I don't just mean these past two years. But I don't want to wait any more. I want you. Now. And for the rest of my life. Marry me, Katie?'

She nodded, unable to say anything, her heart fluttering like a hummingbird. He took her hand and slid the ring on then stood up and pressed her fingers to his lips. He brushed a tear away from her eye.

'Happy tears, I hope?'

'Yes!' she exclaimed, and kissed him, unable to believe the

night had ended like this, with a silver medal and a proposal under the stars.

He rested his forehead against hers. 'What do you think you're going to do now?' he asked her softly.

She paused for a moment, thinking of Anna's sister, thinking of the pro bono work Harriet did with the women's shelter, thinking there was so much she had to give based on what she had been through.

'I'm not sure, but I know there's a lot out there for me, away from the ice, away from competing. A whole other life to lead,' she said, glancing up at him.

He nodded. 'A life with me by your side,' he said firmly.

She smiled and raised an eyebrow. 'Only if you let me come to your mum's Sunday lunch every week.'

He laughed. 'It's a deal.'

Katie smiled, her heart brimming with happiness. At her last Olympics, all she had was an empty hospital room, a broken heart, a broken ankle, and newspapers full of painful rumours about her and Alex that she couldn't correct.

This time she would go home with Jamie, be part of a family, with plans and promises for the future, her reputation restored. She was ready for the next challenge. Whatever it might be.

Thank You

Dear reader,

Thank you so much for choosing to read *Strictly On Ice*. I hope you enjoyed Katie and Jamie's story as much as I enjoyed writing it!

I've long been fascinated by the beauty, physical prowess and artistry of figure skating. The idea for this novel came from hours of dreamily watching YouTube videos of Olympic skaters and *Dancing on Ice* on TV. Like Katie, I also used to skate at Slough ice rink, although I was a terrible skater whose humble aspiration was merely to stay upright – something I didn't always achieve.

If you've enjoyed *Strictly On Ice* I'd be so grateful if you could leave a review on Goodreads or the website where you bought the book. To find out more about me and for updates about my upcoming books, follow me on Twitter, Facebook and Instagram. I'd love to hear from you!

Helen

xx

About the Author

Helen Buckley lives in Bedfordshire with her husband and two sons. After working in the charity sector in the UK and abroad, she turned her hand to writing and her first novel, *Star in the Shadows*, was published in 2019. She writes any moment that she can, enthralled by stories of fame, romance and happy ever afters. Apart from being addicted to writing and enjoying soft play with her sons, she's an avid reader, action-movie fan and chocolate addict.

Follow Helen on social media to find out
more about her work or to get in touch:
Twitter:
www.twitter.com/HelenCBuckley

Instagram:
www.instagram.com/helencatherinebuckley/

Facebook:
www.facebook.com/Helenbuckleyauthor

More Choc Lit

From Helen Buckley

Celebrity SOS

Spotlight series

I'm a celebrity … trying to escape the past!

When Katerina Murphy agrees to take part in Celebrity SOS, a reality TV show where celebrities have to fend for themselves in the Alaskan wilderness, she's up for the challenge. But then she locks eyes with fellow contestant Finn Drayson of 1Dream boy band fame and realises that the show is going to push her further from her comfort zone than she ever imagined.

After all, Finn wasn't just Katerina's co-star in the school play adaptation of Breakfast at Tiffany's where she discovered her acting confidence, he was also her first love – and the first boy to break her heart. Even years later, the secret kisses and shared packets of crisps on park benches are never far from her mind.

Will award-winning actress Katerina Murphy's talents stretch to staying composed in the face of Arctic winds and blasts from the past?

Strictly Christmas Spirit

Spotlight series

From disco balls to Christmas baubles …

Ex-dancer Emily Williams turned her back on the sparkle of popular dancing show Strictly Dancing with Celebs to help those in need. Now the only dancing she does is teaching lonely pensioners to waltz, and the closest she gets to disco balls is making baubles with the homeless people in her Christmas crafts class.

She's certainly not star-struck when Hollywood heart-throb Blake Harris is sent to her at short notice for community service, and has no desire to babysit the arrogant actor with his bad boy antics and selfish ways. Christmas might be a time for miracles, but Blake seems to be a lost cause.

But Emily's reasons for abandoning her dancing passion means she understands the Hollywood wild child more than she'd like to admit. Could their time together, coupled with a dash of Christmas spirit, lead to a miracle change of heart for them both?

Visit www.choc-lit.com for details.

Introducing Choc Lit

We're an independent publisher creating
a delicious selection of fiction.
Where heroes are like chocolate – irresistible!
Quality stories with a romance at the heart.

See our selection here:
www.choc-lit.com

We'd love to hear how you enjoyed *Strictly On Ice*.
Please visit **www.choc-lit.com** and give your feedback
or leave a review where you purchased this novel.

Choc Lit novels are selected by genuine readers like yourself.
We only publish stories our Choc Lit Tasting Panel want to
see in print. Our reviews and awards speak for themselves.

Could you be a Star Selector and join our Tasting Panel?
Would you like to play a role in choosing which novels
we decide to publish? Do you enjoy reading women's
fiction? Then you could be perfect for our Tasting Panel.

Visit here for more details…
www.choc-lit.com/join-the-choc-lit-tasting-panel

Keep in touch:
Sign up for our monthly newsletter Spread for all the latest
news and offers: www.spread.choc-lit.com. Follow us
on Twitter: @ChocLituk and Facebook: Choc Lit.

Where heroes are like chocolate – irresistible!